'Riveting . . . The
a time when it see.
the acts of a handful of brave souls. *The Thirty-One Kings*
is old-fashioned in many ways – which is what makes it such
a reassuring pleasure to read'
Wall Street Journal

'The plot whips along, embellished by dogfights, perilous car
journeys, personal vendettas and plenty of derring-do – plus
a whiff of enjoyable parody'
Daily Mail

'A loving tribute to Buchan . . . and thoroughly good fun'
The Scotsman

'This fast-moving tale will delight Buchan fans . . . gripping
and fun'
Country Life

'Harris revives the lost art of the atmospheric, erudite,
page-turning adventure story'
Anthony O'Neill

A NOTE ON THE AUTHOR

Robert J. Harris was born in Dundee and studied at the University of St Andrews, graduating with a first-class honours degree in Latin. He is the designer of the best-selling fantasy board game Talisman and has written numerous children's books including the Artie Conan Doyle Mysteries, a series featuring the youthful adventures of the creator of Sherlock Holmes. His Richard Hannay series has been acclaimed by critics and readers alike. *The Thirty-One Kings* was listed by *The Scotsman* as one of the fifty best books of 2017. The second book in the series, *Castle Macnab*, was published two years later. Robert lives in St Andrews with his wife Debby.

ROBERT J. HARRIS

REDFALCON

Richard Hannay Returns

First published in Great Britain in 2024 by Polygon,
an imprint of Birlinn Ltd.

Birlinn Ltd
West Newington House
10 Newington Road
Edinburgh
EH9 1QS

www.polygonbooks.co.uk

ISBN 978 1 84697 485 4
eBook ISBN 978 1 78885 661 4

Typeset by 3btype.com, Edinburgh

To Fiona, the Great Woman

CONTENTS

PART THREE: THE REFUGE

PART FOUR: THE FORTRESS

PREFACE

This novel was inspired by the immortal characters and classic stories of John Buchan, particularly the adventures of Richard Hannay and the Gorbals Die-Hards. It was also inspired by the real-life courage of the defenders of Malta, both in 1565 and in 1942.

PART ONE

THE MISSION

A MEETING WITH LAZARUS

I suppose every man at some point in his life wonders what he has got left in him. With a wealth of experience behind him and a shortening future to the fore, he must make certain decisions, whether past achievements have given him the right to leisure and contentment or he is honour-bound to strive against the odds up to his very last breath. There had been a period in my life when I had found peace and fulfilment in running my small country estate while enjoying the love of my wife Mary and the occasional company of good friends, but outside events had broken in on my idyll.

First there was the affair of the three hostages, in which Mary played a crucial role, then the business in the Norlands, where our son Peter John, though still in his teens, found himself at the centre of the action. Finally, with the coming of the war, all thoughts of peace and comfort had to be set aside as I was summoned to action once more.

I had returned home wounded from my mission to Paris in 1940, barely escaping the advancing German army. More grievous than any personal injury was the loss of my friend Sandy Clanroyden on that mission, but I knew that his was just one of the many sacrifices our country would have to make if we were to overcome a foe who appeared at that stage to be all but invincible.

Stiffened by the resolve of Prime Minister Churchill,

the country stood firm and the threat of invasion was turned aside by our brave pilots, who drove the Luftwaffe from the skies. Peter John, now a grown man, was one of those fliers, his boyhood love of falconry evolving into an obsession with flight that had led him to join the RAF at the first opportunity.

For me, my contribution to the war effort now took the form of a desk job as a special intelligence consultant. It was a high-sounding title, but it meant being shut in my Whitehall office day after day, studying intelligence reports gathered from agents overseas as well as from the government's secret decoding station, the location of which was known only to a few. I was to review this bewildering array of information and pass on my assessment of enemy intentions, possible infiltration and potential targets.

It didn't sit well with me to be occupied in safety and comfort while other men were out there taking all the risks. Granted that my speed and physical stamina were somewhat diminished, I still felt that my ability to endure hardship and battle my way out of the most hazardous corner was as strong as ever. I consoled myself with the thought that over the years I had seen more than my fair share of action, and if this was how Richard Hannay could best serve his country, then I would carry out these desk-bound duties with all the determination of a soldier fighting to hold the front line.

All that was about to change when I entered my office on a particularly overcast July morning. It was now 1942 and I had in my pocket a letter from Peter John which arrived the previous day. In February he and his squadron had been sent to Malta to defend that beleaguered outpost.

He was forbidden, of course, to touch directly upon military matters in his correspondence, but even reading between the lines it was clear that things were very rough out there.

The dull weather had cast the office into such a deep gloom that I was forced to switch on the overhead light in order to find my way around. I saw at once a fresh pile of folders heaped high on my desk, a sight which drew a sigh of resignation. I sat down in my chair and glanced at the photograph of Mary which sat off to my left.

She too was now in uniform, heading up the newly formed Royal Nursing Auxiliary. I was one of the few who knew that as well as its genuine medical duties, that organisation also acted as a cover for certain activities of the Special Operations Executive. Churchill had ordered the SOE to 'set Europe ablaze', hitting the Germans hard with acts of sabotage and local resistance until such time as we could turn the tide of battle by more direct means.

Mary's role became especially crucial when the bold and controversial decision was made to train women as agents who would be dropped into occupied France to organise and encourage resistance there. With her background in military intelligence during the last war, she was the ideal person to supervise the training of these new female operatives. She was based now at the SOE's heavily protected centre at Foxton Castle in Norfolk, and it had been weeks since we had been together. How I longed for the day when all three of us could be reunited once more.

Setting such thoughts aside, I turned my attention to work, massaging a crick in my neck while I reached for the topmost folder. During the night my sleep had been disturbed by the noise of planes passing overhead and one or two distant detonations. My dreams thereafter had been the sort that leave a man tense and unrefreshed in the morning.

I had barely scanned the first page of the file when one of my aides, young Corporal Howell, entered my office and saluted smartly.

'A message has come in for you, sir.' He added meaningfully, 'On the blue phone.'

I was well aware that particular telephone number was known to only a select few. 'A message from whom?'

'The caller didn't say, but he was very insistent that you go at once to this address.'

He handed me a piece of paper and I recognised the location at once. I pushed aside the stack of reports and stood up. 'Fetch a car, please, Howell, and drive me there.'

Howell saluted again and hurried to obey the order.

Minutes later we were headed directly to Traill's bookshop in Mayfair, which was owned by my American friend John Scantlebury Blenkiron, who used it as a front for his secret intelligence activities. I had seen little of him since my return from France, and even at Sandy's funeral he had stayed well in the background, emerging only to offer comfort to Sandy's widow Barbara, who was also Blenkiron's niece. I was well aware that in the eyes of our enemies he was a marked man and so had to be circumspect in all his movements.

As soon as we pulled up, I leapt from the car and felt my stomach lurch in shock at the horrifying sight. The bookshop had been utterly destroyed by a German bomb and in its place was a pile of shattered rubble. Somewhere under that heap would be the collapsed remains of the secret inner room where I had more than once met with my old friend to plot and plan. The breeze kicked up handfuls of charred pages from the burnt books and sent them twirling through the air like dead leaves. The area had been roped off and through a haze of dust I saw the rescue workers picking their way through the mound of bricks and mortar. It was clear from their weary movements and gloomy expressions that they held out no hope of finding anyone alive.

People passing in the street had witnessed so much destruction, and some of it much worse, that they scarcely spared a glance for this latest evidence of the ongoing enemy assault. One thin figure, however, stood alone on the other side of the road, his hands buried in his pockets, his eyes fixed upon the desolate scene. I recognised him at once as the austere clerk who looked after the shop and served as Blenkiron's first line of security.

I dismissed Howell, telling him I would make my own way back to Whitehall. Then I approached the grim watcher. He recognised me at once and shook his head in glum resignation to the unkindness of fate.

'Henry, isn't it?' I said by way of greeting.

He nodded. 'A sad day, sir, a very sad day.'

I glanced over at the ruined bookshop and scarcely dared give voice to my fears. 'Mr Blenkiron?'

'He was working late last night, sir, at his confidential business. He would surely have been in his inner office when the bomb fell. I have been to his apartment to check, and he never returned home.'

Contemplating the shattered building, I clenched an

angry fist. It seemed impossible that the enemy could be so precise in their bombing, and yet Blenkiron had long been a prime target for them. There was something not right about this, I felt, some sense of a deeper plot at work that made me uneasy.

I was stirred from my suspicions when Henry directed my attention to a café at the end of the street. 'Might I suggest, sir, that we share a coffee, a sort of toast to Mr Blenkiron's memory?'

This invitation from so austere a man was as welcome as it was unexpected and I readily agreed. The thought of going back to my office to work my way through an endless stream of complex reports did not appeal. In my present state of grief and frustration, my judgement was likely to be seriously impaired.

There were only a few customers in the café and none of them paid us any attention as we entered. The clatter of plates, the low murmur of conversation and the sharp hiss of a heated urn brought a comforting sensation of domesticity into this most solemn of mornings.

Henry directed me to be seated at a small wooden table while he fetched our beverages. He returned with two cups of hot black coffee which he set down as deftly as a waiter at the Ritz. Straightening, he appeared strangely hesitant to be seated when I waved him to the empty chair. 'Perhaps we can share a few reminiscences,' I suggested.

Henry answered with a strange expression on his hollow-cheeked face. 'I don't think that will be necessary, sir.'

I was quite baffled by this response, and then I heard a familiar sound behind me. It was the riffling of a thumb being drawn over the edge of a deck of cards and it immediately jogged an image in my memory.

The recognition prompted me to turn about sharply towards an adjacent table. Here I saw a large, stout man in an overcoat toying with a well-worn pack of playing cards. His features were initially concealed beneath the brim of his fedora, but now he looked up to reveal a face that, despite the lines of age, still retained that cherubic quality I knew so well.

'Blenkiron!' I gasped under my breath.

I was so relieved and delighted to see my old comrade alive, it was all I could do not to leap up and embrace him. I realised that his apparent death must be part of one of those devious schemes he was so fond of devising, and that the last thing I should do was draw attention to him.

With a mischievous twinkle in his lazy eyes, John Scantlebury Blenkiron hoisted up his substantial bulk and transferred it to the seat opposite me, bringing his coffee with him. Henry had already vanished without a sound.

My old friend laid the playing cards to one side. 'I got through five games of solitaire waiting for you to show up,' he drawled. 'Here, let me sweeten that a bit.'

He pulled a hip flask from his pocket and added a dash of brandy to each of our cups. 'I know it's still early enough for the birds to be wiping the sleep out of their eyes, but this is in the nature of a farewell toast.'

'I'm just relieved it's not a wake,' I said as we clinked cups and took a swallow. The bitter taste of the coffee was indeed much improved by the added ingredient. 'So the bomb . . .'

'. . . was an explosive I set myself before sneaking out the back way. Let's face it, it's pretty much how my detractors would have wanted me to go, blasted to smithereens by one of their five-hundred-pounders.'

'I suppose it was you who made the phone call that brought me here,' I guessed. 'I must say it was a bit of a filthy trick, giving me a turn like that.'

'It was,' Blenkiron acknowledged, 'but it guaranteed that anybody keeping watch on the shop to make sure I was dead would have taken your reaction as confirmation that I was a stone goner. I flattered myself that my friendship rides high enough in your estimation for my decease to hit you pretty hard.'

'I should say so,' I agreed ruefully.

'So you'll appreciate that I've kept your period of mourning to a bare minimum. Though I do need you to keep up a glum show for everybody else's benefit. The fewer souls who know I'm walking around like Lazarus, the better.'

2

A SURPRISING INVITATION

'But Henry was in on the trick all along,' I surmised.

Blenkiron indulged in a low chortle. 'Sure, but that stony face of his never gives anything away. Take my advice and never play poker with that gent.'

I tapped the side of my cup. 'You said this was in the nature of a farewell toast.'

He took a swallow and smacked his lips. 'You know better than anyone, Dick, that over the years I've done our enemies more than a few bad turns. Now that the gloves are off they've been itching to pay me back in spades, so it seemed like a smart move to make them think I've shuffled off this mortal coil.'

'And where exactly are you shuffling off to?'

'Well, not to Buffalo,' he joked. 'I'll be on a flight to Washington tonight. Mr Roosevelt wants to pick my brains about how things stand here in Europe. He's also mighty interested in any notions I have about stiffening up the security of our own country.'

'You're going to be a very busy man,' I predicted.

'Just like you, Dick. I hear they've loaded you with a job as a heavy thinker too.'

'That just goes to show how fallible the military mind can be.' I laughed.

Blenkiron scrutinised me through narrowed eyes. 'It suits a fellow of my bulk well enough to just settle into an easy chair and put his brain through its paces, but I know it doesn't sit well with a man like you.'

I gave a grunt of resignation. 'You know what those sheafs of reports are like. It takes the patience of a saint and the eye of an eagle to pick out whatever's worthwhile in them.'

'Well, if you're getting restless, I may have something for you.' He slid an envelope across the table to me. On it was typed my name: *Major-General Sir Richard Hannay*.

As I laid a finger upon it, I felt a tingle of excitement, as though whatever was inside carried a perceptible electrical charge.

'Is this another job?' I enquired.

'It's an invitation,' Blenkiron replied. 'What you choose to do with it is up to you. I'm sorry I won't be here myself to see it through, but I do have a parting gift.'

He picked up his deck of cards and laid it down in front of me beside the mysterious envelope. The pack was frayed and worn and held together with a rubber band, and yet I was touched by the gesture.

'Are you sure you can get by without them?'

'It's time I picked up a fresh pack. After all, I need to look my best when I meet the President.'

I scooped up the cards and turned them over in my hand, recalling how calmly my friend had played out a hand of solitaire as he explained to the German spymaster von Schwabing how he had exposed and overturned his whole network.

'I appreciate this, John, I really do. I'm sure they'll bring me luck.'

'There is that,' said Blenkiron. 'But even more important is this: whenever I find myself stymied, I play out a few hands. It relaxes the mind, so that any inspiration lurking about down there will rise to the surface. It's a trick that's served me well.'

'I'll remember that,' I assured him. If Blenkiron was sending me off on another mad jaunt, I was quite sure I would need all the inspiration I could muster after being out of action for so long.

He swallowed the last of his coffee and dabbed his lips with a folded kerchief. 'Maybe now and then you'll play out a hand or two just to remember your old friend John S by.'

'I'm sure I shall. And I fully expect us to meet again. In this world,' I added emphatically.

Blenkiron rose to his feet with a sigh. 'I'd better get moving. I've got a few last pieces of business to put to bed before my flight.'

He leaned over and we shook hands, wishing each other the best of luck.

'It'll be safer if we leave separately,' he advised. 'Henry will be on watch outside to make sure neither of us is followed.'

As he walked out of the door, I was conscious of the sincere hope that this would not be my last meeting with my wise and cunning friend. After a long pause I picked up the envelope and slit it open with my pocket knife. Inside was an embossed card which read as follows:

You are cordially invited to tonight's meeting of the National Antiquities Council. 9.00 p.m. British Museum.

It was signed by hand *C. Stannix*.

It was a very unusual invitation, to be sure, and on the face of it suggested little to do with the sort of intrigue

I associated with Blenkiron. However, I had heard of the National Antiquities Council some time back under interesting circumstances. I knew it provided cover for a number of activities that had little to do with historical artefacts. Moreover, though I had met Christopher Stannix only once, that name was enough to persuade me that this meeting would have little to do with the museum's usual line of business.

I had been wondering for some time if I had one last adventure in me. It looked as though I was going to find out.

My old friend Charles Lamancha had pointed Stannix out to me during the drinks that followed Sandy's funeral two years ago. Lamancha himself was a member of the War Cabinet, with special responsibility for the supply of munitions to our forces.

'That chap Christopher Stannix is an intriguing fellow,' he had told me, indicating a modestly dressed figure who was currently declining a refill of his whisky glass. 'Whatever official post he holds is hidden behind a thick hedge of code words and cover names, but he pops up from time to time to coordinate operations between the intelligence services and the military.'

'He looks ordinary enough,' I observed.

'Even so, a lot of important people reckon he's got one of the sharpest minds in the country,' Lamancha assured me.

Whether or not Stannix had been aware that he was the object of our hushed conversation, we had somehow caught his eye and he had made his way directly towards us. He was a tall man whose broad brow suggested a large brain behind it. The dark grizzled hair, worn longer than was fashionable in these circles, further enhanced his sage-like appearance.

'Lamancha,' he greeted my friend. 'I hear you have your hands full keeping the steel supply moving.'

'There's never as much as we need, Stannix,' Lamancha responded. 'I don't think you've met Richard Hannay.'

'No,' said Stannix, offering me his hand. 'But I believe all of us owe him rather a lot.'

I gave him my left hand, as my right arm was in a sling from the bullet I had taken in France. When we shook, his grip was firm and friendly, but part of him seemed to remain withdrawn, as though being kept in reserve for another day. After a few minutes of inconsequential talk, he had made his apologies, saying he was being called away to an urgent meeting.

'I am very pleased to have met you, Hannay,' he said on departing. 'One day I may have need of your services.'

I reflected on that brief conversation as I arrived at the site of our appointment. The British Museum was certainly one of the last places I would have expected to meet Christopher Stannix again. I climbed the stone steps and crossed the shadowy portico to the front entrance. The building had the imposing, almost sacrosanct appearance of an ancient Greek temple, an effect I was sure was quite deliberate.

I rang the doorbell and after a few moments was admitted by an elderly, grey-whiskered attendant with the stiff bearing of a former army sergeant. He examined my invitation then touched it to the peak of his cap by way of a salute. 'You'll be Mr Hannay then. If you'll follow me this way, sir.'

The great halls he led me through were always impressive, but now, with no visiting crowd and only the barest selection of items on display, it felt as though we were walking through a series of echoing subterranean caverns. The scaffolding erected to repair bomb damage added to the rather derelict look of the place. The few stone carvings and modest display of flints and coins were set against framed reproductions of more impressive exhibits and photographs of major archaeological excavations, like the recent find at Sutton Hoo.

'I'm surprised there's anything left behind here at all,' I commented. 'I thought everything had been shipped out to safer locations.'

'It's true that all the really valuable stuff is packed away in underground quarries in the middle of God knows where,' my guide affirmed, 'but when they tried to close the place down in thirty-nine there was such an uproar they decided it would be better for public morale to keep her open – as a reminder of our heritage, so to speak. I suppose it's part of what we're fighting for really.'

'When your back's to the wall, it's a good thing to remember the history you have behind you,' I agreed.

'Not that there's much to be inspired by among this lot,' said the attendant, casting a disdainful eye about the vast room we were passing through. 'Mostly it's duplicates of better quality stuff that's in storage. Some of it's even fakes.' He suppressed a low chuckle. 'The fact is, a lot of folk around here have taken to referring to all this as the Suicide Exhibition. Because it's expendable, you see.'

'Yes, I understand.'

'Personally,' he added, 'after all the hits she took in the Blitz, I'm just glad the old lady's still standing.'

Presently we entered a dimly lit back passage where he led me to a door that bore the plainly printed words *The National Antiquities Council*. 'I'll leave you here, sir,' said the attendant. 'I believe you're expected.'

The door opened easily and I found myself in a large, brightly lit office. It was furnished very simply with only a few photographs of the temple at Hathor and the Pyramid of Giza by way of decoration. The walls were lined with filing cabinets and at the far end of the room Christopher Stannix rose from behind his neatly organised desk to greet me.

'Glad to see you've got the use of your arm back,' he commented as we shook hands.

'I won't be doing any fast bowling,' I said, 'but it's working well enough.'

I accepted his offer of Scotch and soda and we sat facing each other across the desk in mutual scrutiny. In the two years since I had last seen him, Stannix had taken on the round shoulders of a man perpetually hunched over documents and plans, and the wrinkles around his eyes were evidence of long nights of anxious concentration.

'I hope you're not planning to send me off to dig for tombs around Cairo,' I joked. 'I hear things are pretty hot down that way at present.'

Stannix smiled thinly. 'Archaeological expeditions and the transportation of antiquities provide an excellent cover for a variety of intelligence activities. I suppose you've already guessed that.'

'I assumed as much.'

He leaned forward across the desk, both hands cupped around his glass. 'Then you won't be surprised that I haven't invited you here to talk about historical relics. The fact is, I believe we have a strong mutual interest in the fate of the island of Malta.'

3

THE RED HAWK

———

I could tell that Stannix was waiting for my reaction. Though my heart had skipped a beat at the mention of that island, I was determined to remain impassive.

'My son is stationed on Malta,' I responded evenly. 'I'm sure you're aware of that.'

'So, I take it you will be personally invested in the fate of the island.'

'You put it very mildly. I've hardly thought of anything else for months. I know the place is taking a terrible pounding with no sign of relief.'

Stannix nodded soberly. 'It's the most heavily bombed patch of earth on the entire planet, which demonstrates how much store the Axis forces set by capturing it.'

'I understand the situation.' I raised my glass and waved it from left to right. 'We have Gibraltar at the far west of the Mediterranean and Alexandria at the opposite end, with Malta in the centre holding it all together.'

'As you implied yourself, Hannay, Rommel's been making things pretty hot for us in North Africa, and we've only been able to hold out because of our planes and ships operating out of Malta. They've wrecked enough of his supply lines to keep the fight even, at least. But if Malta should fall, the Med will become Hitler's private lake, surrounded by the Germans and their allies.'

'Is an invasion imminent, then?' I hunched forward in concern, thinking of Peter John caught in the middle of a Nazi assault.

'After the heavy losses he suffered during his conquest of Crete, Hitler's not keen to repeat the experience with a direct assault on Malta. Instead, the island has been subjected to a ruthless and protracted siege with the object of starving it into submission.'

'I assume we've been making every effort to get supplies through.'

'Of course. But the Germans have been regularly bombing Malta's airfields to make them unusable, and destroy planes on the ground, so we can't provide adequate air cover for incoming convoys. The few ships that do make it through with food and fuel are as often as not bombed in the harbour before they can even unload.'

I took a deep swallow of my drink. 'You paint a very bleak picture, Stannix.'

'Without spare parts and fuel the aircraft will be grounded. Without food the people will starve.' He set aside his glass and rubbed his face with both hands. It was clear to me that he was getting by on very little sleep. 'Unless we can engineer a miracle, by the end of September Malta will have no option but to surrender.'

The prospect was so personally horrifying to me that finally my emotions boiled over. I shot to my feet and slammed a hand down on the desk. 'Look, if there's anything I can do, anything at all, then send me right now. I'll do whatever you want if it will help bring my son home safely.'

The words tumbled from my lips unbidden, and I was aware that the most primitive of moral instincts – to protect one's kin at any cost – had completely possessed me, overriding all other considerations.

Stannix was momentarily taken aback by my impassioned outburst but quickly regained his composure. He gestured to me to be seated again and spoke in a slow, measured voice, intended to assuage my heated feelings.

'As it happens, we are working on a miracle. The sort of miracle that consists more of ships and aircraft than of prayer. Not that I'd say no to the Almighty if he feels like lending a hand.'

Taking a calming breath, I lowered myself back into the chair and fixed my gaze upon him. 'Tell me about it.'

'We're putting together an operation code-named Pedestal, which, with a bit of grit and a huge helping of luck, will allow us to supply the island long enough to turn this thing around. But it's taking time, and meanwhile we're playing a pretty weak hand. It is absolutely vital that Malta holds out until the convoy arrives.'

'No doubt the Germans are just as aware as we are that things are at a crisis point.'

'You're absolutely correct. Whether they've got wind of our plans or they've just anticipated them as an obvious move, they've started acting with some urgency to find a way to crack Malta before our Pedestal convoy gets there.'

'You said they were reluctant to launch an invasion. What else can they do?'

'I can only think they mean to exploit some weakness we haven't guessed at, and strike a sufficiently damaging blow to our defences to enable an assault by sea and air. We've been picking up enemy messages which, as far as we can decode them, mention two specific things in relation to Malta. One is the phrase *der rote Falke*. Does that mean anything to you?'

'The red hawk?' I translated. 'It could be a code word for almost anything – an aircraft, a weapon, or even a person.'

'Yes, that's as far as we've got with it. The other is something more solid – the name Dr Armand Lasalle.'

'I can't say I've heard of him.'

'He's French, of course, and was a pretty big noise in the field of archaeology, particularly as concerns the Mediterranean.'

'An archaeologist? I have heard rumours about Hitler sending off expeditions in search of historical artefacts.'

'Yes, usually something that will back up his claims for the historical superiority of the Aryan races. Sometimes it's a search for some ludicrous symbol of power, like a magic spear. Crazy nonsense, of course, but what else can you expect from a madman?'

'Given that most of that is rot, what makes this business with Lasalle something different?'

'It seems the Germans are trying to find Lasalle in the belief that he personally has the key to taking down Malta.'

'That sounds unlikely.'

'I agree, but if the Germans are taking it seriously, so must we. The last thing we want is to be caught napping. As far as we're aware Lasalle has pretty much fallen off the face of the earth; disappeared while following up some obsessive quest of his own. Fortunately we do have a lead we can follow.'

'What would that be exactly?'

'For a couple of years in the thirties Lasalle was teaching at Oxford. While there he formed a close friendship with a fellow academic, Professor Lucius Owen. We believe they have stayed in touch and Owen may be able to offer a clue to Lasalle's current whereabouts.'

'I hope it's not too forward of me to ask how I fit into all this.'

That brought a smile to Stannix's tired features. 'We want you to go and see Owen, find out what he knows, and if there is a trail, to follow it until you find Lasalle.'

I felt a familiar tingle of excitement at the prospect of leaving my stuffy office behind and being once more on the forefront of the action.

'I'll go, of course, Stannix, but I do have to ask why me? Surely you have younger operatives you could send on a job like this.'

'Not as many as you might think, and none with your experience. There's a thick file on you in Whitehall. Half of it reads like some wild adventure story, with you as the dashing hero.'

'I think if you read closely you'll see that any success I've achieved has been the result of sheer stubbornness and an excess of good luck.'

'However it was achieved, you've got the results where others have fallen short. We both know that this might turn out to be a wild-goose chase and that the Germans are grasping at straws, but if it isn't, if they really are on the track of some weapon or other that can smash Malta, then we need a man who will see the search through to the very end – a man who's as personally invested as you.'

'It strikes me that if the Germans stumble upon this connection between Owen and Lasalle, they may get on the trail themselves.'

'They do still have their sympathisers in this country, it's true – the ones who were prudent enough not to display their affiliation openly when we were locking up those who were being a mite too gleeful about the prospect of an invasion.'

'Yes, I ran into some of that sort on my last assignment.'

'Well, they still represent a real danger. And worse – we have reason to believe that one of Germany's most accomplished agents is on the loose here in England. He goes by the rather dramatic name of Ravenstein, and under a number of ingenious disguises has engineered kidnappings, assassinations and acts of sabotage in several countries before the war. Now he's in our back garden, like a viper lurking in the undergrowth.'

I couldn't help being intrigued by this description of my potential opponent. 'Do you have any more information on this Ravenstein other than the fact that he is clearly very capable?'

Stannix paused before answering. 'We believe he was one of the original Black Stone gang that you had such a big hand in breaking up just before the last war. Somehow he slipped through the net, only to reappear a few years ago.'

'The Black Stone,' I murmured, recalling how it was their activities that had first propelled me from a life of discontented boredom into a career of intrigue and danger. 'I thought we'd seen off the last of them.'

'You might say,' Stannix suggested, 'that this assignment gives you the chance to finally mop them up for good.'

I sat back and drummed my fingers on the arm of my chair, all too aware of the heavy responsibility I was taking on. 'Look, all that stuff you've read about me makes me sound a lot more capable than I am. I had allies back in those days: Peter Pienaar, Sandy Clanroyden, Blenkiron – all of them gone now.'

'Of course I don't expect you to take on all this by yourself. I've already activated your team.'

I gave him a quizzical stare, wondering who on earth he could be talking about. 'My team? I'm afraid I don't follow you. What team is that?'

'Why, those Scottish chaps, of course.'

'You mean the Gorbals Die-Hards?'

'If that's what they call themselves, yes. Two of them are already on Malta ready to support you when you get there. The other two will catch up with you as soon as they can.'

Those four young men had their origins in the rougher parts of Glasgow, but they had been adopted by a retired grocer named McCunn who had financed their education and set them on course for a future that would otherwise have been denied them. They had done courageous service during the affair of the thirty-one kings and had actually saved me from a watery grave. I felt faintly encouraged to know that I would have them by my side, though it was news to me that those in Stannix's circle regarded them as my team.

'Until they show up,' I said, 'I had better get on the trail right away. You say that this Professor Owen is a don at Oxford. Is that where I'll find him?'

'Not any more. He retired some years ago to pursue his own private research. He's been in a wheelchair for the past three years following a dreadful fall while climbing in the Alps. He has a cottage in the village of Chaffly Fields in Devon where he lives with his housekeeper. Here's the address.'

He slid a slip of paper towards me. I gave it a quick glance and placed it in my pocket. 'I'll take a train first thing in the morning.'

Rather than hail a cab or take the Tube, I decided that a long walk home would give me time to absorb all the information I had received from Stannix and contemplate what lay ahead. In a world where anyone's days might be numbered, the fact that this mission might take me to Malta and give me the chance to embrace my son once more was all the encouragement I needed to see the matter through.

I remembered how my heart had lurched when we were informed that Peter John's Spitfire had been brought down over Kent by a Messerschmitt 109. Crash-landing in a ploughed field, he had mercifully survived with only a broken leg and a fractured wrist.

When I visited him in hospital he gave me a crooked grin and brandished a tattered copy of *The Pilgrim's Progress*. It had been bequeathed to me by my old South African friend Peter Pienar, who was also a pilot, and after whom we had named our son. The book had brought me luck during my dangerous journey through France, and I had passed it on to Peter John in the hope that it would bring him the same good fortune.

'I'm pretty sure you're right about the luck, Dad,' he said. 'The fact that I had this little volume stuffed inside my flying jacket kept my ribs from snapping. All praise to good old John Bunyan!'

'It's a fine book,' I said, sitting on the bedside and clapping him affectionately on the shoulder.

'To be perfectly honest, I haven't read a word of it,' he confessed. 'I just like to have it with me because it makes me feel as if you and old Peter are right at my side when I'm up there.'

As soon as he had recovered from his injuries, Peter John was back in the air, helping to complete the task of thwarting Hitler's plans for invasion. Now he and his comrades were in Malta, defending that island with the same dedication and courage they had displayed in the skies over England.

Such were my reflections as I walked down the blacked-out streets, thick clouds shrouding the stars as though they were playing their own part in concealing the great city against aerial attack. I had left behind those areas where clubs, cinemas and public houses drew people in to well-lit interiors where they could dance and revel and forget for a while the ghastliness and austerity of the war. The streets I now found myself on were lined with shuttered businesses and banks, so there was little reason for anyone to be abroad in these parts.

There was a low hum of traffic in the distance and the occasional car rumbled past me, its headlights hooded in accordance with the blackout regulations. Yet I had gradually become aware of steady, cautious footsteps some distance behind me. Glancing over my shoulder, I could detect no movement in the all-pervading gloom, but whenever I paused in my stride, those far-off footfalls also came to a halt, waiting for me to resume. I was left in no doubt whatsoever that someone was following me.

4

FOOTSTEPS IN THE DARK

———

Whoever was trailing me surely meant me no good and I was not prepared to be followed all the way to my own doorstep, wondering when the unseen stranger intended to strike. I determined to take the initiative. Quickening my pace, I rounded a corner and drew myself tightly into the concealment of an estate agent's doorway, gambling that my pursuer, fearing he had lost contact with me, would hurry to catch up. All I required of him was one moment of carelessness when I might pounce from my hiding place and force him to give an account of himself.

Minutes passed in such silence that I could hear clearly the ticking of my watch, but there was no resumption of the pursuing footsteps. I finally decided that the mysterious stranger had abandoned the hunt and that there was no further purpose in my concealment. The rest of the way home I continued to keep a sharp ear open, but heard nothing more.

Had it just been my imagination? No, my instincts in matters of hunt and pursuit had always been sound. I was quite certain that I had been followed, but for some reason my shadow had now melted back into the darkness and dogged me no longer.

When I got home to our house in Great Charles Street and let myself in, I expected to find the place cold and deserted. Instead I spotted a light filtering into the hallway from the open door of the sitting room. I was immediately on alert, for our housekeeper Mrs Broyles would be long gone, and I was still keyed up over those mysterious footsteps.

I slipped through the doorway and saw a figure seated in the large armchair by the fireplace, an elbow resting on the leather arm, chin cupped in a small palm. My apprehension was replaced at once by a leap of delight, for it was Mary, her eyes closed in slumber. The gentle touch of the lamplight seemed to melt the years away and I saw her again as I had first spied her in the garden of Fosse House.

She was a young girl then in the blue dress and apron of the VAD – the Voluntary Aid Detachment – with the white cap perched upon her hair of spun gold setting off the most beautiful face I had ever beheld. I soon learned that, in addition to her medical duties, she was also a trusted agent of military intelligence and was to act as my contact. I believe I loved her from that very first meeting, though it was only after many adventures that we were finally united for good.

Though my movements were silent, her eyes opened at my approach and a smile touched her lips. 'Dick! I was wondering if you would ever get home.'

I bent down and kissed her. 'If I'd known you were here, I would have run all the way. I wasn't expecting you for at least another week.'

'Well, we just got back from the Highlands, where the girls were going through commando training,' Mary explained. 'Learning how to operate in rough country, living off the land, and how to handle weapons and explosives.'

I gave a low whistle. 'How are they taking to it?'

'Better than you might think, especially considering the instructors include some rough types. I'm quite sure one or two of them are jailbirds. Once we got back to Foxton, I insisted everyone get at least one day off before moving on to the next stage of their training. That's going to be how to withstand interrogation, so they definitely deserve a break. When I left they'd cracked open a bottle of gin and put on some jazz records.'

I sat down on the arm of the chair and took her hand. 'There are people who would be outraged if they knew we were training women to be saboteurs and assassins.'

'When we started recruiting, I can assure you that we found no shortage of volunteers ready to risk their lives.' Mary frowned and rubbed her temple as though to soothe away the beginnings of a headache. 'This next week will be especially hard on them. They have to learn to stick to their cover stories, even when deprived of sleep, drugged, threatened or beaten. If they can keep up a convincing show of innocence it might just save their necks. One mistake, on the other hand, could mean a prison camp or worse.'

'It seems to me,' I said, 'that you need a break just as much as your girls do.'

Mary nodded sleepily. 'I've got twenty-four hours to myself before I take the train back to Norfolk. Do you suppose we could go on a picnic or something tomorrow and forget about the war for a little while?'

I felt a tug in my gut at having to disappoint her. 'I'm afraid not.' I laid her hand down in her lap and stood up. 'I've just come from the British Museum of all places, where I had a meeting with a chap named Stannix, who's pretty high up in the intelligence community. He has a job for me that I have to start on first thing.'

Mary leaned back in her chair and sighed. 'Does it always have to be you, Dick?'

'In this case it does,' I said. 'You see, there's a chance the fate of Malta might be at stake.'

At this she sat up abruptly, all trace of fatigue instantly banished. 'Tell me about it.'

I gave her the details of my discussion with Stannix and she listened closely, as though receiving an agent's debriefing. When I was done, she stood and nodded emphatically.

'You have to go, of course. No matter how much of a long shot it might be, anything that might help Peter John get home safely is worth the chance.'

I placed my hands lightly upon her shoulders and drew her near. 'Once this business starts rolling, you know, there's no telling where it will lead or how long it will take.'

Mary touched a finger to my lips and spoke softly in my ear. 'No more talking shop. Let's go to bed and pretend that tomorrow we're taking a boat to see the swans at Henley.'

The early train to Devon left little time for me to enjoy any sort of breakfast, so Mary raided Mrs Broyles's pantry and whipped up some meat paste sandwiches for me to take along. I thanked her with a parting kiss and took a cab to Paddington station. I was soon ensconced in a railway carriage with two tittering girls (I never did discover what they found so amusing), a somnolent clergyman and a chatty young soldier.

Feeling about in my pockets for my pipe, I found Blenkiron's deck of cards. Drawing them out, I removed the rubber band and leafed through the pack as though it were some arcane book. Silly as it seems, I was struck by the fancy that if I were to fan the cards in the correct way, Blenkiron would magically appear, like a genie from the Arabian Nights, and bless me with sage advice and visions of the future.

When the cards caught the eye of the soldier, he saw a less mystical use for them and soon we were passing the time in a few hands of Twist. By the time we reached the small station at Waynford, he had won five shillings off me.

From the station I took a cab out to Chaffly Fields. On the way there, the driver evidently felt some obligation to fill me in on all the local news, which included an accident at a local tin mine and a visit from one of the more obscure members of the royal family. He was in the middle of an anecdote concerning a prize bull's frightening rampage at the annual farmers' show as we approached a narrow bridge leading to Chaffly Fields. All of a sudden, as if from nowhere, a bakery van appeared, rushing across the bridge towards us at high speed. With a vehement curse the cabby swerved sharply to the left just in time to escape a head-on collision. He shook an angry fist at the van as it roared past and disappeared over a hill.

'Did you see that?' he exclaimed indignantly, driving on to the bridge. 'He must think he owns the road, racing down the middle like that. It's a bloody disgrace!'

He then calmly resumed his narrative and by the time we reached our destination I was fully apprised of all the most fascinating events in the area.

When he dropped me off, I gave him a generous tip in appreciation of his saving us from a nasty accident, and he set off in search of a fresh set of ears for his inexhaustible supply of newsworthy tidbits.

The professor's two-storey thatched cottage of white stucco was fronted by a vegetable garden and a pair of apple trees. The sign over the door gave the name of the place as Ithaca, further proof, if any were needed, that it was owned by an archaeologist. When I rang the bell the door was opened by a plump lady of middle years whose silver-flecked brown hair was tied up in a tight bun. Her apron bore evidence of recent kitchen activity.

'I'm here to see Professor Owen,' I informed her. 'He should have received a telegram telling him to expect me.'

'Oh, yes, you'll be Mr Harrow.' She smiled pleasantly and ushered me inside.

'That's Hannay,' I corrected her as she closed the door behind us.

She touched a pondering finger to her lower lip. 'I was sure the professor said Harrow. But there it is, just one more misunderstanding in a troubled world.'

She led me down the hallway into a spacious study with a set of French windows overlooking the garden. The room was furnished with a number of glass cabinets filled with antique pottery, two leather armchairs and a broad desk covered in scholarly clutter. The walls were decorated with the memorabilia of years spent travelling the world: wooden masks, ceremonial weapons, religious icons and exotic hangings.

Professor Owen was over by a bookcase stuffed with leather volumes. He turned his wheelchair to face us.

'Thank you, Mrs Withers,' he said, dismissing the house-keeper. 'You will be Mr . . . Hannay, is it?'

Between his shaggy mane of grey hair and his long, tapering beard, a pair of sharp, intelligent eyes gazed at me through the thick lenses of his spectacles.

'That's right, professor. As the telegram said, I'm here under the auspices of the National Antiquities Council.'

He rolled his wheelchair towards me and I leaned forward so we could shake hands. His grip was firm and friendly but something about him struck me as odd.

'I know of the council, of course, and the excellent work it does in the fields of archaeology and anthropology. But what do they – what do *you* want with me?'

'Actually, professor, it's a friend of yours we want to talk to. Dr Lasalle.'

'Lasalle? Armand Lasalle? I haven't seen him in years, you know.'

'No, but you have remained in touch with him?'

'Yes, I receive the odd letter from some far-flung out-post, sometimes occasionally asking me to check through my own research to provide him with some obscure piece of information.'

'And where was he when you last heard from him?'

The professor stroked his beard thoughtfully. 'Let me see now . . . It was some months ago. He was organising a dig in eastern Turkey. Along the shore of the Black Sea, it was.'

'And do you know what it was he was looking for?'

'I couldn't say, but he did ask me for information regarding Trebizondian reliquaries. My primary area of expertise is the history of Greece and Byzantium.'

'No doubt that is why you named your cottage after the island kingdom of Homer's Nestor.'

Owen's eyes twinkled behind his glasses. 'Just a little joke, you know. I promise you, I don't really think of myself as a king or a famous warrior.'

'Could I perhaps see your letters from Dr Lasalle?'

'Oh no, I don't keep such things.' Owen chortled. 'There's quite enough clutter around here, as you can see.'

He waved a hand at the books and papers piled high upon his desk.

'Here, let me pour you a sherry.' He rolled over to a small table where there was a decanter and a set of crystal glasses. 'Yes, Turkey would be your best bet if you want to find old Lasalle. I can probably give you some names to contact there.'

He poured the drink and handed it to me. I took one swallow and set the glass aside.

'There's just one more thing I'd like to ask you, professor.'

'And what would that be?'

I stood directly before him and fixed him with a hard gaze. 'Who you really are.'

'Mr Hannay, I have no idea what you're talking about.'

'A man who's been pushing himself along in a wheel-chair for three years would have developed calluses on his hands by this time, and when we shook hands I could feel that yours palms were quite smooth.'

'Come, Mr Hannay,' he objected with an expression of perfect innocence, 'you surely don't believe . . .'

'And then there's the name of the cottage,' I pressed on.

'Ithaca was the kingdom of Odysseus, not Nestor. The real Professor Owen would certainly have corrected my error.' I seized him by the shoulders and drove him back until the wheelchair slammed up against the wall. 'So if you're not Professor Owen, who exactly are you?'

A ROGUE FOR HIRE

The impostor's features blanched and he shrank back fearfully. 'All right, all right, there's no call to get rough.' He tried to push himself up out of the wheelchair, proving beyond any doubt that he was a fake. I shoved him back down, ready to take a swing at him should he try to fight his way out of his predicament.

'I'll ask you once more,' I said through gritted teeth, 'who are you?'

He raised his open palms to shoulder level to demonstrate his complete surrender. 'I'm just an actor, I swear it,' he whined. 'I wasn't doing any harm. There's no crime in pulling an innocent jape.'

There was no trace of a Welsh accent now. Instead he sounded like a Londoner imperfectly imitating the diction of a country squire.

'Your name?' I pressed him, and clenched a fist to show that I meant business.

'My name's Peregrine Fowler,' he declared swiftly, pulling his chin back out of the firing line. 'Yes, I'm sure you've never heard of me, but I played at Stratford once. My Osric was highly praised in the local press.'

There was something so pathetic about that last assertion I hadn't the heart to menace him any further. Lowering my fist, I said, 'Well, you're not playing in *Hamlet* now. What on earth do you think you're up to?'

'I was hired to do a job, that's all. There not being

much work around, I'd be a fool to turn down fifty guineas. I thought it was all supposed to be a lark, nothing more than that.'

'Hired by whom?' I pressed.

The actor shrank back even further, his hands fluttering nervously. 'He said his name was Ralston, for whatever that's worth. Now I think back on it, there was something shifty about him. He had a funny accent.'

The mention of an accent seemed to confirm that this deception had been planned by the German agent Stannix had warned me about. 'So tell me, and be straight about it, where is the real Professor Owen?'

Fowler abruptly slid his hand under the blanket. Instantly on the alert, I seized his arm and snatched the blanket away. As Fowler recoiled with a startled cry, I saw to my chagrin that he had merely been reaching for a packet of cigarettes stuffed between his leg and the side of the chair.

'There was no call for that,' he protested. 'No call at all. I just need to calm my nerves. You've shaken me up no end.' He pulled out a cigarette, struck a match and lit it with trembling fingers.

'I thought you might be reaching for—'

'A gun?' came a voice from behind me.

I turned to see that the harmless-looking housekeeper had a revolver trained on me. Her mouth was twisted into an expression of sheer malice, quite out of keeping with her earlier character.

With a wave of her hand she motioned me to step away from the man in the wheelchair. As I did so, he got to his feet and pulled himself up to his full height. I was quite certain now – and far too late – that this was Ravenstein in one of his notorious disguises.

'Really, Hannay, I expected you to be a bit sharper.' He smiled in cold amusement. 'I mean, Peregrine Fowler. Surely that was what they call a dead giveaway.'

His voice was no longer that of a Welsh scholar nor of a minor actor putting on airs. Now his words had the cold, precise edge of the ruthless professional.

'Not at all,' I said. 'I congratulate you on coming up with a name few men would have had the gall to invent. That made it all the more convincing.'

'Of course, I might actually have hired an actor to stall you here. I've done that sort of thing before. But before crossing to England I read your most interesting dossier and I was intrigued. I wanted to meet you face to face.' He touched a finger to his false beard and added, 'So to speak.'

He moved smoothly to the housekeeper's side and took the gun from her, keeping it pointed steadily at my midriff.

He motioned me to back away until there was a good fifteen feet between us. I was pressed between the discarded wheelchair and a tall wicker basket filled with odd items of taffeta and silk

'So it wasn't your intention simply to kill me?'

He shook his head in a mocking show of regret. 'Believe me, Hannay, I would have been much happier to think of you trekking through the mountains of Turkey than lying here as just another corpse in a long and bloody war. I'm afraid, however, you have made such a tidy resolution quite impossible.'

He signalled the woman to return to the back of the house. Before she had taken more than a few steps, however, her way was blocked by a lean figure who loomed in the open doorway. Waving the housekeeper aside, the newcomer pointed his own revolver straight at Ravenstein.

'If there are any dead bodies to be left behind,' he commented dryly, 'I rather fancy one of them is going to be yours, old son.'

There was a flare of anger in Ravenstein's cold eyes as they swivelled towards the intruder. The greatest surprise was mine, however, as I stared at the familiar face of my unexpected rescuer.

'Barralty!' I exclaimed. 'What on earth are you doing here?'

'At your service,' Benjamin Bannatyne Barralty responded, keeping his aim firmly fixed on the enemy agent. 'This, I take it, is one of those ill-intentioned Huns who pop up in our back yard from time to time like troublesome nettles.'

I knew from previous acquaintance that Barralty was what might be styled a rogue for hire. The last time I met him he was attempting to abduct me from a train, and he was just about the last person I would have expected to be saving my skin.

'It appears I underestimated you, Hannay,' said Ravenstein. 'You had a trick up your sleeve after all.'

'Oh, he didn't know anything about me,' said Barralty with smug amusement. 'In fact, he would probably have had a fit if he'd known I was shadowing him.'

The woman was moving slowly to the opposite side

of the room from Ravenstein, forcing Barralty to divide his attention between the two of them.

'I'd be obliged if you'd stop right there, madam,' he said with cold courtesy, 'otherwise I'll be tempted to try my luck at picking you both off.'

The woman halted and raised her hands in a placating gesture. Her gaze was fixed on her chief as if in expectation of some signal from him.

'Really?' Ravenstein addressed Barralty. 'What do you suppose the odds are that I am quick enough to shoot you and then Mr Hannay before you can do any such thing?' His pistol was aimed squarely at my heart, and I was in no doubt that his threat was a real one.

Barralty allowed himself a smirk. 'It sounds like a bit of a long shot, but I admit that I am an incorrigible gambler.'

It galled me to be a bystander in this increasingly tense standoff and I could see that each of the two men was only the slightest provocation away from pulling the trigger. For my own part, the last thing I wanted was for a gunfight to break out before I learned what had become of the professor.

'Let's everybody take a breath,' I advised cautiously. 'Ravenstein, all I want is Professor Owen, alive and well.'

'And what will you be willing to trade for that?' the German enquired without enthusiasm.

Only too late did I spot that the housekeeper had manoeuvred herself within reach of an ornamental dagger that hung on the wall in the midst of more harmless paraphernalia. In one swift motion she snatched it down and hurled herself forward.

'Barralty!'

My cry alerted him just in time to turn and swing his gun at her. He caught her a hard crack on the side of the head just as she stabbed the blade into his thigh. With a curse, Barralty staggered back and crashed into a glass cabinet, throwing up a shower of glittering shards.

Ravenstein turned to shoot him before he could recover. By sheer instinct I grabbed the wicker basket and hurled it at the German, throwing his aim so that the bullet shattered a porcelain vase a few inches from Barralty's ear.

I followed up with a charging rugby tackle that brought Ravenstein down under my full weight, knocking the wind out of him. The pistol was jolted from his startled fingers and slid away across the carpet. We rolled over and he gained the advantage, smacking a powerful fist into my temple. As I lay dazed, Ravenstein leapt to his feet, and I saw Barralty raise his gun. Ravenstein dodged the shot, scooped up his pistol and bolted out through the French windows at a desperate sprint.

6

A CLOSE PURSUIT

———

By the time I got to the window Ravenstein had leapt into a compact saloon car and was roaring off down the country road. I turned back to Barralty, who had slumped down into a seated position on the floor. He had set his revolver aside and was using a handkerchief to stem the flow of blood from his wound. Nearby the bogus housekeeper lay unconscious with a livid bruise forming on the side of her head.

'Missed the artery and only got the fleshy part,' he grunted as I joined him. 'Still hurts like the very blazes, though.'

'Look, I'll bind it up as best I can,' I said, 'but we should get you to a doctor as soon as possible.'

'I'll be fine.' He grimaced. 'You'll recall that I'm a bit of a whiz at speedy recoveries.' He glanced over at his attacker. 'I should have shot her, but I do baulk at that. Looks like she'll be out of it for a while, though.'

I fetched a handful of scarves and kerchiefs from the overturned basket and set about wrapping the ugly wound.

'The last time I saw you—' I began.

'You were throwing me off a train,' Barralty recalled ruefully.

'I was about to say, you had just pulled a gun on me.'

'Well, no hard feelings, eh? I'm the one who ended up at the bottom of an embankment with a couple of cracked ribs.'

'I should say that's the least you deserved,' I commented, tying a tight knot around his thigh.

Barralty winced and forced a thin smile. 'Fair enough. But can't we just let bygones be bygones?'

'If I recall correctly, you were in the pay of men who wanted to make a deal with Hitler.'

'That's still a far cry from working for the Nazis,' Barralty asserted. 'Look, old man, there were even people in the government who thought that was our only chance for survival. But now that the old country's proved her mettle, I can assure you that I'm batting for England just as much as you are.'

I stood up and surveyed my handiwork. It was not the first time I had been forced to dress a wound in the field, and I was confident my makeshift bandage would hold until we found proper medical attention. 'Can I ask what brought about this change of heart?'

'Not long after my bruising encounter with you, I was picked up by some determined men who wouldn't take no for an answer.' Barralty pulled out a cigarette and lit it. He took a long draw that seemed to ease his discomfort. 'In the course of a rather testing time spent in a bare room somewhere in the depths of the Tower of London, they persuaded me that it was in my best interests to shop my former associates, many of whom are now languishing at His Majesty's pleasure. After that I was offered some fresh employment.'

'And what would that be exactly?'

'Most recently watching your back, old fruit. You do have a reputation for charging headlong into the most hairy situations, and I gather that you're currently of too much value to be allowed to suffer the consequences of your own recklessness.'

'So it was you following me the other night after I left the British Museum,' I surmised.

'No, it was someone of less benevolent intent who was trailing you that night. I was the chap who was following him until I judged the moment was ripe to teach him a lesson about minding his own business.'

I thought it best not to enquire into the exact nature of that lesson.

'I'd better take a look around,' I decided. 'It's possible the real Professor Owen is somewhere in the house, bound or unconscious.'

Barralty stuck the cigarette in the side of his mouth and picked up his gun. 'You go ahead. I'll tie up Sleeping Beauty here and keep an eye out for any further trouble.'

I moved briskly through the downstairs rooms, confident that if any of Ravenstein's men were still in the cottage, he would not have fled as he did. When I stepped into the kitchen I noticed an overturned chair and some pots that had been knocked to the floor. I realised that the professor's real housekeeper must also have been replaced by an impostor.

I discovered that poor lady in an upstairs room, laid out upon a bed. She was younger and slimmer than the woman who had met me at the door. She had been bound hand and foot and gagged. She started as I entered the room and her eyes grew wide with fear.

'Don't worry, Mrs Withers,' I assured her, recalling how the false Professor Owen had addressed his companion in deception. 'I'm with the police.' That statement calmed her at once, and it was a simpler explanation of my presence than the full truth.

As soon as I had freed her, she grabbed my arm urgently. 'The professor – did they take the professor?'

I nodded, for I had found no trace of him. 'Please tell me what happened. How many of them were there?'

'Well, there was the one with the grey hair and beard. I'm sure he was in charge. Then there was a pair of evil-looking ruffians who dragged me up here and tied me up. There was a woman too.'

'Have you any idea where they might have taken the professor?'

She shook her head with an expression of utter misery. 'I wish I knew. I can tell you this, though – the two bullies arrived in a bakery van and another car pulled up right after them.'

I almost slapped a hand to my brow at the realisation that my taxi had passed the very vehicle that had been carrying off the kidnapped professor. The other car must have been the one Ravenstein drove off in.

'Listen to me,' I said. 'You have been very brave. Now, if you're up to it, I need you to call the police and tell them what happened here. But please, stay out of the study. There's an unconscious woman in there who'll be well tied up by now.'

The housekeeper's eyes grew wide. 'A woman? Who?'

'She came with the kidnappers and took your place alongside a bogus version of Professor Owen.'

The lady took a deep breath to steady herself. 'What are you going to do?'

'I have a friend downstairs' – how strange it sounded to my ears to describe Barralty as a friend – 'and we're going to give chase. If we can catch up with that bakery van, we may be able to rescue the professor.'

'Then go,' she urged. 'I'll be fine.' She added in a murmur, 'I have some brandy in the kitchen.'

I hurried back to the study, where Barralty had got to his feet and was helping himself to some cigars from a humidor on the desk. I saw that he'd made a very efficient job of tying up the senseless woman.

'They've taken Professor Owen away in a bakery van,' I told him. 'I passed it on the way here. You have a car, don't you?'

'I'll say,' Barralty responded proudly, lighting a cigar. 'She's a real beauty, parked in the orchard on the far side of the house.'

'Then let's go. With a spot of luck we might catch up with them.'

I dashed out of the front door but had to slow down to let the limping Barralty catch me up. When we reached the car, I suggested that, in view of his injured leg, perhaps I should drive.

'What, let you get your hands on my Bentley?' he retorted mockingly. 'Fat chance of that, my old egg. You leave the driving to me.'

I could see his face was pale from the loss of blood and his wound was paining him pretty badly. Nevertheless, he pulled smoothly out of the orchard and took us on to the main road.

'You see, Hannay,' he said, forcing a smile, 'I told you you could trust me at the wheel.'

'Frankly, given our history,' I reminded him, 'I'm amazed that I can trust you at all.'

'Changed times and all that,' Barralty responded with a casual shrug. 'Remember it's not so long ago the French were our dear old pals. Now their Vichy gang are tucked up in bed with the Germans. Makes my little volte-face look like a mere flip of the cards.'

For all I disliked his mercenary ways, I couldn't help warming to the rogue. He wouldn't be the first man to be recruited from the shadier side of life to do good service for his country, and by now he had certainly proved his worth.

'That van was headed south when I passed it in my taxi,' I said. 'If we go down that way we can stop and ask some of the locals if they've seen any sign of it.'

'I wouldn't advise stopping just at present,' said Barralty, glancing up at the rearview mirror.

'Why not?'

'Because somebody's coming up on our tail, and the only reason the chap can have for driving so fast is that he's trying to catch us.'

I twisted about and saw what he meant. A black Daimler was topping a hill we had just crossed and looked to be after us like a hound on a fox.

'I suppose Ravenstein might have set some of his minions on our trail,' I speculated.

'In that case,' said Barralty, 'the best thing we can do is shake them off.'

With that he gave a savage twist of the wheel that swerved us left into a narrow road. The Daimler turned to follow, though the speed of Barralty's manoeuvre had allowed us to pull ahead. Devon is criss-crossed with roads running between high hedgerows, so that parts of the county resemble an elaborate maze. It was through this maze that Barralty raced now, gripping the wheel so tightly that his knuckles stood out white.

Right and left he jerked the Bentley, but still our pursuer followed, keeping us in sight in spite of all Barralty's efforts.

'He's a persistent blighter,' the rogue grated, 'but I'll lose him or . . .'

At that moment he made a savage turn, and a patch of fresh mud flung the car into a spin. Barralty fought for control but we went front wheels first into a ditch. The two of us toppled into the dashboard and the rogue let out a stream of harsh curses.

'Quick, we need to get out before they reach us,' he gasped, throwing open his door. He tumbled out, drawing his gun, and took cover behind the bonnet of the car. I climbed out and joined him, our eyes fixed on the Daimler which had pulled up about twenty yards away.

'If they've come for a fight, we'll give them one!'

In spite of his bold words, I could see his eyes were misting over from the pain of his wound and the obvious damage the crash had done his left shoulder. He was certainly in no condition for a battle.

'Just hold your fire until we see what they want,' I advised.

The doors of the Daimler opened. Two young men emerged and immediately came loping towards us. I was as astonished as Barralty to see that they were dressed in full Highland regalia: kilt, sporran, brocaded jacket with silver buttons, right down to the sgian-dubh tucked into the sock.

'What in God's name is this?' Barralty wondered. 'A new Jacobite rebellion?'

One of the young men was a burly, red-haired fellow, the other dark-haired and wiry. I recognised them both at once as my old friends from the Gorbals Die-Hards – Dougal Crombie and John 'Jaikie' Galt.

Dougal, a journalist by trade, was now an army officer on special assignment to the Ministry of Information. Jaikie had followed a number of adventurous occupations around the globe before becoming an agent of the National Antiquities Council, for whom he gathered a range of valuable intelligence while acting as a guide to various archeological expeditions.

Barralty was drawing aim on the two Scots, but I laid the flat of my hand on the barrel of his pistol and eased it down. 'Don't worry. They're on our side.'

'If that's true, then you've got some dashed queer allies, old bean,' he remarked with a baffled shake of the head.

'I've no idea why they've come dressed for a ceilidh,' I conceded, 'but believe me, you couldn't have two better men at your side.'

7

THE JACOBITE RISING

———

We came out from behind the cover of the car to meet the two Scots.

'Are you all right, sir?' Jaikie asked me with a mistrustful glance at my companion's lowered gun.

'I'm afraid when we saw we were being followed, we assumed the worst,' I explained. 'But I'm very glad to see you, Jaikie. You too, Dougal.'

'And we're right relieved to see you, sir,' said Dougal. 'We were told to get to that Chaffly Fields cottage and join up with you as soon as possible. We'd stopped just in sight of the place and were checking it out through field glasses before moving in – just to be canny, you see.'

'That's when we saw you and this chappy jump into a car and speed off,' said Jaikie. 'We thought we'd better catch up and let you know we were here.'

I introduced my young friends to Barralty as he slipped his gun back in his pocket. He cast a quizzical eye over the colourful pair. 'I suppose you're on your way to London to stick the Young Pretender on the throne and that's why you're decked out like Harry Lauder.'

'Not exactly,' said Jaikie. 'We've hot-footed it here straight from my wedding. That's what we were dressed up for.'

I was delighted to hear the news. 'So you've married the splendid Miss Alison Westwater at last. No more shilly-shallying.'

Jaikie had the grace to look abashed. 'Yes, sir. I finally took your advice about not waiting until the war was over.'

'And mine,' Dougal interjected. 'I've been telling him for years to wife that woman.'

'But surely your honeymoon . . .'

'Will just have to wait,' Jaikie stated firmly. 'Alison understands. She's that sort of girl.'

'I'll wager this isn't the first time you've been torn away from her side at short notice,' I guessed.

'That's true, sir,' Jaikie acknowledged, 'though never before under circumstances quite so extreme.'

'You be sure to bring her back a right bonnie present,' Dougal suggested. 'That will make things up fine.'

'I expect seeing her husband safe and sound again will be present enough for the new Mrs Galt,' I said.

'I hate to interrupt this nuptial chit-chat,' said Barralty, 'but don't we have business to attend to?'

'Right,' I agreed. I explained the situation to the two Die-Hards as briefly as possible.

'It looks like your car's done for,' Jaikie observed.

'Aye, we'd better use ours and get after that baker's van of yours,' said Dougal.

Barralty slumped over the hood of the Bentley and moaned, more from pain than the sad condition of his car.

'I'm all in,' he grunted. 'The crash wrecked my shoulder and I can barely stand on this wounded leg. I reckon I should have let you drive after all, Hannay.'

'You'd best stay here and flag down some help,' I advised. 'If we don't move now, they might have Owen out of the country by nightfall.'

Barralty took out his pistol and handed it to me. 'Here, you'd better have this.'

I tucked it inside my jacket. 'Thanks for your help, Barralty. I can see that against all the odds you really are on the side of the angels now.'

'Don't spread that ugly rumour around,' he groaned. 'I do have my rascally reputation to think of, you know.'

I was following my two young friends to the Daimler when a farm lorry loaded with potatoes came rumbling down the road. I flagged it down and spoke to the ruddy-faced driver.

'We've had a bit of an accident here. Can you get my friend there to a doctor?'

'There be an infirmary at Eccleford,' the farmer offered. 'I could drop him thar for you. He's been through the wars proper from the looks of him.'

'I don't suppose you've seen a bakery van anywhere around here?' I asked without much hope.

'Happen I have,' he replied. 'She were flying along at a right snort back tha-ra-ways on the Westerhock road.'

I could hardly believe my luck. The trail wasn't cold after all. 'Back that way, you say?'

'That be right. She were rushing it on down to Fellbone's old mill. I can't reckon as why. The place has bin empty for years now excepting for the mice.'

He gave me directions which I managed to follow in spite of his thick Devon accent. I thanked him for the information and scrambled into the back of the Daimler behind Jaikie and Dougal. 'I've got a lead on our baker's gang. Let's go.'

As we pulled away I relayed the farmer's directions to

Jaikie, who was at the wheel. As we motored along the narrow country roads, I couldn't help remarking, 'I'm delighted to have you on board, of course, but you aren't exactly inconspicuous in your wedding finery.'

'The message from Mr Stannix emphasised the importance of joining you as soon as possible,' he said.

'So we dashed out as soon as the last speech was over,' said Dougal.

'Dougal was supposed to grab the bag with a change of clothing—'

'But in the rush I clean forgot about it.' Dougal's face was flushed with embarrassment.

'If you think we're dressed up to the nines,' Jaikie went on, 'you should have seen old McCunn. With his feathered bonnet and his basket-handled sword, he looked like the war chief of all the clans.'

'If Hitler caught a glimpse of him,' Dougal declared with confidence, 'he'd be shaking in his jackboots seeing what he was up against.'

Dickson McCunn, I knew, was the retired Glasgow grocer who had taken the band of street boys under his wing and become a surrogate father to them all. As well as sharing some of their adventures, he had seen to their education, opening doors of opportunity to them they would otherwise have been denied. To this day all the Die-Hards idolised him as a figure of epic stature, a man whose character and wisdom were worth more than gold, and I hoped that one day I would have the opportunity to meet this legend and tell him what a magnificent band of heroes he had created.

Peering forward, Dougal tapped his friend on the

shoulder. 'Here, that must be what we're looking for.'

Jaikie pulled over and we stared out to where Dougal was pointing. In the distance, at the end of a long dirt track, was the distinctive outline of a windmill with a copse of beech trees beyond it. We could just make out that there were two vehicles parked next to the mill on a sward of dry grass.

'Better not get spotted,' Jaikie muttered. He reversed to the edge of a hollow in the ground, which was clearly used by the locals as a place to tip their rubbish. It was filled to the brim with old mattresses, rusted cans, broken chairs and other debris.

We got out and climbed a wooded rise from which we could observe our target while remaining concealed. Through a pair of field glasses which the lads had brought along I could see that the motionless vanes were weather-worn and riddled with holes. While the building itself was intact, the door and windows were empty holes and the walls overgrown with brambles and ivy.

One man was stationed outside, making a slow, leisurely circuit of the mill. I watched as he paused by the entrance to light a cigarette before resuming his patrol. There was no way to approach without being spotted by him, and there was no telling exactly how many other men Ravenstein might have inside. I reasoned that for the sake of secrecy he was likely to have kept his group to a minimum. The odds were good that there was only one other besides the sentry and Ravenstein himself.

'If they do have Professor Owen in there, we'll have the devil of a time getting him out,' I said.

I passed the glasses to Dougal, who gazed through them

and grimaced. 'Well, sneaking up on them is right off the table. In these outfits they'll see us coming a mile off.'

Jaikie rubbed his chin thoughtfully. 'Maybe we can use that to our advantage.'

'How do you mean?' I asked.

'I mean that instead of trying to be stealthy we make as big an uproar as possible. Make a real stramash of it.'

'This sounds like one of Yowney's plans,' Dougal grinned. 'They're always about raising a racket.'

Thomas Yowney, now an army chaplain, had since boyhood been regarded by his fellow Die-Hards as the strategic genius of the group. During our mission in Paris, I had seen how the others all turned to him when some clever scheme was required to effect a rescue. In his absence this role had fallen to Jaikie, whose wits were no less sharp.

'I think I've spotted the very thing we need,' he said, trotting down the slope to the hollow and its trove of discarded rubbish. He returned with an old bucket that was pitted with rust.

'I think I see what you're getting at,' said Dougal, with a glint in his eye.

'That's more than I do,' I confessed. 'That bucket isn't much of a weapon.'

'That's not the point,' said Jaikie. 'Do you remember when we were on our way to Paris, Peter told us a story about a soldier with a bucket?'

Peter Paterson was the fourth of the Die-Hards. I cast my mind back, trying to recall the anecdote he had related. 'Wasn't it something about a soldier wanting to milk a cow in the middle of a battle?'

'That's right,' Jaikie confirmed. 'That story's given me an idea that might be half daft, but might just work.'

After a quick discussion we formed a plan which depended on a good deal of stealth on my part, and quite the opposite from my two young friends.

8

GLASGOW BELONGS TO ME

The man on guard outside the windmill was royally bored. He made a circuit of the building every few minutes as he had been ordered to, but he'd rather be inside to see what they were doing to the old codger they'd taken prisoner. His pale, hollow-cheeked face crumpled in displeasure as he thrust his hands into the pockets of his shabby grey jacket and kicked a stone away with the toe of one scuffed brogue.

All at once his tedium was broken by a raucous singing in the distance. He squinted up the rough track to where two colourfully garbed figures were weaving their unsteady way in his direction while caterwauling some guttural gibberish. Another man emerged from the windmill with a jaunty step. His round florid face lit up in amusement.

'Here, Gilson, what's that godawful row?' he enquired.

Both men had the hard-eyed look of professional criminals. They had been recruited from the London underworld and they were the sort who were prepared to do any kind of dirty work so long as the pay was right.

The bored sentry pointed a finger at the approaching strangers. 'Take a gander, Sweeny. It looks like the circus is in town.'

Sweeny took a moment to light a cigarette then peered through the smoke at the distant figures. It was clear now that the newcomers were dressed in the most extravagant Scottish regalia.

'Bloody Jocks,' Gilson growled. 'What do they look like in that clobber!'

He moved to reach inside his jacket for his gun, but the other man stopped him. 'The boss doesn't want any gunplay unless we're pushed to it. From the look of those jokers, they're so blind drunk they'll probably stagger past without even clocking us.'

The two Scots were close enough now for the words of their song to be audible if not actually intelligible.

'I belong tae Glasgow, dear old Glasgow toun,
There's something the matter wi' Glasgow
'Cos it's going roond and roond.
Ah'm only a common all working chap
As anyone here can see,
But when I hae a couple o' drinks on a Saturday
Glasgow belongs tae me.'

On the last line their voices rose in grotesque parody of an operatic chorus.

One of the new arrivals was a brawny, red-headed character who looked as though he could hold his own in a fight, at least on a better day. His companion, by contrast, was pale and dark-haired and of such a slight build you would believe a strong wind could knock him over, especially in his current state of inebriation. With buttons unfastened, their sporrans askew and one sock higher than the other, the pair of them looked very much the worse for wear.

The two stumbled towards the windmill, their vacant eyes raised up in wonder at the great, tattered vanes. The smaller man had a rusty bucket dangling from his right hand which clanked with every wobbly step.

Sweeny halted them with an upraised hand. 'Hold it there, Tam O'Shanter, this is private property.'

'Who the hell are you anyway?' Gilson asked with a sneer.

The big redhead drew himself up and straightened his sporran in a tottering show of dignity. 'Sergeant Dougal Crombie, third regiment, First Caledonian Rifles,' he declared. He swung his arm upward in an exaggerated salute that threw him off balance, so that his slightly built companion had to steady him before he fell over.

'And I'm Corporal Galt,' said Jaikie. 'You'll have to make allowance for the sergeant as he's a mite fu'.'

'I've had no more than a couple o' nips, corporal,' Dougal asserted. 'I'll not have you slandering my good name in front of these gentlemen.' He punctuated this defence of his honour with a loud hiccup.

'And what are you kilted wonders doing here in a civilised country?' Sweeny enquired scornfully.

'Ah, well, we're bivouacked back there,' Dougal explained, thrusting an unsteady thumb back in the direction they had come from, 'back in . . . what is it? Upper . . . ?'

'Is it no Nether something or other?' Jaikie wondered.

'Aye, well anyway,' Dougal continued, 'they're shipping us off to Egypt tomorrow.'

'That's how we've been having a few farewell toasts,' said Jaikie.

'Aye, pretty soon we'll be sipping cocktails wi' Cleopatra,' Dougal declared proudly. He made an exaggerated show of daintily downing an invisible cocktail, then both Scotsmen convulsed with crude laughter.

Sweeny took a draw on his cigarette and blew a puff of smoke into the faces of the Scots. 'In that case you'd best clear off out of here and scrounge up some suntan oil.'

'That's no what we're lookin' for,' said Jaikie with a corrective wag of his finger.

'That's right,' Dougal confirmed. 'Have ye no got a cuh about here?'

Gilson stared at the young Scot as though he were an exhibit at the zoo. 'A koo? What do you mean, a koo?'

'A cuh, man,' Dougal insisted. 'Ye ken, *mooooo!*'

'Aye, *moooo!*' Jaikie repeated after him.

'A cow?' exclaimed Sweeny. 'What in God's name do you want a cow for?'

'Why, tae mulk her, man!' Dougal bashed Jaikie's bucket with the back of his hand to emphasise the point. 'The boys back at camp are needing some mulk for their porridge. They're close tae mutiny for the lack o' it.'

'There's squads of us out searching for some mulk,' Jaikie added.

'And if we're the first back wi' a fu' bucket,' said Dougal, 'why we'll be the cock o' the walk.'

'So tell me, man,' said Jaikie, leaning unsteadily towards the two gangsters, 'do ye have a cuh or no?'

'Does this look like a farm, Jock?' said Sweeny disdainfully. 'Can't you see it's a windmill, and a pretty tatty one at that?'

'Aye, it does look like a shambles,' Dougal agreed. 'So what are you doing here?'

'We're here to . . .' Gilson groped for some explanation of their presence.

'We're here from the council,' Sweeny supplied for him. 'We're inspecting the old ruin before it gets demolished.'

Dougal's features contorted painfully as though he were calculating a difficult problem in mathematics. 'So what yer sayin' is, ye dinna hae a cuh?'

'That's about the size of it, Jock,' said Gilson.

'That's very sad news,' Jaikie lamented with a sorrowful shake of his head.

Sweeny tossed his cigarette on the ground and crushed it under his heel. 'Listen, Rob Roy. Like we said, we're busy here, so shove off and peddle your Highland fling someplace else.'

Jaikie turned to his companion in evident befuddle–ment. 'But, sarge, if they dinna hae a cuh, what am I to dae wi' this bucket?'

'I ken exactly what you should dae wi' it,' Dougal replied in a voice that had suddenly dropped its drunken slur.

In response, Jaikie swung the bucket in a swift motion, smacking Gilson on the side of the head with a loud clang. At the same moment, Dougal lashed out a beefy fist that connected forcefully with Sweeny's astonished jaw.

During all this uproar, I was darting through the gorse and bracken that covered the ground to the rear of the windmill. The distraction my friends had cooked up had kept the sentry from making his usual circuit, leaving this rear approach unguarded at least for the moment. There was always a chance someone inside might take a glance out back.

As I drew closer, I saw an empty window frame that would gain me entrance so long as the two resourceful young Scots could keep up their diversionary charade and no alarm was raised. I could hear their drunken voices loud and clear as they insisted on directions to the nearest cow. They were taking a considerable risk, for I had no doubt that Ravenstein's henchmen were armed and quite prepared to kill at the first indication of trickery.

As soon as I reached the windmill, I pressed my back hard against the mossy stonework to one side of the empty window. I waited long enough to be confident that I had so far not been spotted, but that wasn't to say that this rear entrance was not in plain view for anybody inside.

Crouching down low, I peered over the sill into the dimly lit interior. The only light came from a few holes in the ceiling and the faint glow of an oil lantern somewhere out of my line of sight. Carefully I stood up and climbed inside, dropping to one knee with Barralty's pistol in my hand. The rough stone floor was scattered with dust and crumbled fragments of plaster that had fallen from above.

In the centre of the room was the great millstone, jammed into position apparently and blocking most of my view. A faint nimbus of yellow light was filtering round the edge of this obstacle from a lantern somewhere beyond. Keeping low, I began to work my way sideways, seeking a glimpse of what lay on the other side. The first thing I caught sight of was a small round table upon which were laid out various medical instruments, including a syringe and several small vials. I recognised them as some of the standard items of forced questioning.

'You may as well come out, Hannay,' came a voice. 'I know you're there.'

Keeping to the shadows as best I could, I worked my way around until I could see Ravenstein and his prisoner.

Professor Owen was slumped unconscious on a bare wooden chair. Only the rope that was tied around his chest and under his arms kept him from sliding off. Standing directly behind him was Ravenstein, with a wide-brimmed hat, tinted glasses and a black scarf obscuring his features. His gun was in his hand, the barrel pressed pointedly against the prisoner's temple.

Ravenstein spoke again in a voice that was almost eerie in its lack of emphasis. 'Now keep your distance and throw your gun away, or I'll blast the professor's brains out.'

9

A DEVIL'S BARGAIN

In reply, I raised my gun, pointing it directly at the German, who slouched behind the prisoner to provide himself with a shield. I drew myself into the cover of a barrel while keeping my aim steady. I had already learned that Ravenstein was far too dangerous for me to let my guard down even for an instant.

'I'm afraid the professor is all you have to bargain with,' I told him. 'You'd be a fool to shoot him.'

'You too would be a fool to shoot,' Ravenstein stated coolly. 'No matter how accurately you aim, you can have no guarantee that I will not pull this trigger with my dying breath and put an end to the professor's life.'

At that moment Jaikie and Dougal entered, armed with the guns they had lifted from the unconscious gangsters outside. As soon as they took in the scene, they dodged into cover behind a pair of wooden beams.

'Are you all right, sir?' Jaikie called out to me.

'I'm fine, Jaikie,' I answered. 'I think we've caught up with our rat, thanks to your ingenuity.'

'Ah, you think because you have reinforcements, that gives you the advantage,' said Ravenstein.

'I can't say your position looks any too strong,' I observed. 'You'd be well advised to lay down your gun and surrender. You can be assured that you'll be treated fairly.'

'An enemy spy treated fairly?' Ravenstein responded

sceptically. 'No, I don't think your British justice will extend to the likes of me.'

'In that case, we're at an impasse, and I believe we are better placed to wait it out.'

Ravenstein shifted the position of his pistol so that I could clearly see his finger tensed on the trigger.

'Hannay, I know that what you want above all is the professor here safe and unharmed,' he said. 'I assure you that he will make a swift and full recovery, but not if I put a bullet in his scholarly brain.'

'If you do that, then you will die immediately after him,' I promised.

'I do not think so,' Ravenstein suggested pensively. 'You see, as soon as I have fired the fatal shot, I will instantly drop my gun and raise my hands in surrender. I do not believe for a moment that you will shoot an unarmed man, especially not one who is rendering himself your prisoner.'

'I thought you were wary of our justice.'

'Oh, I am quite the resourceful fellow. No prison has ever held me for very long.'

'Assuming neither of us wants that fatal shot to be fired, then, how are we to resolve this situation? Or are we going to stand here all day pointing guns at each other?'

'It is actually very simple. If you give me your word that you will let me go free, I will lay down my gun, make my way to my car and drive off with no further bother to you.'

'And what about those two men outside?'

Ravenstein gave an unconcerned shrug. 'Do with them what you will. They are merely hired hoodlums and their lives are of no value to me.'

'I wouldn't trust him as far as I could throw him,' Dougal growled, taking an aggressive step forward.

In response Ravenstein pressed his gun directly against Professor Owen's temple. 'Another inch will cost his life,' he promised.

I held up my hand, warning my young friends to stay back and leave this to me.

'I am losing patience, Hannay,' said the German. 'Take your choice now – accept my terms and let me go, or have a dead professor on your hands and me as your prisoner. A prisoner, I assure you, who is expert at every form of escape.'

It was one of the hardest choices I have ever had to make, but I knew if I waited too long, Ravenstein would make the decision for me and pull the trigger. He appeared quite confident that an immediate surrender on his part would prevent me from shooting him, and he was equally confident that if I gave my word, I would be honour bound to keep it.

Ravenstein's eyes bored at me as intensely as the fateful ticking of a clock.

'Very well,' I conceded at last. 'If you lay down your gun, you have my word that you will leave here unharmed.'

The German indicated my two friends with a tilt of his head. 'Make your clansmen swear to it too.'

Jaikie and Dougal's reluctance was only too obvious. 'You need to swear,' I told them. 'It's the only way to ensure the professor's safety.'

Jaikie nodded brusquely towards the German. 'You have our word as well.'

'Aye, we'll let you go, you skulking rat,' Dougal agreed sourly.

Gingerly Ravenstein laid his pistol on the ground and backed away with both hands upraised. 'I am so glad we are all gentlemen here. Until the next time.'

With a nod of farewell, he walked briskly out of the door. I rushed directly to the professor and Jaikie joined me to examine the unconscious scholar. As we raised his eyelids to inspect his pupils, he groaned and began to stir, pulling groggily against the rope that bound his waist.

Dougal stood at the open doorway, watching Ravenstein depart and chafing at the restraint he had been placed under. 'Do we really need to keep our word to a man like that?' he asked me.

'Yes, we do,' I affirmed. 'If we cast aside our honour, we're no better than the men we're fighting.'

At the sound of a car starting up, he rubbed his jaw ruefully. 'I suppose you're right at that. But next time we'll not let him off so easy,' he added in a grim undertone.

10

THE KNIGHTS' SECRET

––––––

Within the hour we had the professor safe in his bed at home with a local doctor tending him. He had drifted in and out of consciousness on the way back from the windmill, but when he spoke it was only to mutter a few incoherent phrases. Thanks to the doctor's careful attentions, he slowly began to emerge from the influence of the drugs Ravenstein had injected into him. Here and there his body bore the marks of more brutal methods of interrogation, but the doctor assured me he had suffered no permanent harm.

Owen's white hair was sparse in comparison to the wig Ravenstein had worn and his beard more closely trimmed. He was a slight figure and the recent ordeal had clearly taken its toll on him. It was a further hour or two before he began to recover full consciousness, at which point the doctor took his leave with our sincere thanks.

As soon as she was granted permission, Mrs Withers entered the bedroom with a laden tray and set it down by the bed. She fussed over the professor for a few minutes, pressing a cup of tea and a jam tart on him before consenting to leave. Her bogus counterpart was already in a police cell along with Ravenstein's two hired gangsters. So far they were all remaining tight-lipped, though I doubted that Ravenstein would have made his hirelings privy to any important information regarding his plans.

Finding myself alone at last with the aged scholar,

I sat down at his bedside as he laid down his empty cup with a weary sigh.

'Professor, I know you've been through a rough time,' I began, 'but I would appreciate it if you could answer a few questions.'

'I'll try my best,' he said, 'but to be honest, it's all a bit of a blur. Shock, I suppose.'

'That and the drugs.' I leaned forward in my chair with my hands clasped before me. 'The man who abducted you was a German agent and he was after important information.'

The professor shook his head with a wince of pain. 'Well, I never thought of myself as the sort of fellow who was likely to get tangled up with a nest of spies.'

Before we could continue, Dougal and Jaikie entered.

'You're looking a lot better, professor,' Jaikie commented encouragingly.

Owen forced a fleeting smile and waved a dismissive hand.

'Speaking of recovery,' said Dougal, turning to me, 'I nipped down to the infirmary to check on your friend Barralty. He's coming along fine, but they're keeping him in for a couple of days. To be honest, sir,' he added, 'he strikes me as a bit of a shady character.'

'Sometimes in wartime that's the sort of man we need,' I said. 'I would certainly have been in a tight fix if he hadn't shown up when he did. And Jaikie, did you make that call to Stannix?'

'I did, sir. From her description, his people have identified the fake housekeeper as a woman named Ilsa Quinn. She's a Nazi sympathiser who went to ground as soon as her friends started being rounded up. It seems Ravenstein knew how to contact her and put her to use.'

'Even if she knows anything of value,' I reflected, 'it will take a long time to prise it out of her. The two men are just hired muscle, of course. Which brings us to you, professor. Can you remember anything that could put us on Ravenstein's trail?'

Professor Owen rubbed his broad brow, as though to soothe an ache. 'All I can remember is being asked lots of questions, though I can only recall it through a haze, as if it were simply a horrible dream.'

I realised that I needed to give him some sort of lead. 'Did he ask you about Dr Lasalle?'

Owen closed his eyes and his brow furrowed. 'Yes, yes . . . Armand. He was most interested in his whereabouts.'

'And what did you tell him?'

'That I can't remember for the life of me. Only that Armand Lasalle's name came up again and again until it was ringing in my ears like the tolling of a bell.'

'Perhaps it would be easier if you just told us what you know about Lasalle,' Jaikie suggested.

'Well, I haven't seen him for years,' said Owen with a shrug. 'Not since we were colleagues at Oxford. We have continued to correspond, as well as one can in the current conditions.'

'What was his area of interest?' I asked, hoping for something specific that might move our mission forward.

'Oh, I would say he is a leading expert in the history of the Mediterranean, from the expansion of the ancient Greeks right up to modern times. However, he has always been especially fascinated by the Knights of St John.'

'And who might they be?' Dougal wondered.

'Their full title was the Knights of the Hospital of St John of Jerusalem, often known as the Hospitallers,' Professor Owen explained. His eyes brightened and his voice grew more animated now that he was discussing a familiar subject area. 'They were among the most stalwart guardians of the Christian strongholds in the Holy Land following the early success of the Crusades. With the fall of the Crusader kingdoms they retreated first to Cyprus then to the island of Rhodes and finally to Malta.'

'Malta!' The exclamation burst from my lips in a sudden surge of excitement, as though a blaze of sunlight had suddenly broken through the clouds of obscurity. Here at last was some clue to the Germans' interest in tracking down a French academic as part of their war plans.

'Yes, they made the island into a fortress,' said Owen, 'and in 1565 they held it in a long and bloody siege, defeating the massively superior forces of the Ottoman Empire. In fact they are often referred to as the Knights of Malta.'

'The island is under siege again now,' Jaikie reflected. 'Could there possibly be some connection?'

His thoughts were working along the same track as mine, though I was still baffled as to how the history of an ancient order of knights could have any impact on a modern war of tanks, artillery and aircraft.

Professor Owen was slowly succumbing to fatigue, his eyes drooping and his head sinking into his pillows. I placed a hand on his arm to summon him back from his slumber.

'Professor, I feel sure that this business of the knights

is somehow the reason the Germans are searching for Lasalle. Is there any more you can tell us?'

Owen's eyes flickered open and he pursed his lips in thought. 'Well, Armand did have a notion, not that I gave it any credit, that among the records of the great siege there were veiled references to a weapon of some sort.'

'A weapon!' Dougal growled.

I exchanged astonished glances with my Scots friends before pressing the professor further.

'What sort of weapon?'

'Oh, it's probably nonsense,' said Owen with a shake of his head, 'a mistranslation, but Armand was convinced that some means had been devised to overcome the strategic superiority of the sultan's forces and that some- where this weapon still existed. He even entertained the rather absurd notion that he might be able to find it.'

'Does that mean then that he is actually on Malta right now?' I asked.

'No, as I recall it was his intention to travel to North Africa and pursue his researches there.'

'Africa?' I murmured. 'That seems rather odd.'

'It appeared that way to me also,' Owen agreed. 'In fact, he needed some more information from the Hospitaller archives in Oxford.'

'What information was that?'

'He wanted someone to track down any possible mention of something called the red falcon.'

My pulse quickened. 'The red falcon, you say?' I had to believe that this referred to the same object as the 'red hawk', which had turned up in Stannix's intercepted German communications. 'Have you any idea what that might be?'

'None at all. As you can tell, my mobility is limited and my health not the best, so I passed Armand's enquiries on to Dr Adriatis.'

'And who might this Dr Adriatis be?' Jaikie asked.

'A pupil of mine at first and then my assistant while I was teaching at Oxford.' Owen smiled at the memory. 'We both worked with Armand Lasalle on some of his researches.'

'It sounds as if we need to catch up with this chap Adriatis,' said Dougal. 'Where can we find him, professor?'

'I'm afraid I must correct you there,' said Owen. 'Dr Adriatis is a Greek lady, Dr Karissa Adriatis.'

'A woman mixed up in this?' Dougal commented grimly. 'I can't say I like the sound of that.'

'Professor, where can we contact Dr Adriatis?' I asked, returning to Dougal's original question.

'She teaches at Clement College, Oxford,' Owen replied. 'But you won't find her there.'

'Nothing's happened to her, I hope,' Jaikie interjected anxiously.

'No, nothing like that,' said the professor. 'It's just that a couple of days ago she told me she was planning to join Armand in Africa. In fact, she had just arranged a passage to Gibraltar.'

My two young friends and I stared at each other.

'Gentlemen,' I said, 'it seems we're going on a journey.'

PART TWO
THE ROCK

11

HMS *GIBRALTAR*

————

'Better hang on tight, chaps,' Archie advised, calling to us from the cockpit. 'When the Levanter is blowing in from the Med, which seems to be most of the time, things tend to get a bit choppy up here.'

Even as he spoke the plane gave a lurch. Dougal stifled a curse, while at his side Jaikie fastened his fingers tightly around the edge of the fold-out bench, his Virginia cigarette clenched between his teeth. On a motorbike racing at high speed through heavy traffic or over rough terrain, Jaikie was a fearless daredevil, but in a plane flown by my old friend Sir Archibald Roylance he turned so pale he must have been willing himself not to be sick.

Seated opposite the two young Scots on my own bench, I felt none of their anxiety. I wouldn't say I was made of sterner stuff, but I had flown with Archie often enough to have lost all sense of fear. Even driving with him in his beloved Hispana was enough to turn the average passenger into a devout pedestrian, but I knew that his apparent recklessness both on the ground and in the air was merely an indication of his expertise. I had heard him liken a safe, uneventful flight to riding a sleepy old horse with no spirit.

Jaikie raised an unsteady hand to pluck the cigarette from his mouth. 'I know Sir Archibald is an old and trusted friend of yours, sir, but was he *really* the only pilot available for this trip?'

Fortunately the roar of the Whitley bomber's engines made his voice inaudible to the pilot in question and I couldn't help but smile.

'We were lucky to get him at such short notice,' I said. 'We haven't a moment to spare in catching up with Dr Adriatis, not if we hope to find Lasalle before Ravenstein gets his claws on him. Going through official channels would have wasted precious hours.'

'First we had to rescue Professor Owen,' grumbled Dougal, 'which now means we have to catch this Adriatis woman, and that's just so we can follow after that Frenchman. It's as if we're chasing after a hare that's always got a head start on us.'

'You're a Scotsman, Dougal,' I encouraged him. 'That means hunting's in your blood.'

We had flown out of Portsmouth that morning and, steering clear of occupied France, had rounded the Bay of Biscay and followed the line of the Spanish coast. The five-hour flight had brought us at last within sight of Gibraltar, much to the relief of the passengers.

Archie's co-pilot Toby appeared to have developed a method of steadying his nerves by sucking intently on peppermint lozenges, of which he kept a plentiful supply stuffed into the pockets of his flight suit. Toby was now on the radio arranging our approach while Archie guided us down.

Swinging round the southern tip of Gibraltar, we banked left, granting us a spectacular view of the east face. From this side it looked as though a giant axe had sheared away half of the ridge, leaving an unscalable cliff to challenge any hostile visitors approaching from the

Mediterranean. Only a couple of small sandy bays showed any sign of welcome.

The whole peninsula was dominated by that great jagged spine of ancient limestone which some have likened to a crouching lion, its face turned watchful and defiant towards the mainland of Spain. Less than three miles long by three quarters of a mile wide, the Rock nonetheless was the most legendary bastion of British imperial power.

Following a complete circuit of Gibraltar, we swooped in from the west towards the single airstrip that ran across the narrow isthmus connecting the Rock to General Franco's Spain. Gazing down through my window, I could see the British fortifications and gun emplacements. They looked daunting enough to give second thoughts to anyone attempting to cross over with hostile intent.

'Brace yourselves, chaps!' Archie cautioned us. 'We're going down pretty steeply.'

Toby engaged the retractable landing gear as we neared the ground. A jarring touchdown was nothing new for Archie and this one was no exception. The wheels bumped twice, causing us to lurch in our seats, before Archie pulled up sharply and the engine shut down with a loud cough. The relief on the faces of my fellow passengers was clearly visible as we disembarked and I half expected them to kneel down and kiss the solid safety of the runway. The air hit us at once, hot and dank, with a light swirl of dust. Luckily my two young friends had retired their Highland splendour in favour of some plain, light civvies, otherwise they would have been poleaxed by the heat.

'Sorry I can't go along with you on this jaunt,' said Archie, hauling off his goggles and squinting in the harsh light. 'Got to refuel and head back home. They've got a fresh bunch of young chaps coming in for flight training. They need my expertise to help whip them into shape before unleashing them on the Jerries.'

'Archie, if they learn to fly like you,' I assured him, 'I'm quite sure they'll put the fear of God into the Luftwaffe.'

Making our farewells to our pilot, my two young friends and I walked past the rows of Hurricanes and Spitfires jamming the airfield. At the bottom edge of the field was an area where an array of cars and trucks was parked. Out of the midst of them emerged a well-built, middle-aged fellow in naval whites and shorts. He waved as he walked up quickly to meet us.

'You'll be General Hannay, sir? We've been expecting you.'

'Glad to meet you. This is Mr Galt and Captain Crombie.'

The seaman tipped back his cap and whipped off a jaunty salute. 'CPO Sidney Stark at your service, sir.'

'A chief petty officer?' said Jaikie. 'Should you not be on a ship?'

'I was on a ship,' Stark answered with a grin, 'but after a bout of Lassa fever I was reassigned to shore duty. Not to worry, though; there's plenty here to keep me busy.'

'I'm glad to hear it, chief,' I said, taking an immediate liking to the man. His pleasantly homely face was open and honest and there was a relaxed confidence in his manner.

'My car's over here, if you'll come this way, sir,' he said, leading us off. 'You know, Gib's a lot like a ship when you think about it. That's the bow up there, tethered to the Spanish coast, and down there's the stern, facing towards Morocco. I like to think I'm doing my bit to keep the old girl shipshape.'

'Where exactly are we going?' asked Jaikie.

'I'm to take you to the Convent,' answered the chief.

'The Convent?' Dougal echoed. 'We're not bunking down with a bunch of nuns, are we?'

Stark uttered a low chuckle that sounded like water gurgling down a drain. 'No fear of that, sir. It used to be a convent belonging to the Franciscans, but since the Brits got here it's been the governor's official residence.'

As we drove off, I could see on the crags above us the tower, terraces and battlements of the old Moorish castle, a reminder that Gibraltar had once been a jumping-off point for the Islamic invasion of Spain. The road took us past the expansive harbour where cruisers, frigates and destroyers were moored along with a variety of merchant vessels. These I supposed would form part of the relief convoy Stannix had referred to under the code name Pedestal.

On our left broad blocks of three- and four-storey buildings rose in tier upon tier up the lower slopes of the Rock. They were every shade of tawny and white, topped with distinctive red roofs. Between them ran narrow streets and steep stairways that plunged vertiginously down from the heights. There was a notable absence of women and children on the streets, most of the civilians having been evacuated some time ago in anticipation of a bloody attack, should Spain enter the war against us. Instead, soldiers of the garrison were very much in evidence, especially those sporting the distinctive dark green plaid of the Black Watch.

After a short drive we pulled up in front of the Convent. Whatever remained of the Franciscan religious house had been built over in a Georgian style with touches of Victorian architecture. The entrance was shaded by a marble portico over which a Union Jack fluttered in the warm breeze.

Once inside, Jaikie and Dougal were served afternoon tea in a downstairs lounge while I was escorted up to the office of the governor, Major-General Noel Mason-MacFarlane. We had met before at a regimental reunion and he came out from behind his desk to greet me with a friendly handshake. On the wall behind him was a detailed map of Gibraltar showing gun installations and new caves hollowed out of the rock to accommodate the expanded garrison, as well as the harbour defences and minefields.

Generally known as Mason-Mac, he had a ponderously handsome Roman head that inclined slightly to the left as the result of a car accident some years ago. He was every inch the military man both in his bearing and in his speech, and I knew from his reputation that he was only completely comfortable in the company of other soldiers, whatever their rank.

I accepted his offer of a vintage Glenfiddich and we clinked glasses.

'Well, Hannay, I've got a notion they only bring you in when something pretty big is in the offing.'

'I should think that applies to almost everything these days,' I said, savouring the fine flavour of the Scotch, 'given the desperate circumstances.'

'Yes, well I'm sure you're on one of those hush-hush jobs. I expect you can't tell me about it any more than I can tell you what's brewing down in the harbour.'

He nodded towards the large square window overlooking the bay. We both gazed down at the bustling activity below. The towering cranes were hoisting nets filled with equipment on to the decks of the ships while brawny dockers rolled fuel drums up the gangplanks.

'At a guess, I'd say a relief convoy for Malta is on the cards,' I observed.

Mason-Mac nodded soberly. 'It's certainly no secret that the place is likely to go under unless supplies reach them in the next few weeks. And as the gateway to the Mediterranean, Gibraltar has to hold firm.'

'Gibraltar has been besieged before,' I recalled, 'and I must say your defences look formidable.'

'The Spanish have some impressively huge guns lined up over on their side,' said Mason-Mac, 'and if they took it into their heads to start a bombardment, we'd be in for a rough time.'

'Then it's a good thing for us that in spite of being chums with Hitler and Mussolini General Franco's chosen to remain neutral.'

'Our chaps in Madrid are busy keeping all the important Spaniards sweet with everything from flattery to out and out bribery,' said the governor with a rueful smile. 'Of course, after the horrors of their civil war, Spain's in a ghastly state. What they want is security to rebuild and food to eat. If they were to be blockaded, it's likely the whole country would starve.'

I waved my glass in the direction of Spain. 'So those

guns out there are likely to stay silent, then.'

'Well, Hitler would dearly love to send an armoured column down through Spain to come blusting across the isthmus.' Mason-Mac flexed his shoulder like a boxer readying for a fight. 'Fortunately the Spaniards have too much pride to simply step aside and let them pass, so we've been spared such an assault so far.'

'From what I've seen at the airfield, you're well equipped for an aerial defence.'

'Those planes' primary purpose is to guard the convoys passing into the Med. We're too far from the Italian airfields for them or the Germans to maintain any sustained bombing campaign against us. Back in '40, after we'd sunk the French fleet to keep it out of Hitler's hands, some Vichy bombers showed up to take their revenge. Since then though they've stayed out of the picture. No, our danger comes from a different direction.'

He gazed down at the waters of the bay. 'If you look out over to the mainland you can see Algeciras. The Italians have set themselves up in a villa there where they keep a very expensive pair of binoculars trained on our harbour. Somehow they've managed to establish some sort of base under the noses of the Spaniards and they use it to send divers out to plant explosives under our ships.'

'That's a long way to swim.'

Mason-Mac took a moment to refresh our drinks before explaining further.

'Well, it seems one of their chaps is a bit of a genius at this underwater stuff. He's designed a two-man torpedo they can ride under the waves. It has a detachable explosive head that can be attached by magnets to the hull of a ship. We do our best to catch them with depth charges, and our own divers work like blazes to find the mines and pull them loose before they go off.'

'Perhaps Spain isn't as wholeheartedly neutral as one might like.'

'There are certainly plenty of Nazi sympathisers over there. With eight thousand workers coming across the border every day, we have to be on constant alert for spies and saboteurs. That isn't why you're here, is it, to help us weed out the bad 'uns?'

'I'm afraid not. I'm here to find a Greek archaeologist, a Dr Adriatis.'

'Adriatis?' Mason-Mac raised a vexed eyebrow. 'Well, she's here all right, and frankly she's a right bloody headache.'

12

AN ENCOUNTER WITH ARTEMIS

This comment of the governor's did not sound promising.

'How do you mean, a headache?'

'At this point we simply don't know what to make of her.' Mason-Mac made a disgruntled noise at the back of his throat. 'She arrived here aboard a Polish freighter and started making enquiries about transport to Morocco.'

This seemed to confirm what Professor Owen had already told us. 'But she wasn't able to get away?'

'When an unknown foreigner turns up on Gib trying to get into Vichy territory, it sets off a few alarms, so we brought her in for questioning. All she would tell us was that she wanted to carry out some archaeological excavation, but exactly where and with whom she wouldn't say. Some of our security chaps are afraid she might be a spy. You'll appreciate what a concern that is, so we've confined her to the Regent Hotel while we look into her background.'

'I can tell you that she did graduate from Oxford with a first class degree in history and archaeology,' I assured him, 'and I believe she is engaged in some sort of historical research.'

'I suppose you can vouch for her, then?'

'I've never actually met her, but I've been told that she has knowledge vital to our operation.'

The governor was sceptical. 'I don't see what archaeology has got to do with the war, but I suppose you know what you're doing.'

'To be honest, it might turn out to be a wild goose chase,' I confessed. 'On the other hand it could mean the difference between victory and disaster.'

Mason-Mac swallowed the last of his Scotch and set the empty glass down on his desk. 'Tell you what, then, I'll have Stark book you and your party into a couple of rooms at the Regent. You can talk to her there yourself, see if you can get more out of her than we could.'

The drive to the hotel took us to the very highest level of Gibraltar town, which granted us a lofty view out over the harbour and the Atlantic beyond. Once inside, CPO Stark left us to make enquiries on our behalf. We did not have long to wait.

'The Greek lady is out in the side garden, sir, indulging in some sort of exercise, so I've been informed,' he told us when he returned.

'You don't suppose she's out there doing calisthenics, do you?' Dougal wondered.

'Whatever she's up to, I think I'd better speak to her alone,' I said. 'From what the governor told me, she's wary of authority and has been keeping tight-lipped about whatever she knows.'

'If that's the case,' said Jaikie, 'then the sight of a whole gang of us would most likely make her close up like a clam.'

'While you find the lady, so to speak, I'll sort out your rooms and get these two gents settled in,' Stark suggested.

'Right you are, chief,' I agreed.

'One last thing, sir,' he cautioned as we parted. 'I hear she takes quite a bit of handling, so you be sure to watch out for yourself. Lay on plenty of the *por favor*, if you take my meaning.'

I gathered his advice was for me to take a gentle approach as opposed to the more pressing interrogations the archaeologist had been subjected to thus far. He even seemed to imply that my own safety was at stake. Only when I stepped out on to the lawn did I fully appreciate the warning.

The sinking sun was casting long shadows across the grass. Beyond them, thirty yards ahead of me to my left, stood an athletic young woman of middle height with a wave of luxuriant black hair pouring down her back. She was dressed in a short-sleeved blouse, khaki trousers and hiking boots, and a quiver of arrows was slung under her shoulder.

In her left hand she gripped an ashwood longbow while her bronzed right arm was flexing back on the string, her narrowed eyes fixed upon a target far off to my right. As I walked towards her she pivoted elegantly about to face me and gave the bow a full draw with the arrow pointed directly at my chest.

I stopped in my tracks and raised both hands to signify my harmless intent.

'Are you another policeman?' she demanded, with only the barest trace of an accent.

'No, I'm not a policeman,' I answered, keeping my hands up and summoning what I hoped was a winning smile. 'I'd like to think I'm a friend.'

Her head tilted quizzically. 'A friend? We shall see.'

With that she swung about and loosed off the shaft, driving the arrow directly into the gold, right in the middle of a cluster of four others.

I took a hesitant step closer. 'You are Dr Karissa Adriatis?'

Lowering the bow, she turned to face me directly. 'Of course I am. Why else would you be bothering me?'

It was impossible not to be struck by that beautiful, olive-toned face. The noble length of her nose suggested a perpetual curiosity, while her wide grey eyes bespoke the broad intelligence which drove that questing nature.

'My name is Richard Hannay,' I told her, judging it best not to mention my military rank. 'It was your colleague Professor Lucius Owen who told me I might find you here.'

'So you have seen Professor Owen. He is well?'

'He is recovering. He was abducted by German agents, though he is now safely back home.'

The girl's full mouth tightened at the edges. 'The professor mixed up with spies? Surely you are joking.'

'I'm deadly serious. I believe you may be in similar danger.'

Dr Adriatis sauntered over to the target and began pulling out the arrows one by one. Over her shoulder she asked, 'Why should I be in danger? I am a scholar pursuing innocent research.'

'Even if you really believe that, it won't protect you,' I warned. 'There are others who think you're on the trail of something very dangerous.'

'Then they are deceived by myths and legends, as many fools have been in the past.' She examined the points of her arrows then dropped them into the quiver. 'Tell me, how long do you intend to keep me a prisoner here?'

Her tone made it more of a challenge than a question.

'It's no intention of mine to make you a prisoner.' With lowered hands I made a placating gesture in the hope of softening her defensive attitude. 'I know you are on your way to meet Dr Armand Lasalle. It's important that I find him too.'

Walking back from the target, Dr Adriatis positioned herself assertively before me with one end of her bow planted on the ground, her fingers grasping the other. I had the impression that in the barest instant she could snatch the weapon up and snap an arrow into place.

She tilted her chin. 'I do not see it so. You are no scholar. Though you did not state your rank, you are quite obviously a soldier.'

Almost instinctively I drew my shoulders back. 'Yes, I have been.'

'In that case you can persuade the other soldiers to let me be on my way. Is that not so?'

'That might be possible,' I conceded mildly, 'but first you have to tell me exactly what Dr Lasalle is looking for.'

She gave me a hard glare, her fingers tapping absently on her bowstring. 'I do not believe I am obliged to do any such thing.'

I drew a deep breath to sustain my patience. 'Look, let me be open with you. I know that you have been helping Lasalle search for something, perhaps a weapon, referred to by the code name red falcon.'

Karissa Adriatis stared at me in silence, her grey eyes wide with surprise. Then she laughed, a long rich laugh such as a goddess might utter in mocking the foolishness of mortals.

'Redfalcon is neither a thing nor a weapon,' she

informed me in a voice bubbling with mirth. 'Redfalcon is a man.'

I was quite taken aback by this unexpected information. 'A man? Then who on earth is he?'

She raised a sardonic eyebrow. 'That I will tell you when you have arranged my passage to Morocco.' With that she caught up her bow and marched back into the hotel.

When I re-entered the lobby, the clerk at reception waved me over and handed me a key. 'Your two friends are in the room next door,' he informed me. 'Coffee has already been sent up.'

I found Dougal leaning on the rail of their terrace, gulping his coffee as he gazed down at the town. With evening closing in, lights were starting to flicker on all over the tight little streets that plunged dizzyingly down the steep flank of the Rock. I poured myself some coffee and joined him.

'Funny, isn't it, to see all those lights?' He gestured with his cup at the scene below. 'No blackout here.'

'No, they're safe from bombing so long as the Spaniards keep out of the fight.' The lighted streets were like the after-image of a bygone age, a reminder that normal life was still a tenuous possibility. 'Where's Jaikie hiding himself?'

'Oh, he and Sid got to talking about motorbikes, so the chief took him off to show him one.'

'The chief strikes me as a good man,' I said. 'I'm glad we have him here to help us out.'

'So how did it go with this Adriatis woman?'

I gave him the gist of my encounter and he shook his head disparagingly. 'She sounds like a stiff-necked sort, a bit like my aunt Aggie. *She* could start an argument in an empty room, she was that contrary.'

'To be fair, she thinks she's just setting out on an archaeological dig,' I explained, 'and we're sticking our noses into something that's none of our business. She doesn't see any connection to the war, and for all we know she may be right.'

Dougal wrinkled his nose. 'Just what you'd expect, I suppose, from some wizened prune who spends all her time among a lot of dusty books. So what do you make of this Redfalcon? Do you suppose it's a code name for another enemy spy?'

'The name turns up in the records of the Knights of St John,' I pointed out, 'so if he's an enemy spy, he must be a few hundred years old.'

'In that case he'd be getting a bit past it, sure enough,' Dougal joked.

At that moment Jaikie hailed us from the doorway and we joined him inside. I settled into the one chair while the two young Scots sat on the edge of their beds. Jaikie sipped his coffee and told us that there was a small garage at the back of the hotel where they kept a motorcycle for use by army couriers.

'It's a Norton 19, and a pretty old one at that. It looks as if they've been taking good care of it, though. What about you, sir? How did your meeting go?'

I brought him up to date on our situation, and a crease of concern formed between his sharp eyes. 'It sounds as though we may be stuck with her if we want to follow this thing through.'

Dougal made a sour face. 'Och, we'll not be wanting

to drag a teacher woman along on a caper like this. It's going to be a hard road and she'll not be up to it.'

I could not help but smile as I recalled the many times my dear Mary had intervened in my own adventures and how often I had depended on her courage and ingenuity. 'Dougal, I think you may be surprised by exactly how much a determined woman is capable of.'

13

A THIEF IN THE NIGHT

———

When later I took to my bed, the room felt stifling, so I left the door to the balcony open in order to let a light breeze waft through. Still stiff from the five-hour flight, I was glad to lie down at last, but my sleep was haunted by dreams of clashing swords and a crimson bird of prey swooping low over a desert blasted by the sun and littered with desiccated skeletons.

I stirred from these nocturnal visions to a gradual awareness that I was no longer alone in the room. Some intruder was creeping about in small, stealthy movements. I had fallen asleep facing the wall and could see nothing when I opened my eyes. I remained perfectly still, feigning sleep as best I could, so as not to alert my unseen visitor to the fact that he was detected. While my vision adjusted to the darkness, I kept my ears attuned to his progress as he roved across the tiled floor, making barely enough sound to alert any but the most danger-honed senses.

Speculation set my pulse racing. Had some agent of Ravenstein followed us from England, or did he have henchmen already established here on the Rock? Whoever my visitor was, I wondered what his intent could be. So far he had made no attempt to strike at me, and so far as I could judge he had halted at the other end of the room by the small table where I had taken my supper. If the intruder were armed, it would serve me best to strike swiftly and without warning, so I braced myself to make a sudden leap and catch him unawares.

Just then my unseen adversary uttered a high chuckling sound, like a chortle of malicious glee. That evil laugh launched me into action. Flinging aside the flimsy sheet, I jumped out of the bed and launched myself across the room with both hands outstretched to seize the interloper and fling him to the floor.

I caught only a flicker of motion among the shadows as he nimbly eluded my grasp, leaving me to slam bruisingly into the edge of the table. Biting back a grunt of pain, I turned to swing at him, but my fist lashed through the empty air as my opponent dodged aside. With astonishing speed he scampered away and hopped out on to the balcony.

Here the wan moonlight gave me my first clear sight of the intruder. I was taken aback to see that he was no more than a child, a small hairy one at that. Squatting on his haunches, he clutched in his little hands a date stolen from the bowl on the table, and as I watched he began gnawing at it with sharp, tiny teeth.

For a few seconds I gaped at the apparition in mute surprise, then the truth struck me and I laughed at my foolishness. The furry shape with the tiny hands and the bright eyes that now blinked at me so innocently was one of Gibraltar's famous Barbary apes. Lured by the scent of unguarded fruit, he had clambered up into my room and was now enjoying his well-earned prize. He once again emitted the chittering noise that I had interpreted as a high-pitched chuckle, then swung over the railing and vanished into the night.

Shaking my head in mingled relief and embarrassment, I walked out on to the balcony to take in a deep draught of night air. How ironic it was that my defensive reaction had been triggered by one of Gibraltar's living tokens of good fortune, a creature some might even count as one of the Rock's defenders.

Popular legend held that if the apes should ever leave Gibraltar, the British would be forced to leave too. In fact their presence was considered so vital to the local morale, Churchill had ordered that their population be supported in every possible way.

Only a few lights still shone in the streets of the town, and the moon cast a pale wash over the red rooftops descending all the way down to the harbour. Suddenly my attention was caught by a movement in the street directly below me.

A pair of shadowy figures emerged furtively into the moonlight. Between them they were supporting the unconscious form of a young woman whom they bundled into the back of a shabby car. Even at a glimpse, I could tell from her long black hair that their victim could only be Karissa Adriatis, subdued no doubt by chloroform or some other drug.

As the two men clambered into the vehicle I gripped the rail in frustration. It was too far to jump, and any outcry I made would only hasten their getaway. Bounding back into the room, I snatched up some clothes and darted into the corridor. I scrambled into my trousers while using my shoulder to bash open the door to the next room.

'Up you get, boys! Adriatis has been grabbed!'

Woken in mid-snore, Dougal rolled out of bed and hit the floor with a thud. Instantly alert, Jaikie sprang to his feet in his undershirt and shorts.

'You mean kidnapped?' he exclaimed.

'I saw her being bundled into a car down in the street,' I confirmed. 'Jaikie, didn't you say there was a motorcycle out back?'

Jaikie slipped on a pair of sandals and headed for the corridor. 'Yes, sir. Let's give her a try.'

'Find Stark,' I ordered Dougal as he clambered to his feet and rubbed his eyes. 'He knows the place and can organise a search.'

'Right you are, sir,' Dougal acknowledged blearily as I hurried after Jaikie and followed him downstairs.

The young Scot vaulted nimbly down three steps at a time, leaving me struggling to catch up.

Over his shoulder he asked, 'Do you suppose they'll try to get her off Gib?'

'I'm sure of it,' I replied. 'If they wanted her dead they would have done it already.'

Jaikie paused briefly in mid-stride. 'Well, they can't drive over into Spain. The border's too heavily guarded.'

'I'll bet they have a boat somewhere,' I told him. 'They couldn't get past the harbour patrols, so that leaves the beaches on the west side under the cliffs.'

Exiting the hotel by a rear door we charged into a small garage where I saw the motorcycle Jaikie had told us about. He plucked the keys from a hook on the wall and flung himself on to the saddle. As he gunned the engine, I climbed up behind and wrapped my arms around his waist. 'Do you reckon we can catch up with them?'

I asked as the machine lurched forward.

'We can if we take a short cut,' Jaikie answered briskly.

We roared out of the garage and whipped around the front of the hotel. A short distance along the road, Jaikie swerved sharply into his short cut. In front of us a flight of worn stone steps plunged steeply all the way down to the waterfront. Nothing daunted, Jaikie pitched us head-long down the precipitous slope. I clung on for dear life as we shot down in a series of bone-jarring bumps, sometimes bouncing into the air before the tyres found purchase again.

'Are you sure you know where you're going?' My voice emerged through gritted teeth.

'I bought myself a map of the place and I've studied it pretty closely,' Jaikie answered confidently.

I was ready to take his word for it. Scouting out new territory was one of Jaikie's major skills.

We continued our downward plunge at dizzying speed. In the back of my mind was the worry that if I was mistaken in my deductions, instead of racing to the girl's rescue we might be speeding away from wherever she was being held. Resolutely I quashed my doubts, trusting to the hunting instinct which had guided me so well in the past.

With a final bruising jolt we reached the bottom of the stairway and swung left on to the main road. Leaning into the throttle, Jaikie sent us rocketing past the harbour's edge where lines of loading cranes stood gaunt against the night sky, looming over us like guardian giants. Peering over his shoulder, I spotted the mouth of a tunnel ahead to the left. When we reached it Jaikie veered sharply into its depths. 'This cuts right through the rock to the other side,' he told me, shouting over the noise of the bike.

Thick lengths of electrical cable ran down the concrete walls, strung with lamps that shot past us in white streaks as we accelerated to full speed. The tunnel amplified the roar of our engine to a banshee howl until we came flying out of the far end. We skirted the narrow coast, feverishly scanning the sandy coves to our right. Abruptly I spotted a familiar car parked on the roadside up ahead.

I gave Jaikie a slap on the arm. 'There they are, Jaikie. On that beach down there!'

On a stretch of shingle that shimmered in the moonlight two men were visible. They were slinging a limp figure into a rowing boat, which they then shoved towards the sea. Fixing his keen eyes on our quarry, Jaikie took us bumping down on to the beach, racing to catch them before they could get afloat.

At the sound of our approach the men pulled up short and jabbered excitedly in Italian. While one continued heaving the boat towards the water, the other waved to us to keep back and yanked a pistol from his belt.

Bending low in the saddle, Jaikie pressed our machine to its maximum speed. Crouching behind him, I saw the gunman take hasty aim. The first bullet went wide, zinging past my ear, but the second blew out our single headlight.

Plunged into sudden darkness, we slewed sideways and struck a rock. The motorcycle bucked like a startled stallion, flinging both of us into the air. We splatted down face first in the sand while the bike keeled over on to its side, its wheels spinning helplessly.

The kidnappers had almost reached the water, and

even as we caught our breath another bullet flew blindly over our heads. 'We can't let them get away,' I gasped, spitting out grit. 'We'll split up and come at him from two sides so he'll have to divide his shots.'

'Right-o, sir,' Jaikie acknowledged. He scrambled a few yards to his right before leaping to his feet and sprinting at the enemy. I jumped up and rushed the gunman from the other direction. He stumbled backwards to keep up with his companion, who had got the boat to the very edge of the sea. As he loosed off another wild shot, something extraordinary happened.

Shaking off the effects of the drug, Karissa Adriatis heaved herself out of the bottom of the boat and rose up behind her abductors. With her dark hair fluttering in the wind like a black flame and her eyes ablaze in the moonlight, she looked every inch an avenging Fury out of Greek legend, poised to visit her vengeance upon the presumption of men.

Snatching up an oar in both hands, she took a mighty swing at the gunman. The oar smacked him squarely across the head and down he went, the gun flying from his numbed hand to splash into the water. As she swayed unsteadily, the second man seized hold of her weapon and snatched it out of her grasp. Losing her balance, Karissa toppled forward and tumbled across the sand.

Seeing that we were almost upon him, the Italian flung the oar into the boat and hauled his companion up by the collar. Together they thrust the boat into the water and hopped aboard. Rowing furiously, they pulled away as Jaikie and I dropped to our knees beside the girl.

She was lapsing in and out of consciousness, and as we

lifted her carefully up the beach I could hear her muttering under her breath in Greek. Whether she was giving thanks for her rescue or calling down curses on her would-be abductors was more than I could tell.

'She doesn't seem injured,' Jaikie observed with some relief. 'I think she's going to be all right.'

I nodded. 'They underestimated her. She's a remarkably determined young woman.'

'There's no doubt of that,' Jaikie grinned, recalling the vicious blow she had struck. 'They should have listened to Virgil's advice to beware of Greeks.'

I was wondering how to get her back to the hotel when Chief Stark's car pulled up beside the kidnappers' abandoned vehicle. Dougal jumped out of the passenger seat and ran across the sand to join us.

'Have I missed all the fun?' he exclaimed, looking out at the rowing boat, which was dwindling into the distance.

'It wasn't what I would call fun,' I answered, 'but we managed to keep Dr Adriatis out of the clutches of Ravenstein's men.'

'Do you think that's who they were?' asked Jaikie.

'I'm sure of it,' I stated flatly. 'Who else would know that she had important information worth taking the risk of abducting her for?'

Rubbing his jaw, Dougal gazed down at the young woman in obvious admiration. 'Whether she knows anything or not, she would make quite a prize.'

Chief Stark joined the party and quickly assessed the situation. 'Well, sir, it looks as though we both worked out where the rats would be keeping their boat. Great minds and all that, eh?'

'Chief, I take that as a great compliment,' I told him.

Bending down, he peered at the girl. 'I don't think I'd be wrong in saying the lady would be a sight more comfortable in her bed,' he advised. 'Once we get her back to the hotel I'll fetch the doc in, just to be on the safe side.'

'Leave this to me,' said Dougal. Before anyone else could make a move, he had gathered Karissa Adriatis up in his arms and conveyed her to the car as gently as a mother carrying a baby. We all followed along as he laid her carefully on the back seat and quietly closed the door.

He turned to face me with a reproachful frown. 'Really, sir, you never let on she was so bonnie.'

14

THE WARRIORS OF GOD

Following a night of little rest, we shared a late breakfast on the hotel terrace with our new acquaintance Dr Karissa Adriatis. She had shooed away the medic who tried to examine her and mixed her own tonic of fruit juice, honey and fresh herbs from the hotel kitchen. As a result she declared herself ready to hunt her attackers down with her bow and stick them with arrows like wild pigs.

'You'll have to turn into a mermaid to do that,' I said. 'They're long gone out to sea.'

'You're supposing then that they rowed in from a ship that kept out of sight,' said Jaikie.

'Either that or a submarine,' I said.

'And what about the car?' Dougal wondered. 'Where did that come from?'

'Chief Stark checked up on that,' Jaikie informed us. 'It seems it was stolen during the night from the home of one of the native Gibraltarians who works at the supply depot. From all accounts he's completely trustworthy and has nothing to do with the enemy operation, other than being a victim of car theft.'

'The Italians!' A cold anger blazed in the Greek girl's large eyes. 'First they attack my country, and when the resistance is too fierce, they call in their friends the Germans to help them. And now, even here, when I am far from home, even where the British stand firm, they dare to attack me again.'

'From what I hear about you braining one of them with an oar,' grinned Dougal, 'they'll not try that again in a hurry.'

The girl directed her gaze at me. 'It seems you were right,' she said, tapping herself on the temple. 'There is something up here that they want.'

'And you've now had more than ample proof of the danger you're in, Dr Adriatis,' I told her.

She waved a dismissive hand. 'No, no more Dr Adriatis. We are not taking tea with the king at Buckingham Palace. If we are to be allies, you will call me Karrie. And I will call you' – she pointed to each of us in turn – 'Richard, John and Douglas.'

'That's Dougal,' the red-haired young Scot objected.

Karrie raised an admonitory finger. 'Douglas, you really must not contradict me over matters of little importance.'

I was surprised that Dougal chose not to argue the point any further. I could only imagine that from the moment he first beheld her on the moonlit beach, the beautiful Greek archaeologist had cast an enchantment over him.

'Well then . . . Karrie,' I said, 'now that we're all agreed that whatever information you have is of serious value to our enemies, perhaps you'd like to share some of it with us.'

'You need to tell us about these Knights of St John,' said Jaikie.

'Yes, who is this Redfalcon,' Dougal pressed her, 'and what is this dratted weapon of his that's got everybody so fired up?'

'Patience, Douglas, patience,' she chided. 'The tale must be told in its proper order, then shall all be explained.'

She sounded now much more the conventional academic preparing to deliver a lecture, but she was right – we needed the fullest possible understanding of what this business was all about.

'To begin with, the Order was founded in Jerusalem by a certain Brother Gerard who was the head of a hospice for pilgrims. With the arrival of the Crusaders, the humble hospice grew into a great hospital and the Order gained the favour of popes, kings and nobles. Their endowments allowed it to establish new centres all over Europe, while in the Holy Land they took on a new duty – the protection of pilgrims passing through their territory. This involved the development of a military arm, knights serving under the monastic rule of St Benedict.'

Jaikie frowned. 'I'm sure this is all very interesting, but does it really answer any of our questions?'

Karrie fixed him with an implacable stare. 'If you do not understand these men, how can you hope to ever penetrate their secrets?'

'You're right, of course,' I said appeasingly. 'Please go on.'

'Over time the kingdoms established by the Crusaders crumbled before the relentless assaults of their Muslim foes,' Karrie continued. 'Acre was the last of the Christian strongholds to fall and with it the Hospitallers were driven from the Holy Land. Now they took on a new role. Instead of charging across the desert plain on their great horses, they took to the sea, harassing the merchant ships of their infidel enemies. They established themselves on the island of Rhodes, aided by the native inhabitants who were already skilled sailors. From this lush and fertile island, the swift galleys of the Order continued the war begun in the Crusades.'

'So now they were just soldiers and sailors,' I suggested.

'Not at all,' Karrie corrected me. 'Wherever the Knights made their home, there would always be at its centre a great hospital for the care of the sick and the help of the poor.'

'But what about Malta?' Dougal cut in impetuously.

Karrie gave him a glare that I imagined had cowed any number of obstreperous undergraduates. Jaikie jogged his friend's elbow and gave a warning shake of the head.

'Twice the great sultan of the Turks laid siege to the Order on Rhodes. The first time the attackers were repulsed. The second time, after a long a weary struggle, the Knights accepted the terms offered. They could leave the island unmolested, taking with them their arms and their ships: an honourable withdrawal. So the leaders of the Order wandered now from place to place until they were granted the sovereignty of the island of Malta.'

I saw my two young friends lean forward intently at the mention of that name. Now, it seemed, we were coming to the part of the story that held the key to the mystery that had brought us here.

'Compared to the beauty of Rhodes, this new island was a barren rock with little to recommend it and no adequate defences. The Knights set to work, erecting castles, thick walls and strong bastions, as they had done back in the kingdoms of the Crusaders. They enlarged the harbours and continued to wage their campaigns by sea.

In time the sultan Suleiman decided he had had enough of these piratical Christians and he resolved to utterly destroy them once and for all.'

'I've heard something about that siege,' I said. 'It was a long and bloody struggle.'

'It was indeed,' said Karrie. 'A huge Ottoman army landed on the island and the inhabitants withdrew inside the stout walls of the twin towns of Birgu and Senglea, which were defended by the Order. The Turks first invested Fort St Elmo, a small fortress isolated at the end of a rocky promontory. They expected it to fall in a matter of days, but they had underestimated the determination of its defenders. During the attack the fort was so engulfed in fire and smoke that it looked like a volcano, but the banners of the Order continued to fly above the inferno. Knights who were too seriously wounded to stand were placed in chairs with their swords in their hands to defend breaches in the walls.'

She clenched her hands in front of her, as though gripping the hilt of a great sword, and the dramatic intonation in her voice seemed to conjure up the scene before our eyes. It was little wonder that her people were famed as a nation of storytellers from the days of Homer onward.

'Finally, after thirty-one days, the fort was taken,' said Karrie, 'but only at the cost to the Turks of many thousands of their men and some of their most famous commanders. It was something of a hollow victory, for shortly afterwards reinforcements arrived, finding a way around the enemy arms to join the defenders within the city walls. The twin towns were on promontories extending into the great harbour, and both came under assault by land and sea.'

Dougal nodded approvingly. 'Those Knights of yours were a tough crew, right enough.'

'After many weeks the Ottomans launched their climactic assault,' said Karrie. 'They were on the point of overrunning the defences when suddenly the retreat was sounded. Their camp, far to their rear, had come under attack, and they feared a fresh Christian army had landed to march against them. In fact it was just a small Maltese raiding party, but the panic they caused saved the Order from being overwhelmed.'

These scenes of battle as she related them were only too vivid for me. I knew what it was like to hold a line against overwhelming odds, clinging to the desperate hope of reinforcement, and I could envisage the terrible struggle only too easily.

'Was that the end of it, then?' asked Jaikie.

'No, there were another three months of hard fighting,' said Karrie. 'By that time the resources of the invaders were dwindling, while the toll of casualties from battle and disease had become intolerable. They were forced to clamber aboard their ships and sail back to the east, where the wrath of their sultan awaited them.'

There was a pause, during which all of us drew breath.

'Well, it's quite a tale,' said Jaikie at last, 'but I didn't hear anything that suggested any sort of secret weapon.'

'Right,' Dougal agreed. 'It seems to have been mostly swords, crossbows and suchlike.'

'They had cannon,' said Karrie, 'and early forms of musket. There was also Greek fire.'

'I've heard of that,' I said. 'Wasn't it developed by the Byzantines?'

'Yes. It was a form of liquid fire used to ignite the ships of the enemy. The Knights often used it in the form of incendiary grenades.'

'That's not something that could threaten Malta now,' said Jaikie. 'Not in the face of modern weaponry.'

'The references to this supposed weapon are few and couched in deliberately vague language,' Karrie explained. 'They do, however, connect it with the name Redfalcon. Armand Lasalle had a certain suspicion about who he might have been, and I was able to confirm it through my own researches.'

'And are you ready to share that information with us now?' I prompted.

Karrie shifted in her seat and her grey eyes swept over all three of us. 'The key to the thing lay in heraldry.'

'That's all about family crests and suchlike, isn't it?' said Dougal. 'A way for rich nobles to show off.'

'More than showing off,' Karrie corrected him. 'It was very important that knights be able to identify each other. Bear in mind that they did not wear uniforms, and in their armour it was difficult to tell one man from another and friend from foe. Each man therefore had his own heraldic symbol painted on his shield. It could be something as simple as a tower or a lion, but was often a combination of several elements each carrying its own meaning with regard to the knight's lineage.'

'And where does this lead us?' Jaikie pressed.

Karrie raised a finger, as though to point to the object of her reasoning. 'To a man whose family bore the heraldic crest of a crimson bird of prey. It was a common enough practice to refer to a man by his heraldic symbol. In this case the man was Sir Thomas Easterly, a Knight of St John who hailed from England.'

'And that is the man Lasalle suspected all along,' I surmised.

'Yes. He was not only a holy knight, he was an expert in the construction of fortifications and in casting cannon.'

'But if he's long dead, how could he have any influence on our war today?' Jaikie wondered.

Karrie allowed a dramatic pause before answering the question. 'Because he left behind a record of his great weapon which was not only for defence. He said that if Malta should fall to the Turks, he had the means by which the Knights could retake the island.'

'And that's what the Germans are after,' I said. 'The means to capture Malta.'

'I still don't follow,' Dougal grumbled. 'If this man Easterly was a knight of Malta, what is your pal Lasalle doing in Morocco?'

'Because that is where the secret of Redfalcon lies.' Karrie slammed her palm down on the table as though closing a coffin lid. 'It is buried with him in his tomb.'

15

THE FOURTH KNAVE

'I take it there's another story behind this,' I guessed.

'You are correct. It is a tale recorded by one of the Order's chroniclers.'

Dougal wriggled in his seat to make himself comfortable and Jaikie took a long swallow of coffee as they prepared themselves for another period of enforced and attentive silence. I was already fascinated by the story, and only hoped that we were on the trail of something tangible and not chasing after some legend that would dissolve through our fingers like mist.

Karrie took a swallow of her personal tonic and resumed her discourse.

'Even though the Knights had won their great victory over the Ottomans, the traffic of the Mediterranean was still harried by the Barbary pirates operating from their North African strongholds. Six years after the siege, Redfalcon was aboard one of the Order's ships when it was damaged in a pirate attack. Forced off course, it was caught in a storm and wrecked on the shores of present-day Morocco. Barely twenty crewmen survived and most of those were captured and made into slaves. Three escaped inland, however, all of them Knights of the Order. Redfalcon was one, Guy de Melancourt, a French knight, was another, and the third was a Spaniard, Rodrigo d'Alcantara.'

'This is all starting to sound a bit Robinson Crusoe,' Dougal commented under his breath.

Karrie continued her tale as though she hadn't heard him. 'They found refuge with a small Christian community which had managed to survive by making their home among the caves and clefts of the mountains. Redfalcon had been badly injured in the wreck, and though his fellow Knights tended him with all possible care, he died only a few weeks after reaching the hidden refuge. With the help of their fellow Christians, Melancourt and d'Alcantara created a tomb inside a cave to house the body of their brave companion.'

'Given how long ago all this was,' said Jaikie, 'and in such an inaccessible spot, how is it that anybody knows about this tomb?'

'I was about to explain that,' Karrie answered curtly. 'After a year the two surviving Knights set out on the hazardous journey back to Christian lands. Along the way Melancourt was taken by a fever and died, but d'Alcantara made it home to Spain and resumed his duties with the Order. The Hospitaller chronicles record the account he gave of his adventures and tell that the greatness of Redfalcon was buried with him in some distant place.'

'Greatness?' I said. 'That could just mean a record of his achievements.'

Karrie shook her head. 'It's very unlikely they would leave a perishable manuscript account of his deeds, or go to the great effort of inscribing them on stone.'

'So you take it to mean that it's this mysterious weapon itself that's buried there,' said Jaikie, 'or some record of what exactly it might be.'

'As so often in history we are dealing with probabilities,' Karrie declared in her scholarly fashion. 'We must hope that the truth lies ahead of us. Dr Lasalle believes it was in the mountains to the south-east of Casablanca that the Knights took refuge and he has searched there as best he can without more detailed guidance.'

'And that's what he wanted you to find for him,' I supposed.

'Correct. I learned that in addition to the tale recorded in the Chronicles, Don Rodrigo d'Alcantara also wrote a private letter to Sir Thomas's brother Frederick Easterly. In this he gave certain clues as to the location of the tomb, so that one day the family might make a pilgrimage there and pay homage to their illustrious kinsman.'

'And you were able to find it?' Dougal prompted.

There was a flash of triumph in Karrie's eyes. 'Yes, among the family records that had been preserved at Dronford Abbey near Exeter.'

'So what are these clues?' Jaikie asked eagerly.

The Greek girl sat back in her chair and folded her arms. 'That information is for Dr Lasalle, not for you.'

'You cannot be serious,' Dougal exclaimed. 'We've come all this way to find you *and* saved you from being kidnapped.'

'I am very serious, Douglas,' she retorted. 'Whatever it might have to do with the war, this is a scientific expedition, a search for an important historical discovery. It is the business of scholars, not soldiers and adventurers.'

Dougal slammed his hands flat on the table in frustration. 'Well, there's hardly much point in us going to find Dr Lasalle without these clues of yours.'

'Exactly.' Karrie's whole demeanour expressed a fixed resolve to have her way. 'Which is why you must abandon any notion of leaving me behind.'

It was clear to me that she had thought this all out before our meeting, and it was going to prove difficult to dissuade her.

'You must appreciate that this is a very dangerous mission,' I cautioned. 'We'll be going into Vichy territory, and if we're caught there they might well hand us over to the Germans. We could be shot as spies.'

'Do you expect me to be afraid?' Karrie unfolded her arms and struck a defiant pose. 'My ancestors defeated the Persian armies of Darius and Xerxes, we threw off the yoke of the Turkish Ottomans, and we shall see off these latest invaders. Greece will always be free in the end because we carry our history with us here.'

She struck a fist against her heart and her whole body seemed to blaze with an almost supernatural fire. At that moment she seemed to me to embody all the glories of Greece, from the age of gods and philosophers to the golden empire of Byzantium.

Abruptly she stood up and pushed her chair back. 'You will let me know when you have arranged passage for us to Morocco, so that we may join Dr Lasalle in Casablanca.'

With that she strode off without a backward glance.

Dougal shook his head ruefully. 'Who does she think she is? Helen of Troy?'

'I hope she won't stir up as much trouble as that,' I said.

'Speaking of ships,' said Jaikie, 'do you think the governor could provide us with a boat of some sort for our crossing to Africa?'

I rubbed my jaw in thought. 'I'd like to keep this as unofficial as possible. We need to travel as civilians and avoid any encounter with the Vichy authorities.'

'And what will we do about the lassie?' Dougal wondered darkly. 'She acts like the boss of the whole business.'

'I'm not any happier about taking her along than you are,' I admitted, 'but it seems that she has us over a barrel.'

'I suppose she's right when she says that she's on a scientific expedition,' Jaikie conceded, 'and we've sort of shoved our noses into it. We can't really blame her for refusing to be left out.'

'Look, why don't you two go and rustle up the kit we'll need for this trip,' I suggested. 'I'll see if I can work something out about transport and figure out how we're going to handle our stubborn Dr Adriatis.'

Back in my room I took time to think and consider our situation. It occurred to me that I had charged into this mission in my usual headlong manner and that Ravenstein had been at least one step ahead of me at every stage. From his interrogation of Professor Owen he must have learned of Karrie Adriatis's departure for Gibraltar and immediately activated part of his network to attempt her abduction.

If we were to head him off in future I would need to clear my head and ponder what further ploys he might have up his sleeve. Feeling in my pocket for my pipe, my fingers touched upon Blenkiron's well-worn deck of cards. As I pulled them out, I recalled his saying that he often used a game of patience as an aid to setting his thoughts in order. It occurred to me that was exactly what I needed at this point.

I sat down at the small table, shuffled the deck and laid out the initial four cards. One by one I built up the sequences, feeling a sense of quiet satisfaction as the patterns took shape before me.

Often a contest between two well-matched opponents has been described as resembling a game of chess, but in chess all the pieces are set out in the open for both sides to see. I fancied that my contest with Ravenstein was more like a card game, one in which you can only guess at what cards your opponent is holding from one hand to the next. You might, however, by studying his play, deduce what his next move was likely to be.

My reflections were proceeding along these lines when I managed to slip the knave of spades into place. Observing that all four knaves were now in play, I felt that I was on the brink of an insight that had set an alarm off in my head. Then I realised that what I was hearing was an actual alarm – the hotel's fire bell.

I shot to my feet and scooped up the cards. Thrusting them back in my pocket, I hurried out into the corridor. The smell of smoke was in the air accompanied by cries of shock which echoed down the adjoining passageways and stairwells. Not wishing to be part of a panic, I walked briskly to the head of the main stairway and made a swift but disciplined descent.

Once on the ground floor, however, I was caught up in a rushing stream of guests and staff which carried me through the hallway and out of the front door. In the street outside the manager was directing everyone to form up in ranks so that he could check off names from his register to ensure no one was left inside. Despite his efforts, however, those fleeing the building were soon mixed up in a jostling mob with onlookers who had gathered to watch the flames and smoke belching out of the windows of the hotel's east wing.

From the direction of the airstrip I could hear the clanging bell of an approaching fire engine. The manager and his senior staff now turned their attention to forcing the crowd to move back and clear the way for the firemen. As we retreated, almost tripping over each other, I pondered what might lie behind this development.

It was too much of a coincidence to be accidental, and I understood now what warning it was that the fourth knave had jogged in my mind. If two enemy agents had been dropped off by boat, might there not be others? Even as I tensed at the possibility, I glimpsed out of the corner of my eye a figure moving purposefully towards me against the flow of the crowd. He was an evil-looking lout, and as I turned to face him I caught the glint of a knife in his hand.

16

THE CROSS OF LORRAINE

Realising I had spotted him, he rushed at me with the blade held high, ready to strike. Seizing his upraised arm, I forced it down and gave his wrist a savage twist. With a shrill howl of pain, he dropped the weapon and tried to wrench himself free.

Hooking my foot around his ankle, I threw my shoulder against his chest. The move toppled us to the ground with my full weight thumping down on top and knocking the breath out of him. As he lay there gasping, I hauled myself up, only to find that a second attacker had shoved the bystanders aside and loomed over me with his blade only a foot from my throat.

Before I could make a move to defend myself, a tall figure in uniform appeared behind my assailant. The newcomer caught the man's elbows in powerful hands and spun him round. Grabbing the knife arm, he slammed it down violently across his upraised knee, snapping the bone. The assassin shrieked in pain and the knife clattered to the ground. My rescuer finished the job with a solid punch to the jaw that dropped its victim in an insensible heap directly on top of the first attacker.

As the shocked onlookers shrank back from the sudden eruption of violence, I got my first clear look at the man behind this welcome intervention. His uniform was that of the Free French forces, emblazoned with the distinctive insignia of the double-barred Cross of Lorraine.

One look at his handsome, aquiline face brought a broad grin to my lips.

'Turpin!' I cried.

It was my old friend the Marquis de la Tour du Pin, whose unwieldy title Archie Roylance had long ago compressed into Turpin, the name by which he was commonly known to those closest to him.

'Dick, *mon vieux*!' he exclaimed, returning my grin. 'You are, as ever, in the thick of the action, as they say.'

'And you, Turpin, are developing a very welcome habit of turning up in the very nick of time.'

When one of the fallen men groaned and stirred, Turpin planted a heavy boot on him to keep him in place.

'Chief Stark told me you were here and of your night-time adventure,' he explained. 'I determined at once to find you and offer whatever assistance I may provide. Even as I spotted you in the crowd I saw these *cochons* preparing to strike.'

As though he had been summoned by the mention of his name, the crowd parted before Chief Petty Officer Sidney Stark. He strolled towards us and cast a disapproving eye over the two attackers lying at our feet.

'A well-placed punch that, monsieur,' he complimented Turpin. 'A few years ago I saw the Bermondsey Kid knock out Thrasher Curtis in the first round in a very similar fashion.'

'Perhaps, chief, you could clear up this mess for us,' Turpin requested.

Chief Stark waved over two privates of the Lancashire Fusiliers who were among the crowd gawking at the scene. 'Come along, lads. You can help me escort these two ruffians to some simply furnished but secure accommodation. Once they've been patched up, I expect they'll have to answer some very pointed questions.'

As the two men were hauled to their feet and dragged off, the officer in charge of the fire-fighting party ordered the crowd to disperse. Between the hoses now being directed at the windows and the staff inside wielding fire extinguishers and buckets of sand, the blaze appeared to be subsiding.

'We must talk,' I told Turpin, 'but first I have to make sure that no harm has come to Dr Adriatis.'

'No worries on that score, sir.'

The assurance came from Dougal. As he approached, he jerked a thumb over his shoulder, indicating a wooden bench at the entrance to the hotel's front garden. The Greek girl was seated there calmly absorbed in a book.

'I thought you and Jaikie had gone off to organise our supplies,' I admonished him.

'Well, bearing in mind last night's spot of bother,' he explained, 'we decided one of us should stay behind and keep an eye on the lady. You know, in case there was any more trouble.'

'And you nobly volunteered.'

'Aye,' Dougal agreed abashedly. 'After all, if anything should happen to her, we'd be stuck for sure.'

I surmised that his vigil was motivated by more than a concern for the success of our mission. Nevertheless, I was relieved to know that Karrie had a guardian angel on hand. I introduced Dougal to Turpin, then left him to his chosen duty while my French friend invited me to join him for a drink in one of Gibraltar's colourful bars.

It rejoiced in the name of the Cloisters, a whitewashed building with the flag of Gibraltar flying outside along with the Union Jack. The décor inside consisted of an unusual mix of religious icons and old music-hall posters featuring the stars of bygone years.

Turpin selected a table by one of the small windows and fetched us a bottle of cognac and a couple of glasses. I lit my pipe and he smoked a strongly scented cigarette as we spoke against the background noise of various hushed conversations being carried on in Yanita, the native language of the Rock, a curious hybrid of Spanish and Arabic. Overhead a creaking fan laboured in vain to dispel the pall of cigarette smoke that filled the place.

'This is a very troubling business,' said Turpin. 'First the kidnapping I was told of, then this fire.'

'When the alarm went off,' I told him, 'I had only just hit upon the notion that the two men who tried to make off with Dr Adriatis might not be the only pair who were dropped ashore. There might be a second team waiting for their moment to strike.'

'*Bien sûr, mon ami*. Without doubt they started the fire to flush everyone out of the building and in the confusion to do away with the very dangerous Richard Hannay.'

I took an appreciative sip of cognac then set my glass down to cast an eye over my old friend's new uniform. 'I knew you had joined de Gaulle's Free French forces, but I never expected to run into you here.'

Turpin threw back his shoulders as though on parade. 'Ah, I am on a special assignment. I am to make contact with certain officers among the Vichy in Morocco and

Algeria, and do all that I can to persuade them to switch their allegiance to the Allies when the time comes.'

'When the time comes?' I was intrigued. 'Do you mean there's to be an invasion?'

He nodded with a wolfish gleam in his eye. 'In a few months' time the Americans will lead such an attack. If the French troops can be persuaded to offer no resistance but instead to join our cause, so much the better.'

The strategy was immediately clear to me. 'I see. From Algeria they can link up with our army in Egypt.'

'And from there launch an invasion of Italy.' Turpin slammed a fist into his palm, as though striking a blow against the hated enemy.

'Do you think you'll be able to persuade your countrymen to cooperate?'

'Pah!' He curled a disdainful lip. 'So many of them have been poisoned by the defeatism of Pétain. That cowardly surrender has enfeebled their souls like a disease.'

I had been in Paris hours before the German army moved in, and still felt a lingering sympathy for those who were forced to deal with the occupation.

'It was a hard choice to make,' I reflected. 'The German advance seemed unstoppable.'

Turpin's expression hardened. Leaning forward, he spoke in a low, forceful voice. 'I will tell you why they surrendered, my friend. They thought that you' – here he tapped me forcefully on the chest – 'you and your people would not stand. They believed that within a matter of months you too would be living under the Nazi flag, making whatever accommodation you could beg of your new rulers.' He gave a bitter snort. 'How wrong they were!'

'I suppose they imagined they were salvaging what they could of what was left of France,' I suggested.

Turpin spat contemptuously. 'What was left of France? Pah! What is France *sans son coeur* – without her heart? They sold themselves like – what is the English word? – trollops. Yes, trollops!'

Turpin had always been a man of strong feeling, but never before had his heightened passion been so entirely justified by such extreme circumstances. His wife Adela was the daughter of the noted American financier Julius Victor and both she and her children would have been stigmatised by the Nazis on the basis of their race. God only knew what fate would have awaited them had they fallen into German hands.

When she and Turpin were still only engaged, she had been stolen from him by the evil genius Dominic Medina to be used as a hostage, and since then her safety meant more to my friend than life itself. As the French defences gave way before the German advance like a mud dyke before a flood, he sent her and their children to New York, where they were now living under the protection of her father. Turpin remained behind to carry on the fight by whatever means possible.

'Sometimes in the darkest hour, survival is all men can hope for,' I suggested.

'They may survive,' Turpin retorted scornfully, 'but they are not men.' He took a calming breath and leaned back in his chair. 'And you, Dick, you are engaged in some new and dangerous escapade, eh?'

'All I can tell you right now is that I need passage to French Morocco for myself and my three companions, and it needs to be carried out in the utmost secrecy.'

Turpin grinned and gave me a hearty clap on the shoulder. 'Why, my friend, I am the very man to arrange that for you. Leave it all to me.'

PART THREE
THE REFUGE

17

THE SHORES OF BARBARY

I could feel the deck of the Portuguese fishing boat bobbing gently beneath my feet as the tide carried us slowly in towards the sheltered cove we had been assured lay ahead. It was a black night with thick clouds smothering the stars, and it was only the beacon of a lighthouse to the east that guided us on our course. Off to the west, invisible in the darkness, lay our destination, the city of Casablanca.

The captain of our vessel, whom Turpin had introduced as Sandor, was a lean, dark-skinned seaman with a gold tooth and a red stocking cap. He had a ready laugh and moved about the tilting deck with the sure-footed elegance of a dancer. Now, however, he was subdued and motionless, as were we all. Our engine was off, as were our lights, rendering us silent and invisible while the sea carried us towards the shore.

It had taken Turpin only a couple of days to arrange this discreet transport to Casablanca. Meanwhile I had noted with some amusement that Dougal was developing a previously unsuspected interest in archaeology as he accompanied Karrie on visits to the Moorish castle built by al Rashan in the eleventh century and to the ancient caves where the bones of primitive humans had been discovered. Chief Stark treated Jaikie to a tour of the Rock's more recent points of interest, most conspicuously its defensive fortifications and formidable artillery emplacements.

I devoted the waiting time to studying all the maps I could find of Morocco, running my finger repeatedly over the great mass of the Atlas Mountains. Somewhere among those peaks and crags lay the hidden tomb of Redfalcon, and within it a secret that might shift the balance of the war one way or the other. It was almost too fantastic to believe, but Ravenstein clearly believed it, and he did not strike me as any sort of fool.

Now I stared ahead into the darkness that shrouded the African shore, trusting that Turpin's contacts had succeeded in making the necessary preparations for our arrival. When I turned back to my companions my eyes had adjusted to the gloom sufficiently for me to be able to make out their features.

'You've been pretty tight-lipped about the trail we're to follow to this knight's tomb,' I heard Jaikie remark to Karrie. We were all keeping our voices low, knowing how easily sound carried over water.

'And about how you intend to contact Dr Lasalle,' I added.

'That is because if I were to tell you all I know, you would leave me abandoned like Ariadne on Naxos,' Karrie retorted. 'You would do so simply because I am a woman and you think me too soft to withstand the rigours of war.'

'You fancy yourself as a bit of an Amazon then,' Dougal joked.

'As you come from a land whose men are famed for wearing skirts, you are ill placed to make jokes about Amazons,' Karrie countered.

'Kilts actually, but point taken,' Dougal accepted wryly.

'Believe me, Karrie, none of us think you're soft,' I assured her. 'But you must understand that, so long as you keep all that information to yourself, your safety must be a priority for us. If anything should happen to you, we would be left blundering around without a clue to follow.'

'I appreciate your concern,' Karrie acknowledged, 'and you may be sure that all will be revealed at the appropriate time.'

We were silenced by a sharp hiss from Sandor and in the dimness I saw him press a warning finger to his lips. At once we all fell silent and I heard in the distance the thrum of an engine. A few moments later a French coastal patrol vessel swung around a headland off to our right, heading directly between ourselves and the land.

As they moved eastward, their searchlight darted here and there across the shoreline, probing for any sign of smugglers or hostile incursion. I found myself holding my breath until they passed out of sight.

'It is good luck for us that they look to shore rather than to sea,' said Sandor, his grin flashing white among the shadows. Starting up the engine, he guided us safely into the shelter of a rocky cove before cutting the power again.

'We must move quickly before their boat returns,' he warned us. 'I should hate to tangle in a fight with fellow sailors, whatever their politics. Worse still, we might be forced to pay them to turn a blind eye.' He shook his head disapprovingly. 'Since war broke out, their rates have been extortionate.'

I marvelled at his skill in timing our approach so that we evaded the coastal patrol while leaving a period of grace during which he could land his passengers and make his departure before the French vessel returned. We slid a small dinghy into the water and Sandor used it to ferry us two at a time over to the shingly beach.

Jaikie and I landed first and scrambled into the surrounding rocks. I was suddenly all too aware of how those shipwrecked knights must have felt, cast up on an alien shore with danger all around. My eyes searched the darkness and my ears strained to pick up any sounds of life nearby. All I heard was the quiet lapping of the waves and the chirping of some nocturnal insects, but I was still very aware that we were on hostile ground. I took some reassurance from the fact that Jaikie appeared confident that we were alone, as I knew from experience that his senses were almost preternaturally acute. Turning, he waved his arms to signal to the boat that it was safe to bring over Dougal and Karrie.

Once they had joined us, Sandor threw us a raffish salute before he and his fishing boat headed off across the night-shrouded waves.

'Well, scout, is there any sign of our ride?' asked Dougal.

'I reckon we've a quarter hour or so to wait yet,' Jaikie answered.

I recalled that each of the members of the Gorbals Die-Hards had his own particular role within the group. Jaikie was the scout, while Dougal himself acted as captain, always in the lead when they charged into action. The others I had met during our last jaunt were Peter Paterson, their medic, and Thomas Yowney, now an army parson, who was the strategic genius of their little band.

The first glimmers of dawn were beginning to break over the distant foothills, slowly lending shape to the surrounding landscape of rocks, bushes and dry trees.

'You'd best keep your head down, Douglas,' Karrie advised solemnly. 'If the sun catches that red hair of yours, it's liable to stand out like a bonfire.'

Dougal glowered at her, then gave a belated chuckle as he realised she was only teasing him.

'You're a right minx for vexing a man,' he muttered. 'I've never known the like.'

'Listen!' Jaikie interrupted.

It was a few moments before the rest of us could hear what his keen ears had already picked up: a car was approaching from the west along a straight, dusty road that was now becoming visible. We crouched down among the rocks and peered out from our hiding place. Soon we saw a green Buick with American consular plates rolling towards us, a miniature Stars and Stripes fluttering on the bonnet.

The big car coasted to a halt and by squinting at my watch I could see that it had arrived spot on time. The flare of a match as he lit a cigarette showed us the silhouette of the driver, who was waiting expectantly. This dawn rendezvous had been arranged by Turpin, using secret radio contacts with the US consulate in Casablanca, and every moment of it had been closely calculated. Even so, I decided it would be best to make sure there was no trickery afoot before revealing our whole party.

'The rest of you stay hidden in the rocks,' I ordered.

'I'll go and have a word with that chap to assure myself that he's sound.'

'But surely he must be our contact,' Dougal objected, 'or he wouldn't be here at all.'

'You're probably right,' I agreed, 'but I've walked into one of Ravenstein's traps once before. I intend to be doubly cautious from now on, even at the risk of being a bit of an old woman.'

Leaving my cover, I walked openly towards the Buick. The driver rolled down his window and took a long draw on his cigarette as he watched me approach. As I drew closer, his features came into focus and I was delighted to find that I was already acquainted with him.

'Willis!' I exclaimed. 'Ellery Willis!'

Willis flung open the door and climbed out. He was dressed in a slightly rumpled white suit and a Panama hat with a Harvard class pin prominently clipped to his red silk tie. Tossing away his cigarette, he offered me his hand and we shook.

'General Sir Richard Hannay,' he exclaimed heartily. 'I'm guess I'm to be your taxi service, sir.'

I had known Willis in the Great War, when he commanded a field battery with the American 2nd Corps, and met him again in the 1920s while he was serving as a military attaché at the London embassy. He had always struck me as an earnest young man, but with a quick sense of humour that kept him from becoming too solemn, and Mary had once assured me that he was the best dancer in London.

Seeing that all was well, my companions emerged from concealment to join us.

'John Galt, Captain Dougal Crombie, and Dr Adriatis,' I told him.

'I'm mighty pleased to meet you all,' said Willis, fetching a large manila envelope out of the car. 'I've got your papers with your new identities here. Since Brits are real unpopular in these parts, you three gents are now American citizens, part of our programme to boost trade relations between Morocco and the USA. Do you think you can pull that off?'

Dougal and Jaikie exchanged grins as Willis handed out the documents.

'Why, I sure reckon we can, pardner,' said Dougal in a thick Texas accent.

'It's a sure enough dead cert,' Jaikie agreed, following suit.

'Okay, tone it down,' Willis admonished them. 'You're supposed to be businessmen, not cattle rustlers. Dr Adriatis here remains her own sweet self but under the auspices of the University of Maryland, who've sent her here to study some of the local archaeology.'

'I'm certain I can "pull that off", as you say,' said Karrie. 'It's close to the truth, after all.'

'We'd best get moving into town,' said Willis, throwing open the car doors. 'It seems to me the lady will be more comfortable riding up front with me, rather than being squeezed into the back seat with you fellers.'

'I suppose so,' Dougal agreed grudgingly. Resuming his American accent, he added, 'It sure is mighty chivalrous of you.'

Once we were all inside, Willis performed a smooth U-turn and took us speeding down the road to Casablanca.

18

CASABLANCA

———

Once we were under way, Willis cast an admiring sidelong glance at his beautiful passenger. In a courtly drawl he said, 'I confess, ma'am, that I'm kind of surprised to see a lady like yourself in cahoots with these desperadoes. Their brand of excitement is liable to get pretty tough.'

'You think I am not tough, Mr Willis?' Karrie turned the full force of her penetrating gaze upon him. 'Perhaps you think I am like one of your American women with their lipstick and mink coats and little poodle dogs.'

I could see that Willis was taken aback. 'I wouldn't say that's all our women,' he protested mildly.

'I am Greek, Mr Willis,' Karrie informed him sternly. 'It was my people who invented the very notions of freedom and democracy, and we have been fighting for those ideals ever since. We fought the tyranny of the Persians, then the Turks, and now the Germans. Greece will be free and I will do my part to make it so, even at the cost of my life.'

'I sincerely hope it won't come to that,' said Willis, dropping his bantering manner. 'Speaking of which,' he added to me, 'that was dashed bad news about old Blenkiron.' Willis was something of an Anglophile, and during his time in London he had consciously adopted what he fondly supposed were some typical English speech mannerisms.

'I suppose in time bad luck catches up with all of us,' I responded noncommittally.

'Of course, Blenkiron always had an extra ace up his sleeve,' he recalled with a smile. 'Maybe, like Mark Twain, reports of his demise are premature.'

'With a man like that, you never know,' I agreed.

Like me, Willis was well aware that Blenkiron had been supposed dead once before, only to reappear in the thick of some foreign gambit. I supposed it would not take long for his presence in Washington to become common knowledge, much to the consternation of his enemies.

'Now, if you'll look over your papers, gents,' said Willis, getting back to business, 'you'll see that you're here as representatives of the Socony-Vacuum Oil Company. It's one of a number of outfits importing American goods into Morocco, along with Douglas Aircraft and Singer sewing machines. In return we're opening up markets to export Moroccan goods like olive oil, almonds, snails and animal hides. The French and Moroccans alike are more than happy to welcome anybody who's lending a helping hand to their economy in these tough times.'

As we neared the city, we passed by an impoverished shanty town. Its ramshackle dwellings had been patched together from rotted planks of wood, ragged patches of tarpaulin, overturned handcarts, and every sort of junk from broken furniture to the rusting doors of wrecked cars.

'Peasants have been drifting in from the interior for ages,' Willis explained, 'looking for work and an escape from the hard life of the countryside. Out there all it takes is a drought or an invasion of locusts to devastate the harvest and leave families starving. In the city they might find jobs in the harbour or the canning factories.'

Once we entered the city proper the contrast could not

have been more extreme. Here, in what our guide described as the Ville Nouvelle, French architects had taken the opportunity to create a model town, with wide boulevards and elegant buildings whose simple style exemplified the efficiency of the French colonial administration. The art deco architecture was more suggestive of the south of France than Africa, though many of the buildings were embellished with colourful Moroccan tilework.

The city had been awake since dawn, and the streets were already filled with coughing motor cars, horses, and wagons drawn by sleepy-looking donkeys. 'Officially the French classify Morocco as a protectorate,' said Willis, 'and the sultan is still the ruler. In actual fact, though, the only thing he has any real authority over is the religious life of his people, who are Muslim, of course.'

We pulled up outside the Hotel Excelsior and entered through a shady portico. A small fountain in the centre of the lobby helped to cool the air while a row of fans whirred overhead. Tapestries made up of brightly coloured geometric patterns hung from the walls, interspersed with glamorous photographs of French film stars.

Willis was clearly acquainted with the clerk at the desk, so we left it to him to check us all in under our assumed identities. Though we had brought only one small bag each, a scrawny porter, whose French came with a heavy Eastern European accent, insisted on carrying them to our rooms for us, while treating us to a stream of incomprehensible local gossip. He departed at last only after receiving a generous tip from Willis.

Following an uncomfortable night on the open sea, the others were all too ready to freshen up and catch up on their sleep. I invited Willis to join me so that he might give me his assessment of the situation in Casablanca. Once we were settled down on a pair of rattan chairs on the veranda of my room, I lit my pipe while Willis tapped out a cigarette from a packet of Marlboros.

The breeze wafting in from the Atlantic carried a salty tang. It mingled evocatively with the dusty haze rising up from the busy streets and the scent of jasmine drifting from the garden below us.

Beyond the orderly boulevards I could see a maze of narrow twisting alleyways interspersed with lively open-air markets. Willis informed me that this was the medina, the heart of the old town, crammed in between the French Ville Nouvelle and the busy harbour. Above the background noise of car horns and the cries of street sellers rose the voices of the muezzins echoing from the minarets like muscular birdsong, summoning the faithful to prayer.

'So,' I began, 'what brings you to this exotic part of the world?'

'I'm stationed here as a cultural attaché.' The American took a long draw on his cigarette, as though considering his words carefully. 'It gives me plenty of scope for sight-seeing.'

From his cautious phrasing I inferred that his duties had more to do with intelligence-gathering than diplomacy. No doubt he was providing Washington with detailed reports on the defensive positions of the Vichy forces.

'I'm sure there's no shortage of interesting things to see,' I remarked. 'I expect it won't be long before there are a lot more American visitors in these parts.'

Willis squinted into the middle distance. 'Yeah. I'm guessing the tourist industry is set for a boom.'

'By then you Americans might not be so welcome,' I suggested. 'Not if your tourists bring a lot more than cameras with them.'

Willis acknowledged the point with a slight tilt of the head. 'The war's a pretty touchy subject around here. The French have taken a licking and they know it, so their pride is smarting something awful. The fact that the Brits have refused to cave in like they did just makes it worse, plus they're real sore about you guys shelling their fleet.'

'It was a hard choice to make,' I said, recalling the various intelligence assessments that had been produced regarding the possibility of the French ships falling into Nazi hands. 'I suppose we can't blame them for taking it badly, though. I heard that the women and children evacuated to Casablanca from Gibraltar were driven out by a hostile mob.'

'Yeah, that was an ugly scene all right,' said Willis with a grimace. 'That's why you need to pass yourselves off as Yanks.' He added casually, 'If you don't mind my asking, where are you folks headed?'

I shrugged. 'Like you, we're just here to see the sights.'

'Well,' said Willis, accepting my need for secrecy, 'I reckon you and your pals will get along fine so long as you don't give yourselves away.'

The drone of an aircraft passing overhead drew our attention skyward. Watching its flight, Willis went on, 'The Cazes airfield is about five miles outside of town and the flights are pretty tightly regulated. With all the security there, no way could we get you out by that route without raising a ruckus. When you're through with this caper of yours, we'll have to cook up a different plan to get you back home without falling into the hands of the local authorities.'

I chewed thoughtfully on my pipe. 'It's hard to judge just how far the Vichy are prepared to go to keep their peace with Germany. We used to be allies, but now . . .'

'Well, they're keen to hang on to what they've got left,' said Willis reflectively, 'and not give the Nazis an excuse to march into their colonies. It gives them the feeling they've still got some shred of *la liberté* left to them. This peace deal is kind of like a friendly handshake where one hand is putting a tight squeeze on the other. It's only a matter of time before some bones get crushed.'

'Are there any Germans here in Casablanca?'

Willis pulled a sour face. 'There's the twelve-man German Armistice Commission stationed here to make sure the French are sticking to the terms of the peace deal. It's an open secret that most of them are actually Gestapo agents keeping an eye out for any enemies of the Reich who might be passing through town.'

'I suppose there are quite a few of those, not to mention locals chafing under this enforced cooperation.'

'You've got that right. There are plenty of people in Morocco who favour the Free French over their Vichy government, and there are Resistance cells here and in Algeria just itching to blow something up.'

'Where do the local authorities stand?'

'They've got their hands full, for sure,' said Willis with some degree of sympathy. 'The city's swarming with refugees from every part of Europe, everything from White Russians to Spanish republicans. The police chief, Colonel Riveaux, tries his best to be fair-minded and keep the peace.' He broke into a smile. 'In fact, even though he's cottoned on to the fact that we're operating an illegal radio transmitter out of the consulate, he's been nice and sloppy about tracking it down, which has got our Gestapo friends pretty hot under the collar.'

'I think he's going to find it harder and harder to stay neutral,' I said.

Willis stubbed out his cigarette and there was a hard glint in his eye. 'Let's just hope that when push comes to shove, most of the French will realise which side their bread is buttered on, whatever they think of Pétain.'

With a final assurance that I could count on him in case of trouble, he returned to the consulate. Following his departure I treated myself to a bath and a couple of hours' sleep, and awoke in the early afternoon feeling sufficiently refreshed to face the hardships that undoubtedly lay before us – above all, dealing with Karrie's stubborn insistence on keeping her vital information to herself.

I joined the others downstairs in a dining room adorned with green and white mosaic tilework. We refreshed ourselves with some of the local sugary mint tea, a basket of croissants and a bowl of figs while we contemplated our next move.

'Well, Karrie,' I said, mustering as much patience as I had in me, 'now we've brought you to Casablanca, what's next?'

She took a sip of tea. Surveying us over the rim of the cup, she said, 'Well, the first thing I must do is go shopping in town for some clothes.' In answer to my nonplussed expression, she explained, 'I'll need to be well dressed when we visit the Blue Paradise.'

'Blue Paradise?' Dougal echoed. 'What's that, then?'

'It's a night club,' the girl replied with the faintest hint of an impish smile.

'We're surely not going dancing, are we?' I protested.

Karrie dabbed her lips with her napkin and reached for a fig. 'No, Richard. We're going fishing.'

19

THE BLUE PARADISE

That night Karrie and I approached the Blue Paradise Club across a tiled courtyard with a small rectangular pool in the centre of it. The entrance was flanked by a pair of palm trees which bowed their heads together over the doorway. Above this arch a neon sign read *Le Paradis Bleu*.

Upon entering, we were greeted by a cacophony of hoots and crashes from a raucous jazz band and the lively chatter of the customers. Painted pillars and Moorish arches divided the large room into discrete sections where blue table lamps illuminated the crowds of revellers partying beneath a floating canopy of tobacco smoke. Ornate brass lamps suspended on chains from the ceiling added to the suggestion of a sheik's desert palace.

The round tables could comfortably accommodate four people and some of them had been pushed together to seat larger parties. The cosmopolitan clientele were clearly out to enjoy themselves, the men in their tailored evening wear, the women in daring dresses that flashed with every shade of crimson, emerald and azure. The air was filled with the buzz of conversation, outbursts of laughter and the clinking of glasses, all of it audible even over the noise of the band.

If a man of my advanced years were to enter a club or restaurant in London accompanied by a girl so beautiful, and so young, there would have been raised eyebrows and loud murmurs of disapproval. We were in French territory, however, so no one batted an eye, although I noticed that one or two of the tables were concealed behind carefully positioned wooden screens, perhaps to hide an assignation that would be considered scandalous even in these exotic quarters. Karrie drew one or two admiring glances before the gentlemen with their roving gaze were brought sharply to heel by their lady friends. Even in the simple white frock she had purchased in the medina, she struck me as the most attractive woman in the place.

A most improbable waiter approached us with a deferential bow. Plump and grey-haired, he peered at us through his thick spectacles like an absent-minded academic who has mislaid his books. Gesturing us forward, he led us across a floor tiled with yellow hexagons to a table that afforded us a clear view of the entire room. In a thick Austrian accent he asked for our order, then set off to fetch a Scotch for me and a brandy cocktail for Karrie. En route to the bar I saw him pause occasionally as if he had forgotten the way.

'This is quite a place,' I said, taking in the décor and the exuberant company.

'Did you not think I would treat you to so good a time?' Karrie enquired teasingly.

Shortly the waiter returned with our drinks. When he had set them down, Karrie drew him in close and spoke confidentially in his ear. 'Please tell Mr Kalimi that Callisto wishes to speak to him.'

Flustered by this very forward behaviour, the elderly waiter adjusted his spectacles, which had almost slipped from his nose. 'Callisto, you say?'

'That's right, Callisto,' Karrie affirmed. 'Tell him it is very important.'

The waiter scurried off and, after halting momentarily to take his bearings, disappeared up a corner stairway to an upper floor.

With her message dispatched, I saw Karrie turn her attention to the band, whose presence it was difficult to ignore. It was a five-piece group and a placard hanging over their heads proclaimed them to be The Louisiana Cats, though I doubted that any of them had ever been within a thousand miles of Louisiana.

They sported a wild variety of facial hair, from the straggly goatee of the clarinetist, via the drooping bandit moustache of the drummer, to the massive bushy beard that rendered the trombonist's features practically invisible. I guessed his anonymity might be deliberate, for I was aware that there were many men in Casablanca who preferred that their faces not be recognised. At that moment they were making a violent assault on a melody normally associated with the more sedate tempos of Glenn Miller and his orchestra. The few couples who attempted to dance to this fevered accompaniment quickly gave up in despair and returned to their tables.

Karrie took a sip of her drink and smiled. 'What is it Shakespeare said about music soothing the savage breast?'

I shook my head in wonderment. 'Frankly, I've endured artillery bombardments that were more soothing. To be fair, though, I can't fault their enthusiasm.'

Karrie grinned at me. 'If you think this is loud, you must let me take you to a Greek wedding sometime.'

Her remark reminded me that I had as yet learned

very little about my companion. 'I'd be interested to know how you came to be an archaeologist,' I ventured. 'I assume that you come from a family of academics.'

'Not at all,' she responded with a shake of her head. 'You may be surprised to learn that my father was a mining engineer.'

I was indeed surprised, and pleasantly so. 'Really? That used to be my line too, before I got drawn into matters even more dangerous.'

'Well then, perhaps you will understand what it was like for me growing up around explosives. Even when I was a child, my father would let me come along to watch him work. I treated it all as my own personal fireworks display and my nerves were hardened by the boom and blast of dynamite. I even considered making the profession my own until one day something changed me.'

I frowned in concern. 'Not a bad accident, I hope.'

'No, nothing like that,' Karrie assured me. 'He was blasting in a quarry, and when the smoke and dust of the detonation cleared I beheld something wondrous. Cleared of the earth that had covered them for centuries, there lay the broken columns of an ancient temple. I ran to it as though summoned by the deity, even with my father calling me back. The inscription I read upon the stonework declared it to be a shrine to Hera, the queen of the gods.'

'That must have been quite a find,' I commented.

'It was for me a moment of revelation. I realised then that beneath our feet lies a world of wonders if we will only look for them.'

'So rather than go in for the family business of blowing things up . . .'

'I have been uncovering and preserving the treasure of ages past, something in which my own country is especially rich.'

Just then Dougal and Jaikie entered, arriving a few minutes after us as we had planned. The young Scots sauntered over to the bar and seated themselves on a pair of stools fringed with gold tassels. I saw Dougal lick his lips as he contemplated the multicoloured ranks of bottled spirits that lined the mirrored shelves.

I had judged it best to split our party in two so as not to draw too much attention to ourselves. While Karrie and I dealt with our business here, the two Die-Hards would keep a discreet distance and watch our backs in case of trouble.

With a touch on my arm Karrie alerted me to the fact that our stout waiter had returned downstairs and resumed his duties, shuffling back and forth between the bar, the kitchen and the crowded tables. A minute or so after, a very different figure descended: a tall, thin man in a fez. He stopped at the foot of the steps to survey the room before strolling towards our table, acknowledging the compliments of his customers with a brief nod and a polite smile as he came.

When he arrived before us, he greeted us with a short bow.

'You are Mr Kalimi, the owner of this establishment?' Karrie asked him.

'Such is my burden,' he confirmed, placing one hand on the back of an empty chair. 'May I join you?'

'Of course,' I answered. 'This is your place after all, isn't it?'

He smoothed down his yellow blazer and loosened his blue ascot before sliding into the seat and studying us with dark, half-lidded eyes. Beneath the fez his head appeared to be completely bald, which, along with his sallow features and sharp cheekbones, gave him the appearance of an ascetic.

He fitted a cigarette to an ivory holder and lit it from a book of matches emblazoned with the name of his club. Fixing his gaze upon Karrie, he asked, 'You are the young woman who wishes so urgently to speak with me? You are Callisto?'

'That is the name by which I was told to identify myself. My name is Karissa Adriatis and I believe you can put me in contact with a mutual friend, a one-time colleague of mine.'

Kalimi took a deep draw on his cigarette and let the smoke drift out in thin streamers from his nostrils.

'And your gentleman companion, who is he?' He turned to me. 'Zeus, perhaps? Or Vulcan?'

I found the man hard to read and that made me wary. 'I won't insult you by giving a false name, Mr Kalimi, but I think it will be wiser all round if I keep my identity to myself.'

'What is one more secret,' said Kalimi, with an open-handed gesture of acceptance, 'in a city that is already home to so many?'

He glanced over at the band and waved his cigarette in their direction. 'They make quite an impression, do they not?'

The combo were currently in the middle of a crazed rendition of what might once have been 'Sweet Georgia Brown', but that was only a guess.

'Yes, quite an impression,' Karrie agreed non-committally.

'They're certainly putting their backs into it,' was the nearest I could come to a compliment.

'Every one of them is from a different country,' Kalimi informed us proudly. 'Hungary, Czechoslovakia, Russia, and so on. They have only been playing together for a short time.'

'I find that easy to believe,' said Karrie, rubbing her thumb around the edge of her glass to produce a squeaking sound that expressed her irritation with this small talk.

I knew she was impatient for Kalimi to put her in contact with Lasalle, but he was clearly giving himself plenty of time to take our measure. To rush him would be to risk losing his trust. I couldn't help wincing when the drummer began thrashing his cymbal as though it had spat in his face.

'I suppose we all have our own taste in music,' I said.

A thin smile touched Kalimi's lips. 'You must appreciate, Monsieur Zeus, that in a city of many secrets, some of my customers do not wish there to be any risk of their conversations being overheard, which makes a band such as this a vital necessity.'

At this point, mercifully, the quintet took a break. They sprawled or hunched in their chairs, sharing cigarettes, downing glasses of wine and chatting in their native tongues. Their rapid speech and expressive gestures felt like a continuation of their frenetic musical performance.

Dropping his voice, Kalimi continued, 'My previous band was somewhat more harmonious, but they broke up when their most musically competent members, the trumpet player and the pianist, managed to obtain travel visas. They are now on their way to Lisbon with high hopes of reaching the United States.'

'Mr Kalimi,' Karrie interrupted in a voice of unaccustomed sweetness, 'your club is very beautiful and the entertainment undeniably stimulating.'

Kalimi briefly doffed his fez. 'I thank you for the compliment, madame.'

'But you are a businessman,' Karrie persisted, 'and you will appreciate the importance of getting to the point.'

Kalimi arched an eyebrow. 'Which is to say, dear lady?'

'My friend assured me in his letter that if I were to present myself to you under the code name of Callisto you would be able to put me in contact with him.'

Kalimi gently tapped his finger on his cigarette holder. 'You must understand that your friend is fearful of those who wish to wrest his secrets from him.'

'He's right to be afraid,' I said. 'We've met those men and they're not to be taken lightly.'

'Which is why you must take me to him now.' Karrie leaned forward insistently. 'Before our enemies catch up with us.'

Kalimi stared at her with the intensity of a jeweller assessing a precious gem. Rising to his feet, he stubbed out his cigarette and slipped the holder into his pocket. 'Very well, dear lady. Please excuse me while I make a brief telephone call.' With a small bow of farewell he returned to his upstairs office.

'Are you sure we can trust him?' I wondered.

Karrie threw back the last of her cocktail. 'Armand's instructions were that I should contact him through

Kalimi at the Blue Paradise. It's the only course open to us.'

As we awaited the proprietor's return, I became aware of two men at a table tucked into a shadowy corner who were observing us with some interest. One of them stood and strolled towards us with an air that was too casual to be convincing. He was dressed in a plain dark suit with a thin black tie and his demeanour was one I recognised all too easily. Prussians have a way of carrying themselves that makes them stand out from less arrogant people like thistles in a flower bed.

When he reached our table he greeted us stiffly. 'Sir, madame, allow me to introduce myself. I am Herr Gerber of the Armistice Commission.'

Even if I had not been forewarned by Ellery Willis, I would have been in no doubt that we were being addressed by a member of the Gestapo.

20

ANTIQUES AND CURIOS

The Gestapo man was standing close enough to enable me to smell the oil on his close-cropped hair and see that his eyes were that cold blue supposedly favoured by the Führer.

'Yeah, I heard about you guys,' I responded affably. 'You're here to smooth along your peace deal, or something.'

Gerber's clean-shaven features, freshly scrubbed to a pink flush, creased into an expression of pained concern. 'Yes, to ensure that there is no violation of the terms of the armistice. You will understand, then, that when strangers come to Casablanca I am most concerned that they should not provoke an unfortunate incident which might disturb the delicate balance of peace. Might I enquire as to your name and business?'

Adopting a bluff manner to mask my true feelings of hostile suspicion, I answered with hearty good humour. 'Why sure – it's no secret. I'm Hank Brewster of the Socony-Vacuum Oil Company. I'm just prospecting for some business opportunities, that's all.'

I was no stranger to assuming a false identity, but I had never before tried to pass myself off as an American. I could only hope that my efforts to imitate the cadences of Willis's speech would allow me to pass muster with this curious German. A quick glance out of the corner of my eyes assured me that Jaikie and Dougal were keeping watch over us from the bar, even while they put on a lively show of joking and drinking.

'There have been worrying rumours,' noted Gerber with unpleasant emphasis, 'that the American consulate has been associating itself with certain dissident elements here in Morocco. I sincerely hope these rumours are untrue.'

I feigned a snort of laughter. 'If you want to talk diplomacy, you'll have to find somebody else. All I know is oil, son.'

The Gestapo man raised a warning finger. 'I advise you, Mr Brewster, to tread very carefully here in Casablanca, especially in view of the fact that our nations are now at odds.'

I decided I'd had enough of the German's hectoring manner. 'Herr Gerber, if I recall correctly,' I retorted in a harder tone, 'your Führer was the one who decided to pick a fight.'

I'd raised my voice sufficiently to turn a few heads at the neighbouring tables. Clearly discomfited, Gerber shifted his ground. 'Let us turn to more pleasant things, shall we? Such as your lovely companion.' He regarded Karrie with an appreciative gaze. 'And you, madame, are . . . ?'

Karrie glared at him coldly. 'I am Greek, Herr Gerber, so you will forgive me if I choose not to indulge in pleasantries.'

Gerber curled his lip. 'There are more than a few here who bear us ill will,' he conceded, 'but the French, ever a practical people, have shown that a friendly accommodation can be reached between former adversaries. I am sure it will be so in future.'

There was no mistaking the flash of bitter anger in

Karrie's large grey eyes. 'I assure you, Herr Gerber, that an accommodation will be reached when Berlin is in flames.'

Whatever response the German was about to utter was interrupted by a cacophonous outburst from the band, who had received a signal to resume their set. Gerber scowled at them, as though wishing he had the authority to arrest them all.

'Pah! This American jungle music!' he spat sourly.

'Not entirely American, I think,' said Karrie.

Puzzled as to her meaning, I turned my ear to the wild combo. Somewhere amid the din, almost strangled by the squeal of the clarinet, the braying of the trombone, and the frenzied beat of the drums, a familiar melody was struggling against the odds to make its presence felt. It took a few moments before I realised that, warped and mangled as it was, the tune they were playing was the Marseillaise.

The other customers rapidly came to the same recognition and began clapping along to the beat. Before long some were even singing the words, difficult as it was to keep in step with the group's frantic tempo. Even Dougal and Jaikie were clapping and stamping their feet with an almost Gallic enthusiasm.

Gerber glowered at the revelling customers, many of whom were openly pointing at him and jeering. With a curt gesture he summoned his companion from his table and they marched sullenly out of the door. There was a ragged cheer at their departure and when the Louisiana Cats finished their number they were rewarded with extended and raucous applause.

While she was clapping, Karrie addressed me with an

arched eyebrow. 'I must say, you make a very convincing American.'

I eyed her suspiciously. 'I do hope that's supposed to be a compliment.'

Kalimi rejoined us as the noise died away. He tilted his head in the direction of the band. 'Officially that revolutionary anthem is banned in Vichy territory, but with musicians' – he shrugged his bony shoulders – 'what can one do?'

I had my suspicions that he had passed an instruction to the combo to play exactly that tune with the full intention of driving the Gestapo men from his club. He was perhaps more closely allied to our cause than I had first expected.

Meanwhile four members of the band had retired to the wings for a smoke and a drink, leaving the pianist alone on the stage. Throwing back his unruly mop of black hair, he commenced a version of Beethoven's 'Moonlight Sonata' that was surprisingly close to what the composer had intended.

As the music rippled in the background, Karrie turned to Kalimi. 'And now, Mr Kalimi?' she prompted.

'Ah, yes, the business,' Kalimi acknowledged. He pulled a small scrap of paper from his pocket and passed it to her; I caught the merest glimpse of an address scrawled in a spidery hand. Karrie read the note and passed it back with a nod. Striking a match, Kalimi set the paper corner alight and dropped it into the ashtray.

'And now that our business is concluded,' he said, 'I plead that you will not make yourselves the object of any further attention in my establishment.'

I took his meaning and rose from my seat. 'It's been a lovely evening, but you're probably right. We really should be going.'

'Yes, and thank you for your help, Mr Kalimi,' said Karrie, standing up beside me. 'I'm really very grateful.'

The proprietor regarded her gravely through half-lidded eyes. 'I must caution you, dear lady, to beware of the many dangers that lurk in Casablanca. I should hate for one so beautiful to come to any harm.'

Karrie tossed back her glorious mane of black hair. 'You shouldn't worry about me. My ancestors were Spartans.'

Once outside, we waited on the corner for Dougal and Jaikie to join us before proceeding down the street.

'So who was that sleekit-looking German that was gabbing with you?' Dougal asked.

'That was Herr Gerber of the Armistice Commission,' said Karrie, her voice dripping with distaste.

'And I'll eat my hat if he's not a Gestapo officer,' I added.

'I think he's got a couple of locals in his employ,' said Jaikie in an undertone. 'Don't look, but there are two shifty characters lurking in the shadows a safe distance behind us.'

A more worrying possibility occurred to me, that they might be in the employ of Ravenstein. The thought that the master spy might be somewhere out in the dark orchestrating another ambush was enough to send a tingle of apprehension down my spine. Through gritted teeth, I said, 'We have to shake them off.'

'Yes. We cannot let them follow us to Dr Lasalle,' said Karrie.

'Don't worry,' said Jaikie. 'There's a canny old trick we can use.'

Dougal grinned roguishly. 'I know just what you mean. We'll be the tail-enders, right?'

Karrie peered at him curiously. 'What do you mean, tail-enders?'

'It's really simple,' Jaikie explained. 'You two walk ahead of us and we'll all keep up a loud conversation. As soon as you see the chance, the pair of you duck down out of sight somewhere while Dougal and I carry on as if we're still talking to you up ahead of us.'

'With any luck our pals back there won't realise we've split up,' Dougal concluded.

I knew that in their rascally youth among the slums of Glasgow the Die-Hards had become experts at dodging trouble, especially when it came in the form of the police. I was confident that they could pull off their trick.

'That's the plan then,' I agreed. 'They'll very likely miss us in the dark. We'll meet up later back at the hotel.'

We began walking faster, forcing our unwanted friends to increase their pace while still trying to remain inconspicuous. At the same time Dougal and Jaikie, in keeping with our false identities, led off a boisterous and mostly ill-informed conversation about American sports.

'Did you hear about that Mets game?' Dougal enquired in a loud Texan drawl. 'What a bust-up!'

'Yeah, they were sure pitching the pigskin on that one,' Jaikie responded.

'The slammer must have hit at least three home runs before tea,' I contributed, wondering if what I said made any sense at all.

Karrie chimed in with, 'Those were some of the best hoops of the season, so I hear. I would bet that Notre Dame will capture the pennant this year.'

'Well, I say that Yale are a dadblamed cert to clinch it,' Dougal asserted belligerently, 'and if some wise guy wants to cross me, he'll take a kick in the caboose.'

So we carried on until we spotted an empty unattended handcart to our left. I caught Karrie by the sleeve and we ducked behind it. Dougal and Jaikie carried on as though nothing had happened and continued to discourse vociferously on various sports of which they knew nothing.

Crouching low, Karrie and I observed a pair of men in hooded robes slinking along in pursuit of the two Scots. Our friends were making such a row it was easy to keep track of them even as they briefly passed out of sight round a corner. As soon as we judged it was safe, we emerged from hiding and headed off in a different direction.

'That was certainly fun,' said Karrie, 'but I hope Dougal and Jaikie aren't walking into any trouble.'

'Oh, I think they can handle themselves,' I assured her, then added, 'Probably nearly as well as you could.'

She led me unhesitatingly to where the streets narrowed to a series of twisted, constricted alleyways, dotted with ancient wooden doors. I realised that she had led us into the medina, the old town. It was a baffling maze of tunnels and passageways, some so narrow that a man with broad shoulders would have difficulty squeezing through.

'You're sure we're not going to get lost?' I asked.

'As an archaeologist, Richard, it's part of my job to familiarise myself with the lie of the land,' Karrie asserted confidently. 'I've found my way around the ruins of

Mycenae and the labyrinth at Knossos. I memorised a map of Casablanca earlier this evening, just as if it were another historical site.'

Her self-assurance was not misplaced. Soon we were standing in front our destination, a small shop with dust-streaked windows. A sign above them declared in Arabic and French *Antiques and Curios for Sale*. A few brass urns and ornamental daggers were visible through the murky glass, none of which looked especially valuable.

'This is the place,' Karrie said. I could tell from the catch in her voice that she was as excited as she would have been if she had been standing before the entrance of a newly discovered Egyptian tomb.

I yanked on the bell pull hanging by the door and heard muffled clanking from inside. After a few moments the door was opened by a squat figure in a skull cap. His bulging eyes stared up at us out of a frog-like face.

'I believe we are expected,' said Karrie. 'Mr Kalimi said I would find my colleague here.'

'Yes, Kalimi, of course,' said the little man in a voice so hoarse it was almost a whisper. 'This way, please.'

He ushered us inside through a shop cluttered with all manner of knick-knacks. In the dim light I glimpsed figurines pitted with age, strings of inexpensive baubles, and tarnished brass candlesticks. The little man directed us to a rickety wooden stairway then disappeared through a bead curtain into a back room.

I led the way up the creaking steps to a plain white door. Here I hesitated, suddenly recalling my initial mistrust of Kalimi. Knowing there was a chance we might be walking into a trap, I signalled Karrie to stay behind me and she reluctantly complied. Turning the knob as quietly as possible, I slowly opened the door.

The first thing to meet my gaze was the last thing I expected to see – a policeman.

21

THE GAME PLAYERS

He was a compactly built officer in the dapper uniform of the local gendarmerie. Ignoring my arrival, he shook a pair of dice in a cup before tossing them nonchalantly on to a backgammon board. Sitting opposite him was a very different figure in a loosely fitting burnoose. His bald head and Van Dyck beard, along with his arched eyebrows, lent a faintly Satanic cast to his features. On the table between the two men sat a near-empty bottle of cognac from which they had been filling their crystal glasses.

As soon as Karrie entered the room, the bald man leapt from his chair with a cry of recognition. Embracing her warmly, he kissed her on both cheeks before stepping back to admire her.

'Ah, Karrie, *ma chérie*, you look so well,' he exclaimed. 'And yet you must have made a hard journey.'

'It wasn't without incident,' Karrie admitted. Gesturing towards me, she added, 'This is—'

'Hank Brewster,' I interposed, wary of revealing my true name in the presence of the Vichy police. 'I'm very pleased to meet you, Dr Lasalle.'

The historian's gaze remained fixed on Karrie. 'I cannot tell you with what excitement I have anticipated your arrival.'

Stubbing out his cigarette, the officer stood and straightened his tunic. Tucking his cap under his arm, he greeted us each in turn with a small bow. 'I am very pleased to meet any friends of the good doctor,' he said in accented but impeccable English. 'Colonel Marcel Riveaux, prefect of police, at your service.'

Ellery Willis had told me that the prefect was doing his best to maintain a fair-minded neutrality in difficult circumstances, but I still felt uncomfortable in his presence. It was tricky to judge just how much he might be under the influence of the Gestapo men overseeing the armistice.

'The colonel and I were comrades in the Great War,' Lasalle explained. 'We meet occasionally for a friendly game of backgammon.'

'And once again the dice have favoured me most generously.' Riveaux scooped up a pile of banknotes from the table and slipped them into his pocket. 'I would be delighted, *monsieur le docteur*, to stay here all night winning your money, but alas, duty calls.'

Tossing off the last of his drink, he placed his cap on his head and secured it with a light pat. 'I have made the shocking discovery that some enterprising rogue has been smuggling cases of cognac into Morocco. I must at all costs get to the root of this infamy.'

'I understand perfectly,' said Dr Lasalle.

Riveaux's eyes passed appraisingly over all three of us before focusing again on the historian. 'My powers of premonition, which have never failed me yet, tell me, my friend, that you will soon be setting out on another of your archaeological expeditions.' He smoothed his moustache with a delicate fingertip. 'Be assured that I will see to it personally that all the necessary permits are properly signed.'

'I am very glad to have that assurance.' Lasalle smiled.

On his way to the door, the prefect paused to address Karrie. 'And you, mademoiselle, if during your time in Casablanca you should find yourself in any sort of difficulty, please do not hesitate to call on me.'

'You are very kind,' Karrie responded guardedly.

Riveaux accorded her a brief courtly salute then made his exit. Listening to his receding footsteps, I inwardly breathed a sigh of relief.

'Has he really gone to investigate a case?' Karrie enquired.

Lasalle indulged in a short laugh. 'Not unless the mistress he keeps in the rue Veronne is also an underworld informant.'

'You keep very interesting company,' I noted, dropping my American accent.

'When one wishes one's presence in Casablanca to remain a secret,' the archaeologist observed with a wry grimace, 'it helps to be in the good graces of the prefect of police.'

'From the look of his winnings, his good graces don't come cheap,' said Karrie.

Lasalle gave a fatalistic shrug. 'In these difficult times, even old friends cannot afford to do favours for free. Fortunately, since selling the family vineyard I inherited some years ago, I am not without resources.' He turned to me with a frown. 'And you, sir – I take leave to suppose that your name is not Hank Brewster.'

'My name is Richard Hannay,' I told him. 'I'm here on behalf of the National Antiquities Council of Great Britain.'

'Ah, yes, Mr Stannix and his little band of spies.'

The Frenchman wrinkled his nose. 'I have crossed paths with them before. They have more interest in advancing armies than in advancing science.'

Noting his disapproval, Karrie said, 'Armand, without the help of Mr Hannay and his friends, I doubt I would have made it this far.'

'And unless I have been misled,' I added, 'your researches into the Knights of St John may prove crucial to the future of Malta and perhaps the whole of Europe.'

'The war!' Lasalle gave a melancholy sigh. 'There is no escaping it, even when one is delving into the distant past.' He threw Karrie an appealing look. 'My dear, can we not discuss our work without the presence of this Englishman?'

'Armand, this is no time to be concerned with nationalities and past wrongs,' she rebuked him.

'Bear in mind, doctor,' I pointed out, 'that if Malta falls, Britain may fall too, and with it any hope of freedom for your own people.'

Lasalle gave a reluctant grunt of acceptance. 'You are right, of course, both of you. I have been working alone for so long, so suspicious of everyone, that I have become, what would you say – soured?'

Karrie laid a sympathetic hand on his shoulder. 'You are not alone now. I promise you that Mr Hannay is the best friend you could have.'

I was surprised by the compliment, but the doctor appeared to take it to heart.

Lowering his head, he said, 'Very well then, *ma chérie*, I am satisfied.'

There was an air of weary resignation about him,

as that of a man worn down by age and declining health. Then, fixing his eyes on Karrie, he seemed to recover his vigour.

'Now tell me, tell me please,' he asked eagerly, 'did you find the route to the tomb?'

Karrie reached out and clasped his thin hand. 'What I found was a series of clues,' she told him. 'I only hope you can see the meaning in them. They were in a letter I found in the Easterly family archives. I was not allowed to remove it, but I have all the information stored here.' She tapped her temple.

Lasalle smiled broadly. 'Tell me then, and I shall do my best to elucidate the mystery.'

Karrie took a moment to collect her thoughts then recited from memory. 'First, you must pass the night beneath the eagle's beak, then look through the eye of the sun to find the way to Kedesh.'

'It doesn't sound like much to go on,' I commented. 'And what is this Kedesh place?'

'Kedesh is a city in the book of Joshua,' Karrie explained to me, 'appointed as a place of refuge. Here a man pursued by enemies could find sanctuary under the protection of God.'

I did not find this particularly enlightening. I had expected the information we had risked so much to bring here would be of more solid and practical use, not a series of poetic allusions.

Lasalle demonstrated no such disappointment. He snatched up a pencil and paper and eagerly noted down the obscure phrases while Karrie repeated them.

'I have come across such instructions before,' he said,

tapping the pencil against his lower lip. 'They represent markers along the route, whether natural or man-made, and thus form a sort of verbal map.'

I was beginning to understand. 'You mean it's sort of like *turn left at the farmhouse*,' I suggested, '*carry on to the elm tree and go straight through the cornfield.*'

'Something along those lines, yes,' the historian affirmed.

'That is what I suspected,' said Karrie, 'though I am at a loss as to how to interpret these particular markers.'

Lasalle rubbed his brow. 'The vital part is to identify the starting point, the eagle's beak.'

'If that refers to an eagle's nest, then we really are in trouble,' I said. 'Those instructions are hundreds of years old and any nest built then will be long gone by now.'

'Bear in mind that these words are meant to guide the family of Sir Thomas Easterly to their kinsman's tomb,' Karrie reminded me, 'even if that turned out to be a future generation. We are dealing with something that would still be present after many years.'

'Just so,' said Lasalle. 'Please follow me.'

He led us into an adjoining room that was evidently his study. The shelves were packed with antique books and scrolls while various maps adorned the walls, many of them annotated by hand and marked with circles and crosses. In the centre of the room stood a large table with wooden boxes stacked beneath it. Its surface was completely covered with notebooks, manuscripts, photographs and samples of local art.

Lasalle waved a hand over his collection. 'I have been visiting Morocco for many years, and over the past months I have made several excursions into the mountains searching for traces of lost Christian settlements. I have mapped peaks and valleys never before explored and made many detailed notes, all in hopes of finding my way to the tomb of Sir Thomas Easterly.'

I couldn't help but be moved by the tenacity of this frail scholar whose thirst for knowledge had driven him to exploits that would have daunted stronger men.

'And you're hoping,' I said, 'that this infernal beak can be found among all this.'

'If I remember right, then perhaps so,' he agreed.

He began rifling through the notebooks on the desk, snatching up one, casting it aside, and flipping open another.

'Somewhere, somewhere,' I heard him mutter under his breath.

Karrie meanwhile was making an enraptured survey of the maps and books on display. Her slim fingers traced a reverent journey along shelves laden with leather-bound volumes of obvious antiquity.

Abruptly Lasalle cried out, 'See! See!'

He was holding out an open book. With a trembling forefinger, he pointed. There, in the middle of a disordered cluster of hastily scrawled notes, was the sketch of a sharp hook of rock, rendered in skilful detail.

'In my notes here,' Lasalle declared excitedly, 'I have named this distinctive formation the Talon. But you see, do you not?'

The thrill of discovery in his words was echoed in my own. 'Yes, I can understand why you would name it the Talon. But it could just as easily be the beak of a gigantic bird of prey.'

'But where is it?' asked Karrie, hardly daring to believe that we had indeed found the first step in our journey, 'Do you have a location?'

'Yes, yes, these numbers here refer to a particular map.'

As he spoke, Lasalle laid the book down and rummaged about on the desk. Finally he pulled out a map with frayed edges and swept a clutter of native ornaments aside so that they crashed unheeded to the floor. He unfolded the map across the empty space and smoothed it out. Karrie and I watched as he trailed a quivering finger across the Atlas Mountains to where a particular spot was marked with a symbol and a number.

'My friends, this is where we must go,' he declared, almost breathless with anticipation. 'It is here that the eagle's beak awaits us, and with it, let us pray, the lost secret of the Knights of Malta.'

22

THE PLAGUES OF EGYPT

———

Back at the Excelsior hotel that night Karrie and I brought Dougal and Jaikie up to date on our meeting with Lasalle. The Frenchman was going to contact us as soon as he had made the necessary arrangements for our expedition into the mountains. The two Die-Hards had led our unskilled pursuers on a merry dance through the streets of Casablanca before bringing them to the edge of a rather smelly canal. Here the Scots caught the two Arabs from behind and shoved them in for a highly unpleasant plunge.

I revelled in the comfort of my bed that night, knowing that there were to be some rough times ahead. I had hiked through the Highlands of Scotland many times over the years, but the Atlas peaks were much more challenging and I no longer had the resilience of youth on my side when it came to the hardships of trekking across the heights.

A dream came to me of Mary, Peter John and myself standing on a rocky shore, gazing out to sea. We were watching the approach of an elegant sailing ship that was gliding lightly as a feather across the calm and sunlit waters. In the skies above circled a flock of doves, their outspread wings glistening like a fresh fall of snow.

I awoke with that image still fixed in my mind. It gave me hope that one day the three of us would be together again and that peace might finally come to us all.

Later that morning I received a phone call from Ellery

Willis inviting me to join him for coffee at l'Etoilerie, a café overlooking the harbour. I arrived to find him alternately sipping espresso from a small cup and nibbling an almond pastry. He ordered the same for me and lit a cigarette with a glance towards the harbour. I guessed he was hoping that the smoke would do something to mask the pungent odours of fish and sweltering vegetables wafting up from the docks.

The busy harbour was quite a sight, expanded and built up by the French to turn the city into a major centre for trade. Huge loading cranes were swinging cargo containers to and from the various foreign freighters crowded there. The flags of Spain and Portugal were prominent among them, while further out I could see a French naval cruiser. I wondered if it had been one of those damaged in the notorious British attack.

We kept our voices low in order not to put too heavy a strain on my uncertain American accent. When the waiter brought my cup Willis pulled a wry face.

'It's not great,' he apologised, 'but it's about as near as you can get to real coffee around here. Best not to ask what they make it from.'

My first taste proved him right. It was a bitter brew, forcing me to throw in a couple of spoonfuls of sugar. I gave him the gist of our encounter with the Gestapo man and he smiled ruefully over my account of the Louisiana Cats bursting into the Marseillaise.

'This really is the darnedest place,' he chuckled. 'I think I'm actually going to miss it when they move me on.'

I noticed that he was keeping one eye on the harbour below us. There was no doubt in my mind that he was gathering information for his next report to the US intelligence chiefs.

'While I appreciate the coffee, such as it is,' I said, 'I'm sure you didn't invite me here to look at the view.'

'This is a spot where I know we won't be overheard,' he explained 'and I wanted to give you a heads-up. The fact is, there's been a bit of a buzz in the German security traffic since you got here. I think Casablanca is about to get hot for you and your friends.'

I nodded sombrely. 'I suppose that's to be expected. You'll be glad to know that we're leaving later today. All I can say about the mission is that we're headed into the Atlas Mountains.'

Willis gave a low whistle. 'I expect even the Gestapo will be slow to follow you there.'

At that moment I was taken aback by the sight of three uniformed Germans walking past us only about twenty yards away, as boldly as if they were strolling down the Koenigstrasse. They were headed in the direction of a customs house. Abruptly they burst out laughing as if one of them had just topped off a hilarious joke.

Willis eyed them narrowly. 'Under the terms of the armistice,' he informed me, 'the Germans are allowed to refuel and repair their U-boats here, so for all its Gallic-African charm, Casablanca serves as a base for attacking our Atlantic shipping.'

I followed the Germans with a sour gaze until they passed out of sight. 'They're certainly not leaving their French hosts in any doubt as to who's actually in charge.'

'There was a time they were more discreet,' Willis reflected, 'but now they like to flaunt their presence by marching around in uniform. Given the increase in Reich activity around here, you might want to avoid coming back this way, especially as you've caught the eye of Gerber.'

'If you can find us another route, I'd be very grateful.'

He pondered a moment. 'I'll tell you what, I'll make a few calls and have travel documents and tickets waiting for you at the El Nouri hotel in Fez. The manager is one of our contacts and he'll see you on to the train to Tangier.'

'Tangier is still neutral, I hope.'

'Sure. The Spanish have moved in for the sake of security, so they say, but the place is still run by an international committee, so neither the Germans nor the Vichy can touch you there.'

I was glad to hear Willis sound so confident and wished that I shared his optimism. Although Tangier might prove a safe refuge under other circumstances, I was sure that Ravenstein was on our trail and absolutely nowhere was beyond his long reach.

When I got back to the hotel, Lasalle had arrived in a battered Citroën 11B, an old six-seater that looked as though it had seen plenty of miles over rough terrain. Dougal and Jaikie were already loading our modest luggage into the back while Karrie and the Frenchman were poring over a map spread across the bonnet of the car.

'Glad to see you, sir,' Jaikie greeted me. 'It seems everything has been cleared for us to move out.'

'From the sound of it, it's going to be quite a trip,' Dougal added eagerly.

I joined the two historians and Lasalle explained his plan.

'We're going to follow this road south-east to the town of Kamsoura,' he said, tracing the route with his forefinger. 'This will be what you might call our jumping-off point for the Atlas Mountains. I have a contact there I have used many times before and he will supply all we need for our expedition.'

'I'm glad to hear it,' I said. 'From what Ellery Willis tells me, the sooner we get clear of Casablanca the better.'

Lasalle folded up his map and we all climbed into the car. Soon, to my great relief, we had left the outskirts of the city far behind. Lasalle and Jaikie shared the driving – Lasalle because he knew the route and the idiosyncrasies of his well-travelled vehicle, and Jaikie because he was keen to get behind the wheel of a car he regarded as a classic.

The first stage of our journey was along one of the modern highways constructed by the French to link up the far-flung regions of their protectorate. Initially the terrain was colourless, a flat expanse of barren rocks and dust-covered phosphate mines. By degrees, however, we began to encounter stretches of pasture where herds of grazing goats were watched over by lean mongrel dogs who had been trained to guard them.

Presently, under Lasalle's direction, we left the main road and struck a rough, gravelled track that led to higher ground. Ahead of us loomed the vivid foothills of the Atlas Mountains. As we ground our way over the stony byway, our venerable Citroën gave a sudden alarming choke. The next instant it jolted to a dead halt.

Lasalle spat out a stream of French profanities as he climbed out of the car. Throwing open the bonnet, he peered at the engine with a growl of vexation.

Jaikie hopped out and joined him. 'I think the alternator's cut out,' he surmised. 'Have you got a tool box handy?'

Lasalle nodded curtly and pointed to the boot.

While Jaikie rummaged about for the tools, Dougal, Karrie and I got out to stretch our legs. Tier upon tier, the Atlas Mountains rose majestically before us. Even in summer, crowns of snow capped the highest peaks and glistened under the sun. I took a deep breath, savouring the herb-scented atmosphere. After only a few moments, however, I found myself coughing as a dramatic change struck the air.

From the arid lowlands to our rear a wind was kicking up, carrying with it a stream of dust. With an eerie howl it swept towards us, causing the ranks of evergreens on the nearby slopes to shudder like frightened sheep. Watching the roiling cloud bear down on our little party, I was reminded of the plagues of Egypt from the book of Exodus. This, however, was no curse from God, but nature's own fury.

Bent over the engine, Jaikie became aware of the ominous shadow drawing over us. Immediately on the alert, he pulled himself up straight and slammed down the bonnet.

'Sandstorm!' he yelled.

'*Vite! Vite!*' cried Lasalle. 'Everyone into the car at once!'

We bundled inside and quickly rolled up the windows.

Dougal pressed his nose against the glass, wide-eyed. 'How can there be a sandstorm?' he objected incredulously. 'I thought the Sahara was on the other side of the mountains.'

'There are other deserts to the west of us,' Lasalle informed him, 'and when the winds rise from that quarter . . .'

There was no need for any further explanation. Twisting funnels of sand, ten to fifteen feet high, were now whirling around us like crazed dervishes. The howl of the wind rose to a banshee screech as it enveloped us in a smothering shroud of sand. It rasped over the paintwork and seeped in through vents and cracks to cover the car's interior in a layer of terracotta dust.

It caked over the windows, entirely blocking out the world beyond, and plunging us into a lightless obscurity so absolute it was as if we had been swept out of this world and cast into a bottomless Stygian pit. We huddled together, as though seeking safety from some ravenous lion that had come roaring out of the western desert to devour us.

After what seemed an eternity, the shrieking wind dwindled away, and a few feeble rays from the dying sun began to filter through the dusty air. Even through the murky window I could see that the road had utterly vanished beneath deep layers of sand. It was piled up in solid dunes against the car doors, trapping us inside.

23

'YOU ARE A GAZELLE'

———

Jaikie laboriously cranked down his driver's window then squirmed outside. The rest of us could only look on as he crawled his way over the dune until he found firm footing. With long, slow scoops of his hands he eventually cleared the door and hauled it open. One by one we emerged, relieved to be free of the dusty confines of our trapped vehicle.

Even working as a team, it took us some time to dig the car out, and by the time we were done night had fallen. Working by the light of an electric torch, Jaikie and Lasalle laboriously cleared the carburettor intake and dusted off the engine. Only then did they dare to start the motor, which wheezed worryingly at the first few attempts before growling into renewed life.

Lasalle switched it off and gave the Citroën a fond pat. He looked up at the stars, which were now penetrating the hazy remnants of the storm, and cleared his throat.

'We are still some hours from Kamsoura,' he informed us all.

'It's going to be hard enough to keep to the track,' said Jaikie, 'let alone trying it in the dark.'

'Look, it seems to me that after all we've been through, we're pretty much all in,' I said. 'Why don't we get some sleep and see if we can find our way in the morning?'

This suggestion was met with weary murmurs of assent. After cleaning out the inside of the car as best we could, we made ourselves as comfortable as possible with the blankets we had brought and settled down for some welcome rest beneath a sky now brilliant with diamond-sharp stars.

Dawn broke blue and clear. Dragging ourselves stiffly from the car, we breakfasted on dates, biscuits and water. Karrie shook some grit from her luxuriant hair and peered out at the sand-covered landscape before us. All trace of the road had been covered over by the storm.

'I hope you can find the route, Armand,' she said. 'It feels as if we're in the middle of a desert right now.'

Lasalle fished a set of field glasses from the glove compartment and carefully surveyed the landscape. Standing beside him, I searched with naked eyes for some indication of where our road might lie buried. I was completely baffled, but the Frenchman gave a sudden cry of delight.

'Look, over there!' he urged, thrusting the glasses into my hands and pointing dramatically.

Peering intently, I was able to make out a rough stone obelisk a few hundred yards away poking up above the sand. 'It looks like a small monument of some sort,' I observed. 'Are you saying that you recognise it?'

'It is one of a series of markers laid down every hundred yards by the Berbers centuries ago,' Lasalle informed me. 'They mark out the caravan routes, and if we follow them they will lead us to Kamsoura.'

'Well, thank goodness for history!' Dougal declared with a laugh.

We gathered up our things and began packing them back into the car. We were just about to set off when

Lasalle gave a sudden grunt of pain and staggered up against the vehicle, laying a hand on the bonnet to steady himself.

Karrie flew to his side. 'Are you all right, Armand?' she queried anxiously.

He patted her hand reassuringly. 'It is just a touch of heartburn. No need for concern.'

As he turned away from us, I saw him take a small tube from his pocket and slip a pill into his mouth. After a few deep breaths he gave us a smile.

'You see, it is nothing at all. Come, let us go!'

Before climbing into the driver's seat, Jaikie drew me aside.

'I'm not a doctor,' he said, 'but I'll swear those are glycerine capsules he's taking.'

'Yes,' I agreed, 'exactly what would be prescribed for a man with a heart condition.'

With nothing more to go on, we let the matter rest.

After an hour of following the ancient caravan route we saw the road emerge from beneath its sandy covering. A welcome stretch of greenery opened up ahead and soon we were travelling through lush woodland that lifted our spirits immeasurably.

The road took a winding path through a flowering forest which gradually gave way to lofty stands of cedar, some of the trees measuring close to two hundred feet. At last we reached Kamsoura on the banks of the Oum el Rada river, driving through an ornate gate of obvious antiquity. The houses were painted carmine red, while the woodwork of the windows and doors was a vibrant turquoise. As we drove down the street, bands of barefoot children ran after us, cheerfully waving and yelling at the foreigners in their big car.

We parked at a hostel Lasalle had used before and took rooms there for the night. It was simple and clean and we were glad of the chance to freshen up before setting out on foot for the home of the Frenchman's friend Zouvier.

'Even a small car could not pass through the narrow alleys of the medina,' he explained. 'Besides, it will be a chance to stretch our legs after that long drive.'

When we reached the centre of the old town, a broad square opened up before us, filled with the hubbub of a busy market.

It was the smell that hit me first, a heady mixture of horse refuse, charcoal smoke, perfumes and spices. Then came the noise, the rhythm of drums and castanets and the voices of hawkers crying out their wares, everything from orange juice to gaudy jewellery. Standing out from the rest of the din came the braying of donkeys and the excited sounds of barter.

Visually it was a seething mass of colour – patterned rugs, shimmering silks, gold, silver and sparkling gems. There were fruit stands filled with oranges, lemons and pomegranates. Meat stalls too, one of which, from the severed camel's head suspended over it, I guessed to be selling cuts from that particular animal.

In an open space by a fountain, an aged but animated storyteller was weaving his tale before an enraptured audience. His recitation was lent additional drama by the accompaniment of a drum and a guitar. I wondered if his thrilling yarn was something from the Thousand and One Nights or some more local legend.

While the others were distracted, I drew Karrie in for a private word. Nodding towards Lasalle, I said, 'You do realise your old mentor is a sick man, don't you?'

Several yards ahead of us the Frenchman was enthusiastically pointing out to Jaikie and Dougal a group of Gnaoua musicians in their distinctive blue robes and caps decorated with shells. They were playing on three-stringed instruments like long-necked lutes which produced a sound that was almost hypnotic.

Karrie's jaw tightened, as if she were unwilling to speak. 'Yes, I know,' she said at last.

'If the man is in poor health,' I suggested, 'he should let us carry on without him, for his own good.'

Karrie shook her head emphatically. 'That is impossible.'

'Karrie, aren't you afraid that the hardships that lie ahead might well kill him?' I asked gently.

Her large grey eyes turned on me with a heartfelt appeal. 'Richard, you could not be more wrong. Don't you see? The journey, the quest, this is all that is keeping him alive.'

I had known such things before, men whose bodies were giving out on them, being driven by an ambition, a dream, a destination, to rise above any physical weakness. Armand Lasalle appeared to be just such a man.

Beyond the market we followed a cobbled alleyway to a pink-painted riad, a typical Moroccan townhouse fronted by a walled courtyard. We edged around an ornamental pool, the cool surface of which was liberally sprinkled with rose petals. It was clear from the welcoming attitude of the servant who admitted us that Lasalle had sent word on ahead and we were expected. Bowing and smiling, the servant led us inside and up a stairway to the flat roof where our host awaited us.

From here we were treated to a splendid view over the town, all the way to the olive groves that spread across the plain right up to the outlying crags of the Atlas range. There, built into the rock face, was an imposing kasbah, a rugged fortress raised up ages ago in defiance of the invading Europeans.

The spacious rooftop was spread with carpets and cushions to provide comfortable seating, with small tables laid out here and there at knee level. Zouvier, the owner of the house, rose to greet us warmly. He was a stout man with a cherubic face and enormous eyebrows which twitched expressively as he spoke. Once the servant had presented us to him by name, Zouvier sent him off to summon food and refreshments while we seated ourselves.

Settling down on his capacious cushion, Zouvier leaned towards Armand Lasalle with intense interest. 'You are well, my friend? And in good health?'

'Apart from those pains which are the inevitable harbingers of age. And you, Zouvier? You are well? And your children?'

'I am as robust as the great oak.' Zouvier grinned and beat a fist against his chest while his impressive eyebrows hoisted themselves high on his forehead. 'The children thrive like a garden in the spring rains.'

'And your business, does it also thrive?'

Their conversation continued in this manner for several minutes while the rest of us sat patiently listening. These lengthy enquiries after health, family and business appeared to be an indispensable prelude to any discussion of more pressing matters. Lasalle had evidently acquired a fluency in such extended small talk and left our host satisfied that all the proper forms of greeting had been duly observed.

Zouvier then turned to me, presumably as I was the oldest of our group and therefore to be most respected. 'And you, sir, Mr Hannay, your family is well?'

'I believe they are,' I answered, without betraying any of the anxiety I actually felt about Peter John. I decided to change the subject rapidly, since any further talk of my family might lead to some mention of Malta and therefore touch upon our confidential mission.

'My friend Mr Galt here is only recently married,' I declared, presenting Jaikie as grandly as if he were a foreign prince.

'Ah, a thousand blessings upon you and your bride, handsome sir,' Zouvier enthused. 'And may all your many children grow up healthy and strong.'

'I certainly hope so,' said Jaikie. He showed obvious relief when the Arab shifted his attention to Dougal.

'And you, my fine friend with the flaming hair, do you too have a bride preparing your home for your return?'

'No, sir, I'm not married,' Dougal stated stiffly.

Zouvier assessed him with shrewd, narrowed eyes. 'That is because you are a warrior born, too busy fighting to entertain thoughts of love.'

'I wouldn't say that,' Dougal demurred, with an uncomfortable sidelong glance at Karrie.

Zouvier followed his eyes to the girl, and regarded her in unabashed delight. 'You, madam, you are a gazelle!' he exclaimed.

This apparently was the highest compliment that could be made to a woman. Karrie seemed to understand that and lowered her eyes modestly.

'You are very kind.'

'And yet I am troubled.' Zouvier's eyebrows plunged into a frown. 'I see no mark of marriage upon you.'

Karrie shook her head. 'No, I am not married. My life is dedicated to my work.'

Zouvier reeled back in shock. 'What? Here you are in the full flower of your womanhood and yet, even at such an age, you are not married? This must not be.' He considered the matter gravely then raised a magisterial finger. 'For your honour's sake I will make you one of my wives. It is the very least I can do.'

'I am flattered, but no,' Karrie responded demurely.

I had the impression that this was not the first proposal she had declined, though I imagined it was the most abrupt and unusual.

Zouvier was not so easily rebuffed. 'I pray you to think again. I have money, I am a handsome man, and I make good children.'

'When the time comes,' Dougal interjected gruffly, 'she'll marry who she chooses.'

'Ah, so you make claim to her,' said Zouvier. 'Why was this not said before?'

'No one has any claim on me,' Karrie clarified in a surprisingly calm and collected manner. 'Though you would honour me, sir, you must know that I would make you a very bad wife. First because I am a Christian, but also because I am hard-headed and stubborn. I would not wish to bring shame upon your house.'

For all her strong will, and occasional stubbornness, it was evident that in her travels Karrie had developed the ability to conform politely to the customs of another land without in any way compromising her own character.

'Ah so, the gazelle must run free, eh?' Zouvier sighed resignedly. 'But let me say this: it is better to be the wife of Zouvier than to go chasing ghosts in the mountains.'

This warning was given with a doleful glance at Lasalle, who made no response. Fortunately, as Zouvier's unsuccessful wooing came to an end, the mood was immediately lightened by the arrival of a troop of servants bearing dishes, platters and jugs, a veritable feast to be placed before the honoured guests.

We were each presented with a bowl of stewed lamb with apricots in spicy sauce, poured over a bed of couscous, a local rice made from semolina. This was accompanied by loaves of tannour bread and the inevitable cups of mint tea heavily sweetened with sugar.

Zouvier saluted us with his cup and toasted: 'B'saha wa raha!'

This, I learned, translated as 'In health and rest'.

We all joined in the toast and set to our meal with a good appetite. After our meagre breakfast, this was indeed a rich banquet.

While we ate, Lasalle discussed with Zouvier the supplies and equipment we would need for our expedition into the mountains – sturdy clothing, several lengths of rope, small shovels for digging, rations, flasks of water and so on. Zouvier appeared to note all this mentally, without the need to write it down. Clearly he had long experience in providing for travellers and had access to everything that was necessary.

Gradually, however, I saw his brow cloud and his enormous eyebrows droop sadly. 'It troubles me that you again go searching for tombs,' he told Lasalle dolefully. 'The dead have earned their rest, my friend, and you should leave them in peace, lest they come to haunt you to your grief.'

'Pah!' Lasalle waved his forebodings aside. 'I've told you before not to vex me with superstitions. Such ideas grow around lost places like ivy and must be cut away.'

Behind his words, however, I sensed a certain apprehension, like a premonition of perils yet to come.

24

THE PILLARS OF HEAVEN

———

Three days later we were in a different world, one as ancient as Casablanca's Ville Nouvelle was modern. We had followed a series of rough sheep trails over slopes dressed in thick forests of oak and cedar, with waterfalls tumbling dazzlingly from the heights. Tortoiseshell butterflies flitted among the greenery and small birds darted from tree to tree, piping their lively songs. We passed small villages whose Berber inhabitants waved gleefully and offered us food and refreshment. By contrast, we sometimes had to press our way through herds of unwelcoming goats who butted us when we came too close. Perhaps their owners had trained them not to trust strangers.

Rather than accept any offers of hospitality, we had chosen to shelter for the night in caves or under canvas. In this way we avoided being questioned as to our purpose and destination, knowing we would be forced to respond with silence or a lie, by which we would be dishonouring our hosts.

Zouvier had provided us with stout boots and warm clothing for the cold mountain heights and we were soon grateful for both. In our packs we carried cooking gear, water bottles and tinned rations as well as pup tents and blankets. Without the Frenchman being aware of it, Jaikie had carefully arranged the loads so that Lasalle's burden would be the lightest.

Though I was an experienced climber, the higher we ascended, the more I began to feel the weight of years that lay upon me. The cold thin air chilled me through whenever I paused to catch a breath. Clapping myself warm with both hands, I forced my body to carry on in spite of an almost overwhelming fatigue. However, I was more concerned about Lasalle.

On occasion he succumbed to an attack of weakness, leaning on his alpenstock, and feeding a capsule between his lips when he fancied no one was watching. As soon as he saw any signs of concern in the faces of his companions, he moved off with a determined briskness of step, refusing any suggestion of rest or help. I marvelled at his miraculous stamina and could only imagine the force of the impulse that drove him on: the urge to discover the fabled tomb of Redfalcon.

Now we were entering a land more stark and unforgiving, picking our way along crumbling paths that took us over rocks of mustard brown and umber, shot through with streaks of yellow. Water cascaded dizzily down the cliffs to splash into isolated patches of greenery far below. Wildlife became scarce and our most constant companions were the birds of prey who rode the wind currents in the lofty sky above.

Ahead, beyond the hard, ruddy landscape, rose the blue, snow-tipped peaks of the mountains which had lent the Atlas range its name. It was easy to see why they had been identified with the mighty Titan of Greek mythology who was tasked with supporting the sky upon his broad and straining back. They seemed to reach up to the very vault of heaven with a grandeur worthy of the gods of Olympus.

Deeper we advanced into the interior of the range, and our surroundings became increasingly austere, taking on an almost primeval magnificence. The mountains soared up in ramparts all about us, like the ancient bones of the earth itself, rearing up in gargantuan defiance against the vivid cerulean blue of the heavens. It was as if we had come face to face with the very roots of creation.

Now, however, in the late afternoon of our fourth day, an icy wind was scouring the bare slope above us and sullen grey clouds were boiling across the sky. A storm was imminent and we were fully exposed to whatever fury it might unleash upon us. There was no sign of shelter on this bare rock face and occasional drifts of shale slipped beneath our feet, threatening to pitch us down into the shadowy depths below.

When the first sheets of rain hit us, it was almost a relief from the tension of awaiting the storm. Lightning flashed in the distance, followed by rolls of thunder that echoed in great detonations all around the gaunt cliffs. The rain swelled in its rage, as if egged on by the lashes of lightning, dashing whips of icy sleet into our faces.

'First a sandstorm and now this,' Dougal growled. 'You'd almost think somebody didn't want us to find this blessed tomb.'

'I'd pay three months' rent in advance for a good cave right now,' said Jaikie through gritted teeth. 'I wouldn't even demand running water.'

'I thought you Scots were made of sterner stuff than that,' Karrie challenged them. 'Do you really want to be caught hiding in a cave like Robert the Bruce and his spider?'

'That spider was no mug,' Dougal informed her gruffly. 'It was probably raining outside.'

With such hard bitten humour to bolster our spirits, we pressed on doggedly, scanning our rain-shrouded surroundings for any sort of overhang that might lend us some semblance of shelter. As the lightning drew closer, flaring across the sky in blazing white sheets, our pace slowed and our footing grew ever wetter and more treacherous.

'Maybe we should just stop here,' Jaikie suggested, 'and huddle together until the storm's passed.'

I knew that he had the experience of many a hazardous expedition behind him, and I was half-minded to take his advice. I was certainly feeling the pace and even Karrie, whose powers of endurance were quite astonishing, was finally beginning to wilt. Lasalle, however, was having none of it.

'No, we must press on,' he insisted hoarsely, stabbing a determined finger directly into the face of the tempest.

He glared at each one of us in turn, daring us to contradict him. I could see a feverish glint in his eye that would brook no denial. Dougal and Jaikie directed their attention to me, as if to say yes, this was the doctor's expedition, but it was my orders that they would follow.

'Perhaps just a little further,' said Karrie, ending the brief stalemate. She took the Frenchman by the arm. 'For all we know, there might be a refuge of some sort just around the next bend.'

As we trudged on, heads low, backs bent, the storm seemed to redouble its efforts to drive us back. I recalled Dougal's earlier protestation about someone not wanting us to find the tomb, but quickly dismissed such gloomy fancies. Whatever ancient gods might once have dwelt in these mountains, they had slumbered through too many long ages to bestir themselves over such minor intruders as the five of us.

Our pace by now was little more than a crawl, and we were surely on our last legs. Lasalle was staggering and would have fallen without Karrie's support. I was about to insist on a halt when a streak of lighting, flashing directly over our heads, illuminated an extraordinary sight.

Ahead and above us, standing tall upon a ledge, was a man wreathed in grey robes, with a long white beard hanging from beneath the shadow of his hood. He leaned upon a gnarled staff and with his other hand beckoned us to follow him.

For a moment we were too startled to obey, but Lasalle, suddenly revived, urged us on.

'He's one of the Berber folk,' he gasped. 'They know these heights like no one else.'

'He looks like a wizard to me,' said Dougal.

'At this point I'd be ready to follow him if he was just a bus conductor,' said Jaikie, adjusting his pack and lurching forward.

By the time we had clambered on to the ledge, our unexpected guide was several yards up a twisting path that led around a jagged spur of rock. As we rounded the bend, another sheet of lightning revealed an even more astounding sight. On the cliff face ahead was a series of terraced dwellings, two and three storeys high, built right into the rock. As we drew closer, they looked so much a natural part of the mountain you might have imagined they had grown up organically, rising up from pools of lava in some antediluvian epoch.

Opening the door of one of these dwellings, the bearded man led us inside, threw back his hood and set aside his staff. His long hair was pure white, framing a lean, handsome face the colour of newly burnished leather. The large room before us was lit with oil lanterns and the welcome glow of a fire crackling in the hearth.

'My friend, my friend, a thousand blessings upon you for guiding us here,' gasped Lasalle, bowing so low I was afraid he might fall flat on his face.

Karrie caught him by the shoulder and helped him straighten up. The rest of us echoed the Frenchman's words of thanks, all of which were waved modestly aside by our host.

'By all that is holy, what were you doing out there in the midst of such a storm?' Karrie asked.

'It came to me in a dream that there were strangers lost in the mountains,' the Berber answered in heavily accented but perfect French, 'and that the storm would not abate its anger until they found their way to shelter.'

He seemed quite unabashed to lay this mystical explanation before us, and we, at this point, were not minded to argue with the ways of providence.

'We are very grateful,' I told him, 'both for your dream and for your hospitality.'

At this point our host turned to face the interior of the cliff-house and clapped his hands. Immediately, with squeals of delight, a bevy of boisterous children surrounded us under the stern supervision of their diminutive mother. They helped us out of our sodden outer garments and hung them to dry before the fire. Once we were seated on the soft woollen carpet, they brought us cups of hot herbal tea flavoured with a hint of spice.

As we drank, a pleasant warmth filled my chilled body and the menacing thunder seemed to pass away into the distance. Lasalle introduced each member of our party in turn, explaining that we were on an archaeological expedition, but revealing no more than that.

Our host's name was Yattuy, which in his language – not surprisingly – meant the tall one. He told us that the spirits of the mountains granted certain gifts to those who honoured them, and this was the source of his prophetic dreams. He then issued a soft-voiced command to his tiny wife, who immediately chivvied their chattering brood into the kitchen to help with the preparation of the evening meal.

'Your people are very brave to dwell among these rocky heights,' Jaikie complimented the Berber.

'We are the Amazigh,' said Yattuy, 'which in our tongue means the free men. We were here before the Romans came, before the Arab invaders, and long before the men of France and Spain crossed the narrow strait. When all of those have passed away like sand scattered before the wind, we shall yet remain, for this land has been ours from the first dawn of time.'

This prophecy might have sounded grandiose coming from other lips, but Yattuy spoke with such sure authority that his words carried a ringing conviction of truth.

Soon our supper arrived in the form of what we learned was called a tagine. This consisted of goat meat cooked in a spicy sauce, surrounded by layers of carrots, turnips, potatoes and courgettes, forming a sort of volcano shape that was topped with red chilli. Lasalle, who had been entertained in this fashion before, explained to us the etiquette of such a meal.

First we were all required to say '*Bismillah*' (in the name of God) as a blessing. Our host then divided a loaf between us, with which, pinching the bread between our fingers, we were first to scoop up the juices from the bottom of the tagine before using it like a spoon to help ourselves to the vegetables. The meat was divided evenly between us all by Yattuy and every piece of it consumed.

I must say that it was delicious, and restored our party to what was almost a second life after the trials of our ascent. As we washed down the food with more tea, Yattuy enquired as to our destination. Lasalle took out his notebook and showed him his drawing of the Eagle's Beak. The Berber gave a knowing nod.

'You are not far from this place. In the morning I will take you there.'

Waterstones

12 George Street
Oban
Argyll and Bute
PA34 5SB
01631 571455

SALE TRANSACTION

LADY'S ROCK	
9781915089922	£9.99
REDFALCON	
9781846974854	£9.99
Balance to pay	£19.98
VISA	£19.98

WATERSTONES PLUS CARD
YOU HAVE JUST MISSED OUT ON 1 STA...
ON ITEMS WORTH £19.98
JUST ONE OF THE MANY BENE...
OF THE WATERSTONES PL...
Apply on our app, online ... shop

*** CARDHOLDER COP...

P:W3433036
M:***76632
28/06/...

Waterstones

BUY ONE
GET ONE
FIVE

nes

RA

se wil
oods wi
scretion
is recei
here a
oke
direc
this

anges
efund or exchan
30 days or at
Please bring them back
this receipt and in resalable conditio

25

THE WAY TO KEDESH

Yattuy was as good as his word. After a breakfast of barley cakes, fresh figs and honey we set off across the mountainside, where all traces of the storm had vanished like the wispy memories of a bad dream. The sun shone with a hopeful radiance from a sky of purest blue and there was a sweetness in the air wafting from the wild flowers that decked the slopes about us. Even the cries of the hunting birds had lost their harshness and sounded more like a welcome than a warning.

It was as if Yattuy's generosity in coming to our rescue had assuaged the savagery of the elements and brought us into a kinder world. He strode boldly at our head, deep in conversation with Lasalle, who had gained a renewed vigour in the Berber's company.

After half a day's hike we saw looming ahead of us the very landmark we had been seeking, a sharp peak that looked as if it had been bent downward by some colossal hand to form the grey beak of a giant bird. Quickening our pace, we arrived at a shelf of rock directly beneath that pointed overhang, our faces directed to the darkening mountains of the east.

After making a formal farewell, Yattuy raised a majestic hand over us and spoke a blessing in his own Berber tongue. It was a humbling moment and when he turned to stride back to his precipitous village we felt all too keenly the loss of his presence. I could not shake off the notion that our new friend was somehow kin to the great prophets of old and had seen us through hardship and danger like a modern-day Moses.

'I still say he's a wizard,' muttered Dougal. Hands on hips, he surveyed the surrounding terrain. 'All right, we're here, but what the devil is the eye of the sun supposed to be?'

'Perhaps some sort of crystal,' I suggested, though how we were to find it was beyond me.

'Well, this isn't a bad spot to camp while we figure it out,' said Jaikie, slipping off his pack.

'The instructions do say that we're to pass the night here,' Karrie agreed. 'Maybe the meaning will be clearer in the morning.'

Lasalle nodded his weary assent, and we settled ourselves down, breaking out some food and drink. After days of near ceaseless exertion, it felt good to enjoy a few hours of simple relaxation.

Once he had eaten his fill of bread and tinned sardines, Dougal leaned back against a bank of moss and fell into a deep slumber. His low, rhythmic snoring was somehow strangely restful. Karrie and Lasalle were engaged in a deep conversation in French about what sounded to me like some rather obscure archaeological controversy. Jaikie had pulled a book from his pack and was absorbed in one of Haggard's well-spun yarns.

I toyed idly with Blenkiron's worn deck, rehearsing almost absent-mindedly some of the card tricks I had learned as a boy. When the queen of hearts flipped over between my fingers I could not help but think of Mary and that smile I so longed to see again.

We spent the night wrapped in blankets against the cold. When the dawn came, I cracked an eye and saw the neighbouring crags silhouetted against the sun's first rays.

Rolling out of his bedding, Dougal hauled himself upright and stretched his stiff limbs. 'Well, we've followed orders,' he yawned. 'So what do we do now? Search about for this daft eye?'

Jaikie was already on his feet, his brow furrowed as his eyes fixed on the broad eastern landscape. There was a tension about him, as though his well-honed traveller's instincts had alerted him to something none of the rest of us had guessed at.

Suddenly he stiffened. 'I think we've found it,' he breathed. 'Look!'

The whole party surrounded him and followed his pointing finger. Some miles to the east, almost in the dead centre of a distant mass of rock, the dawn was shining bright crimson through a round hole, gleaming at us like a dragon's baleful eye.

'You are right, my young friend!' exclaimed Lasalle, clapping Jaikie on the back. 'That is the sign we are looking for.'

'I don't suppose there can be any doubt?' I wondered, scarcely able to believe that the meaning of the mysterious phrase *the eye of the sun* had manifested itself so clearly.

'It must be,' said Karrie, her face shining with sheer delight. 'We are to go there and peer through the hole. That will show us the way to Kedesh.'

We downed our breakfast with haste and set off across a rocky valley towards our beckoning goal. By now the sun had risen above the level of that wondrous portal, but the position of it was fixed in all our minds. Jaikie in particular, I felt sure, could make his way directly towards it, even if he were blindfolded and spun around three times.

Having found the eagle's beak, and with the eye of the sun directly ahead of us, our confidence was now high that this was no mere game of riddles, but a map that would lead us to the destination we sought. A few hours of rough hiking brought as to the base of the great crag and we all stood staring upward.

'There!' said Lasalle, pointing at the round opening that was only just visible in the face of the rock. 'I must get to it!'

So saying, he slipped off his pack and attempted the climb before anyone could stop him. Almost at once his boots slipped and he slithered down the few feet he had attained.

Jaikie steadied him with a gentle hand. 'Here, doctor, that looks like a treacherous climb. You'd better let me have a go.'

Lasalle accepted the inevitable with obvious reluctance while Jaikie slipped off his encumbering gear and set off up the rough wall, feeling out the handholds and fixing his feet carefully on solid outcroppings. The historian chafed impatiently, and to him, I was sure, our young friend's progress must have seemed painfully slow. In fact, however, it did not take Jaikie more than ten minutes to make the ascent. Gripping the edge of the portal with both hands, he hoisted himself up and thrust his head and shoulders into the gap.

'What do you see?' Lasalle called out eagerly.

I hoped his question would not distract Jaikie, who was still poised upon a perilous height. Seconds later he had disappeared from view, drawing his feet in after him. After some anxious moments we saw him reappear and commence a careful descent. Back in our midst he took a deep breath and consulted his compass while we gathered eagerly around him. Lasalle was by now almost bursting with anticipation.

'Did you see it?' he demanded. 'Did you see the way to Kedesh?'

'What I saw,' Jaikie reported, 'was a waterfall a few miles across the next valley. A real beauty it is.'

'Then the settlement must lie somewhere beyond that,' Lasalle concluded, smacking a fist emphatically into his palm.

'Can we make it through that hole, do you think?' Dougal asked, scowling up at the height.

Jaikie shook his head. 'It narrows as it goes, clearly framing that one exact spot in the distance. It's too tight even for me. We'll have to go round. But don't worry, I'm sure I've got my bearings fixed.'

Once again his unerring sense of direction proved a blessing, and by evening we stood at the foot of a waterfall that cascaded down the mountainside in a crystalline flurry of frothing waters. I cupped my hands to catch some of it, and when I drank there seemed to be a striking sweetness about it – though I was ready to concede that this might simply be because it had brought us so close to our goal.

Dougal peered dubiously at the curtain of tumbling water. 'I don't see any sign of a doorway,' he grumbled.

'It must be up there,' said Karrie, indicating a steep trail leading to the head of the falls. It promised to be a hard climb.

'It will be difficult, no doubt,' Lasalle conceded in a cracked voice, 'but we must go.' The unhealthy fever we had seen grip him before appeared to seize him yet again, so that he began to shake spasmodically.

'No, sir, it's nearly dark,' Jaikie cautioned him. 'It would be sheer folly to attempt so hard a climb without the sun. We don't want to lose anybody when we might be so close.'

Lasalle chewed his lip in frustration, and I moved close enough to grab him should he be mad enough to start off on his own.

'We will go in the morning,' Karrie promised quietly, as though reassuring a child. 'Then you will be the first to see the wonders of Kedesh.'

'Yes, in the morning,' Lasalle agreed, his body finally sagging from the day's long hike.

Weary as I was myself, I could well understand his impatience. Soon we would know at last what awaited us and whether the legendary knight had left us a treasure worthy of our long journey.

In the morning, once the sun had cleared the eastern peaks, the light sparkled over the waterfall that marked our way upwards to our hidden destination. We exchanged glances of thrilled anticipation as we gathered for this final effort.

Jaikie, who was certainly the most sure-footed among us, took the lead, his keen eyes probing ahead, and his steady tread testing the steep ground. Dr Lasalle went second, a privilege to which he was justifiably entitled. In spite of the lapses of health we had all witnessed, he now seemed fired with a fresh vigour.

After him came Dougal, whom I judged to be the most capable of supporting or catching the Frenchman should he slip or fall. Karrie suppressed her own hunger for discovery to take up the position directly behind the red-haired Scotsman, to whom she had become increasingly attached, as evidenced by her frequent playful teasing of him.

I brought up the rear so that I could follow the trail picked out by the others while still being alert for any signs of danger or pursuit in the surrounding landscape.

Jaikie clambered up skilfully, shrewdly assessing which route would prove easiest for those following. Occasionally he reached a narrow shelf where he could stand straight and scan the rock face above, mapping out in his head the most promising passage.

The downward rush of the waters cast up a cool spray that dappled us like a welcome dew as our aching limbs became soaked in perspiration. Occasionally a stone knocked loose by one of those above came clattering past me, and I flashed an anxious glance upward to check that none of my companions was in distress. Sometimes Jaikie's voice would waft down with words of advice on the best way to negotiate a particularly tricky part of the slope.

I lost all sense of time as I concentrated on the rough, mossy surface directly in front of me. I was an experienced climber, to be sure, but never before had I been tested with so arduous a journey, not even when I had the unquenchable strength of youth on my side. Determined not to fall behind, I drove the pain and fatigue from my mind even as I wiped the beads of sweat from my eyes with the edge of my sleeve.

Finally there came a whoop of triumph from above to announce that Jaikie had reached the summit of our climb. He hauled Lasalle up after him and called down the good news.

'It's easy going from here! There's a path behind the waterfall!'

Soon we were all gathered on a ledge just large enough to accommodate us. Every one of us was panting, our faces flushed with exertion and excitement. As Jaikie had said, there was a path, wide enough for a man to walk along, vanishing into the shadowy depths behind the roaring cataract.

Taking a deep breath of the chill, high air, I said, 'Well done, Jaikie. I suppose now comes the moment of truth.'

'If there's nothing ahead but a rock wall,' said Dougal, 'I for one will be properly scunnered.'

'Dr Lasalle,' said Karrie, 'you should be the one to lead the way.'

The Frenchman's smile shone through all the weariness of his tired, sick body. 'Thank you, Karrie.'

'On you go, sir,' said Jaikie, gesturing towards the path.

Lasalle nodded gratefully, and took his first tentative steps into the unknown.

26

HOLY GROUND

———

As we followed the passage through the rock, the roar of the waterfall behind us echoed down the tunnel like thunder. When I emerged from the darkness to join the others, I found we were perched on a wide shelf overlooking the far side of the mountain, where a wondrous sight greeted our eyes.

It was an enormous basin surrounded on all sides by high, sentinel peaks. Great ructions in the earth had thrust the mountains upward and hollowed out this sheltered valley, like a fragrant garden cupped in a hand of stone. To the east was a small lake surrounded by willows and reeds. The waters were dotted with outcroppings of rock from which herons, wildfowl and lapwings launched themselves into the air.

On the flat ground to the west were a score of dwellings formed of rocks and pebbles with roofs of wood and slate. None looked inhabited and all had fallen into some degree of disrepair. They were overgrown with ivy and gorse, and lush grass carpeted the ground between them. At the far end of the valley, the high cliff wall was dotted with caves and birds' nests.

So this was Kedesh, where those fleeing Christians believed they had found a place of refuge under God's protective wings. Clearly the place was long abandoned, but it retained a lush, Edenic beauty.

'You were right, Armand,' said Karrie in breathless wonder. 'It really exists.'

'Yes, yes,' Lasalle nodded. 'I wager no human foot has trod this ground in centuries. We are the first to uncover it.'

Dougal grinned and ran his fingers through his tousled red hair. 'I admit I had my doubts, but here we are right enough, in our own little Lost World.'

'I hope not,' said Jaikie. 'After all we've been through, the last thing I want to do is tangle with a dinosaur.'

Gazing out over the deserted settlement, I tried to work out where Redfalcon's tomb might lie, assuming that part of the legend was also true.

'We'd best get down there,' I suggested. 'We won't achieve much by standing here gawking.'

An easy slope led down to the valley floor and we spread out across the abandoned village. I was drawn towards the most distinctive structure, a small stone-built chapel topped by a slated roof and a simple carved cross. Karrie was by my side as I drew near the open doorway. It was clear that at least some of the original settlers had been French, for inscribed on the lintel was the name of the little church: *Notre Dame des Montagnes* – Our Lady of the Mountains.

The interior was dimly lit by the sunlight filtering in through the thin lancet windows. Empty alcoves were evidence of statues and vases removed, and the vaulted ceiling was pitted with holes. A series of worn benches faced a plain stone altar behind which hung a large wooden cross. An age-worn image of the suffering Christ had been painted upon it in a few simple colours which rendered it all the more striking. Here the Saviour kept vigil over his abandoned realm, patiently awaiting the return of the faithful.

Crossing herself, Karrie bowed before the altar and

murmured a melodious Greek prayer. When she rose I followed her outside and once more took in our surroundings. Here by rock and foes surrounded, by desert and wind beset, here amid the cedars and the running waters, those Christians of old had built their sanctuary. Though the settlers were long gone, I had a sense that some faint trace of their presence still lingered, like incense hanging in the air.

I heard Karrie speak in a soft, musical voice.

'Tread softly! All the earth is holy ground.
It may be, could we look with seeing eyes,
This spot we stand on is a Paradise.'

She looked at me with a smile. 'Christina Rossetti.'

'I thought I recognised the words.' I was somehow gratified that her thoughts so closely echoed my own.

She seemed relaxed and happy here, as if this was where she belonged, her true home: the past. Indeed, despite the dilapidated dwellings, there was a timeless serenity about the place, a freshness in the mountain air and a quiet barely disturbed by the piping of the birds and the sighing of the breeze. It felt like an oasis of peace, a million miles and a dozen centuries from the war being waged far beyond the mountains.

On a patch of ground beside the chapel was a small cemetery, each grave being marked with a block of stone inscribed with a cross. Certainly none of these could be taken for a knight's tomb, and there was no sign of a sepulchre as far as the eye could see.

Lasalle was scurrying from place to place, examining first the empty cottages, then the edge of the lake and finally the ground beneath his feet.

'This soil is too dry to support much in the way of agriculture,' he informed us when we joined him, 'and the ground is too rocky to provide pasture for more than a few animals.'

'It couldn't support much of a population, then,' I surmised.

'No. If the original settlers took in more outsiders,' said Karrie, 'or even had children of their own, their resources would soon become stretched.'

'On top of that,' said Lasalle, waving at the lake, 'the bands of dried sediment around the shore are clear evidence that the lake has been shrinking steadily over the years. The diminishing water supply would also set a limit on the population.'

'I can't say I've spotted any signs of burning or looting,' commented Dougal.

'As a Viking you would notice such things, of course,' Karrie stated with scholarly seriousness.

'All I'm saying,' Dougal pressed on, undaunted, 'is that it doesn't look as if folk were driven out by force.'

'I judge that many of these dwellings were already abandoned when the final inhabitants departed,' said Lasalle. 'My guess would be that their numbers had dwindled to the point where their community was no longer viable. Perhaps in imitation of the knights, they decided to put their fate in God's hands and set out to find a route back to their Christian homelands.'

Karrie gazed about her, as though her eyes could penetrate time and behold those past events. 'I suppose we'll never know if they succeeded, or died in the desert or the mountains.'

'It will take years of close study and much digging to unravel the complete story of this remarkable site,' said Lasalle.

'Fascinating as all of this is, I see no sign of a tomb,' I said.

'Maybe Jaikie's found something,' Dougal suggested, looking about for his friend. 'Hey, where's he flitted off to?'

As if in answer, we were hailed by a loud cry from the far end of the valley. While we had explored the village and its environs, Jaikie had gone scampering up into the heights, drawn by the allure of the mysterious caves. He was waving to us from one of the paths that zigzagged their way up the cliff face.

'I think you'll want to see this!' he yelled. 'And you'd best bring a lantern!'

Spurred on by his obvious excitement, we hurried across the valley floor and clambered up the track after him.

'There's not much in these caves,' he told us, 'but from the markings on the walls, I'd guess that when the first Christians arrived they took shelter here before building their cottages down on the valley floor.'

'But you've found something more interesting, my young friend,' Lasalle prompted him eagerly.

'I have that,' Jaikie confirmed.

He led the way further up the slope and halted by a flat slab of stone that covered the entrance to a cave, the only one that had been shut off in this way.

'See here.' He tapped his finger against a sign that had been engraved into the rock at eye level. It was an eight-pointed cross, the symbol of the Knights of St John, commonly called the Maltese cross.

'If this isn't a knight's tomb,' Dougal declared with a grin, 'then I'm a knock-kneed Morris dancer!'

27

THE MESSAGE

Dougal and Jaikie set their shoulders against the slab and pushed, forcing it gratingly aside to expose the cave mouth beyond. Lasalle took up the lantern and stepped inside, illuminating the interior. The cavity was no more than twenty feet deep and at the far end lay the unmistakable shape of a sarcophagus.

It was fashioned of plain grey stone that had been carefully smoothed. There was no decoration except for the Maltese cross engraved upon the flat lid accompanied by the words *MORS JANUA VITAE* – Death is the doorway to life.

Lasalle set the lantern down in an alcove and laid a reverent hand upon the tomb. He appeared quite overcome, as though this contact had opened a channel of mystical communication between himself and the knight enclosed within. 'It was all true,' he murmured. 'The shipwreck, the refuge, the whole story. It must be that we will find here the great secret that holds the fate of Malta.'

The rest of us were almost equally affected by being here in the very presence of Redfalcon, the man whose name had drawn us across sea, desert and mountains. Karrie stood beside the Frenchman, her grey eyes wide, a hand pressed to her heart as she shared in his sense of wonder.

Lasalle set both hands against the side of the lid and pushed with all his might. 'Now we will see,' he declared.

It was a heavy weight, and he had barely shifted it a half-inch before his face contorted in pain and his breath rasped sharply. Dougal stepped past Karrie.

'Here, sir, you'd best let us do that for you,' he offered.

'No!' Lasalle pushed him away. 'This is my time – my task to complete!'

We all exchanged anxious glances, but it was clear that Lasalle would not be denied his moment of glory. With a throaty grunt, he continued shoving the stone lid back.

It moved with dreadful slowness, and every inch was costing the historian some fraction of his life. The sight of part of the exposed interior appeared to fire a fresh, frantic energy in him and his entire body strained with the effort. The scraping of stone on stone and Lasalle's ragged breath filled the small chamber with sibilant echoes. Fearing for his safety, I was about to pull him away by force when the lid passed the tipping point, tilted over, and dropped behind the tomb with a booming crash.

Lasalle gripped the exposed edge with both hands and leaned heavily against it as he sucked in one desperate breath after another. I joined him in staring down at the skeletal remains of the knight. The tattered remains of a shroud were all that covered the bare bones, but what drew our eyes was the object enfolded in his arms.

It was a bronze tablet, the size of a large dinner plate, but dilated into an oval. There appeared to be markings upon it, but it was impossible to make them out in the dim light.

Slowly and delicately Lasalle drew the skeleton's hands and arms aside, being careful to do them no damage. Once the tablet was exposed, he took it in his hands and lifted it up out of the tomb. The lamplight washed over the bronze treasure as he raised it up, and the Frenchman's eyes shone with the sheer marvel of it all. He turned to face us, with the tablet pressed to his chest. Then a tremor shook him, his eyes glazed and with a startled cry he collapsed against the sarcophagus and slid to the floor.

'Oh dear God!' Karrie exclaimed in shock.

I bent to check the man's breath and pulse, but his long journey was over. He was dead.

We carried him back down to the valley floor, Karrie following behind with the precious tablet in her arms. Dougal and Jaikie dug the grave and we buried Lasalle outside the little chapel among those other souls who had passed away in this hidden fastness.

When the last scrapings of earth had been laid upon the deceased, we gathered around the grave and Jaikie wiped a hand across his sweating brow.

'He was a plucky old bird,' he commented.

'He was that for sure,' Dougal agreed. 'If I'd been half as sick as he was, I doubt I'd have made it as far.'

Since Karrie had known him best, I invited her to say a few words, but she raised a hand to her mouth to stifle a sob and shook her head. It seemed it was up to me then, as the most senior member of the party, to make some sort of parting speech. I wished I had a Bible or a Book of Prayers to read from, but I was cast back upon my own resources.

'Through two wars,' I began, 'I've buried more friends and comrades than I like to recall, but never in a spot like this. Here among these mountains it's like stepping into a fabled land, a place out of myth and legend that has somehow miraculously come alive. It's a worthy setting for a brave knight to lie at peace and for a wise scholar to find his final rest.

'A friend once said to me that every man must find his own Jerusalem. Sometimes it's a place we build for ourselves, sometimes it is only found at the end of a quest. Armand Lasalle has surely found his holy place and the sacrifices he made to get there have not been in vain.'

As I concluded, I heard Karrie softly begin a prayer in the lilting tongue of her native land. 'Χαίρε, Μαρία, κεχαριτωμένη, ο Κύριος είναι μαζί Σου.' I recognised enough of the words to understand that this was the Eastern version of the prayer commonly called the Ave Maria in the West. Her eyes moved from the fresh earth of the grave to the pure sky over our heads as she recited that ancient plea. At the conclusion she added in English, 'Pray for us now and in the hour of our death. Amen.'

We all echoed the amen and turned away from the grave towards our makeshift camp. We lit a fire against the chill of the coming night and ate a few simple rations washed down with water drawn from the stream that flowed into the mountain lake.

Karrie had already spent some time studying the bronze tablet and I had given it some attention of my own.

There were ten symbols etched into the metal, each one about the size of a small coin, each finely detailed and utterly mysterious: a tree, a shepherd's crook, a boat, a rose, a fish, a lion's head, a lightning bolt, a sword, a shield and a hand. They were not laid out in any sort of order, not in lines or columns, but placed irregularly with no particular relation between them. If anything, the arrangement appeared frustratingly random. Now we passed it around and offered our thoughts.

'It looks to me like some sort of puzzle,' said Dougal.

'Some of these are religious symbols, surely,' Jaikie speculated.

'Correct,' said Karrie. 'The fish, for example, is an ancient Christian symbol for Jesus, while a boat is often used to represent the church as an ark riding upon a storm. The shepherd's crook is like that carried by a bishop; the lion is the symbol of St Mark.'

'That's all very interesting,' I said, 'but where exactly does it lead us?'

Karrie's mouth quirked in irritation. 'I don't know. I wish Armand were still alive to tell us what he thinks.'

'I must say the whole thing leaves me feeling like a complete duffer,' Jaikie admitted. 'I know it must mean something, but I can't see what.'

'Give it time,' I said. 'Sometimes these things work themselves out through what psychologists call the unconscious.'

'Is it maybe some sort of code?' Dougal wondered.

'I can't see the point of putting a message into a code that's impossible to interpret,' said Karrie, tugging at a lock of her hair in frustration.

'The best thing we can do,' I advised, 'is to get a good night's sleep. We need to start out in the morning and it's a long way back.'

'I hope that without Armand we can still find the way.' Karrie sighed.

'Don't worry about that,' said Jaikie. 'All the way Dr Lasalle has been letting me study his maps and notes. I can retrace our steps as easily as I could find my way down Sauchiehall Street to the Brewer's Arms.'

'I hope you are as sure as you sound.'

'You can count on Jaikie,' Dougal assured her. 'Why, I once saw a homing pigeon stop and ask him for directions.'

'Ah well, he'd got his head turned round by a very glamorous dove.' Jaikie laughed. It was hardly a secret that he was alluding to how his friend's head had been turned in a similar fashion.

The excitement and tragedy of the day had left us weary in body and soul, and we passed a night of deep sleep beneath the stars. We still had so far to go, and all we had to show for our trouble was a conundrum we appeared to have no hope of solving. I could only hope against hope that Malta would hold out and that Peter John would stay safe until we reached that distant island.

PART FOUR

THE FORTRESS

28

THE LIFELINE

Far away in London there was tension in the atmosphere of a spacious office in Whitehall. The office in question belonged to Sir Charles Lamancha, one of the most senior figures in the wartime government. As a soldier, a businessman, a diplomat and a politician, Lamancha had proved his qualities as a leader of men many times over. He might have become the head of a major party, and even Prime Minister, but that was a choice he had declined.

He had witnessed how the constraints and burdens of such a position could weigh a man down, forcing him into hard decisions and cruel compromises that took their toll on the soul. He chose instead to stand to one side and lay his considerable talents at the service of those who dared to hold their ground at the very centre of the storm. He would be their shield against betrayal, and, when necessary, he would be their sword.

He had served the current Prime Minister with unswerving loyalty right from the beginning, lending his full support to the man's determination that a life or death struggle with the enemy was the only honourable option, even when many in the highest offices advised, indeed all but demanded, that an accommodation be made with the dictator.

The iron nerve of the Prime Minister had steeled the sinews of the nation, and the threatened invasion had been seen off by courage, resolve and, some insisted, a miracle.

Now at last the time had come for the turning of the tide, but all depended on one tiny island whose defenders were holding out with dwindling resources against the most brutal and efficient war machine in the history of the world.

A large map spread over the north wall behind Lamancha displayed the whole of the European theatre of war and also showed North Africa. The extent to which it was dotted with small flags bearing the swastika was enough to give pause to even the most stalwart. The Union Jack protruding from Malta looked pitifully isolated.

A few feet away, on the other side of a desk neatly laid out with documents, charts and photographs, Christopher Stannix stood toying with a dying cigarette. 'I expect the Prime Minister wants an update on the progress of Operation Pedestal.'

'He will when he returns,' said Lamancha. 'Right now he's in Moscow meeting with Stalin. He insisted on going there in person to break it to the old brute that there will be no second front in Europe this year.'

Stannix rubbed his jaw, as though to soothe away an ache. 'I don't imagine Stalin will take that very well. He's been bashing the table and howling for that second front like a wolf baying for blood.'

'I think we can count on Winston to smooth things out over vodka and cigars,' said Lamancha with the barest shadow of a smile.

Stannix came round the desk to join the other man in front of the great strategic map where a long line of swastikas was spread across western Russia. 'Can't say as I'd blame him for being upset, considering what the

Germans are doing to his country. Still, I agree that our best option is for the Americans to go into North Africa and link up with our forces there. Once we've polished off Rommel, we can direct a thrust straight into the soft underbelly of Europe.'

Lamancha's gaze followed Stannix's gesture towards the boot shape of Italy. Endless hours of intense labour spent coordinating a range of intelligence activities with larger scale military operations had paled Charles Lamancha's tanned, aquiline features, but nothing had dimmed those hawk-like eyes, which still glittered with the same bold intelligence that was so obvious to anyone who had watched him as a young officer walking through the gates of Jerusalem at the side of General Allenby.

Picking up a document from the desk, Lamancha slipped on his spectacles and scrutinised the typed list. 'Let's see,' he murmured. 'More than a dozen merchantmen; four aircraft carriers, *Victorious*, *Indomitable*, *Eagle* and *Furious*, the battleships *Nelson* and *Rodney*; the cruisers *Sirius*, *Charybdis*, *Nigeria*, *Manchester*, *Kenya*, *Cairo* and *Phoebe*; plus a fleet of destroyers, with oilers and corvettes in support. It's the biggest convoy we've ever sent to Malta.'

'And the biggest gamble,' said Stannix. 'Every convoy we've sent out there has taken an absolute hammering, and this is the juiciest target yet that we've offered to the Germans.'

'I suppose they're bound to have got wind of an operation involving this many ships,' Lamancha said ruefully.

'Their friends in Spain have been keeping an eye out

for Pedestal, ready to pass on the warning,' Stannix confirmed. 'Field Marshal Kesselring has the job of taking Malta and securing the Med, and he's determined that not a single one of our ships will make it through.'

Lamancha gave a fatalistic nod. 'I expect he has the resources to make good that threat.'

'As far as we can determine, he's put everything he can lay his hands on into smashing Pedestal. By our estimates he has six hundred and fifty-nine front-line aircraft, six cruisers, fifteen destroyers, nineteen fast torpedo boats, sixteen Italian submarines and three German U-boats to throw at us. And the Med isn't like the open ocean. Out there there's nowhere to hide.'

Lamancha laid the paper aside and folded his spectacles back into the breast pocket of his jacket. 'I suppose I can assume that progress has been difficult.'

'Between bombardment from the Axis navies,' Stannix reported grimly, 'relentless bombing from enemy planes and repeated attacks by submarine, our losses are already serious.'

'You might as well give me the worst. I wasn't planning on sleeping tonight anyway.'

'The aircraft carrier *Eagle* was torpedoed by a German U-boat,' Stannix related. 'She went down in eight minutes with a hundred and sixty-three of her crew. We also lost the Hurricanes she was carrying, so that's a big part of the convoy's air cover gone.'

'What about *Furious*?'

'Safe so far. She got all her aircraft off and they've arrived on Malta to reinforce the squadrons there. The other carriers have by now turned back to Gibraltar, so the convoy is without air cover until they come in range of Malta's airfields. The cruiser *Manchester* has been disabled, so to keep her out of German hands the captain has abandoned ship and scuttled her.'

Stannix, who had poured so much of his own energy into organising this operation, looked as though every loss from the convoy had personally diminished him. Lamancha was quite certain that his thick hair was greyer and his heavy features more deeply lined than they had been only a week before.

'The escort's taken a battering, then,' he said after a moment. 'Pretty much as we expected. What about the supply ships?'

'So far four of the merchantmen have definitely been sunk: *Glenorchy*, *Wairangi*, *Almeira Lykes* and *Santa Elisa*. A couple of others we've lost track of, the *Dorset* and the *Brisbane Star*. With any luck they've just become separated from the convoy and will make their own way to Malta.'

'Yes, with any luck,' Lamancha repeated under his breath. 'And what about the *Ohio*? I think it's fair to say that the success or failure of the whole operation lies with her.'

The *Ohio* was a massive oil tanker donated by the Americans and was larger than anything the Royal Navy could muster. Packed from end to end with food, fuel and machine parts, she was the very heart of the rescue mission.

'We've received reports that she's taken several hits,' said Stannix, 'but as far as we know she's still afloat.'

'What a bloody mess!' muttered Lamancha, raking his fingers through his hair. 'And on top of all this I have reliable intelligence that the Germans have built up a force of airborne troops in Palermo. There's no doubt that they're intended for Malta.'

'Yet they're being held back,' said Stannix, 'as if they're awaiting some sort of signal.'

'Presumably a coup being planned by their man Ravenstein. Any news of him since he managed to sneak out of England?'

'He covers his tracks pretty well,' said Stannix, 'but we picked up some chatter that he's been in contact with a group of Nazi sympathisers in Madrid.'

'There's no shortage of those,' said Lamancha, 'but what in damnation can he be up to?'

A frustrated silence hung between the two men as off in the distance an air-raid siren commenced its banshee wail. Lamancha decided to calm his nerves by lighting a pipe. After a few soothing puffs he asked, 'What about Dick Hannay and his party? Do you know if they actually found anything at the end of this mad quest you sent them on?'

Stannix answered with a sombre shake of his head. 'The last we heard from our American friends is that they made it safely to Fez and were on the train to Tangier.'

Lamancha took the pipe from between his teeth and waved it at the map. 'All those ships and planes, all that firepower, and the whole thing might come down to a few brave souls on the loose somewhere in North Africa. It almost makes you want to pray.'

Before Stannix could make any further comment, there came a rap at the door and the blushing face of a junior officer appeared.

'I'm sorry, sir,' he apologised sheepishly to Lamancha.

'I know you gave orders that you weren't to be disturbed, but I couldn't stop her.'

'Couldn't stop who?' Stannix demanded irritably.

'Me, I'm afraid.'

Mary Hannay shooed the young officer away as she entered the room and closed the door behind her. Although the Royal Nursing Auxiliary was not officially part of the military, it had been granted military ranks. Mary now stood before them in a khaki uniform with captain's stripes, which lent her a commanding air of authority.

'You, I suppose, are Mr Stannix,' she said, addressing the man who had spoken, before turning to Lamancha. 'Hello, Charles. It's been ages, hasn't it?'

'Kit, this is Mary Hannay,' Lamancha explained. 'You know I'm always glad to see you, Mary, but we're mired in some deep business right now.'

'Yes, I know,' Mary informed him brusquely. 'You've sent my husband off on some desperate mission that will take him to Malta, God willing. I'm sure you know my son is already stationed there. Well, now you're going to send me.'

Confronted by a pair of faces blank with astonishment, she went on, 'I'm sure you could use my services as a military courier, and once there I could take up a post at the hospital.'

The two men exchanged dubious glances and Lamancha struggled to articulate a response. 'Mary, I appreciate how you feel . . .' he began.

'But really, Mrs Hannay, there are proper channels for this sort of thing,' Stannix asserted gruffly.

Mary's eyes grew as hard as diamonds and she fixed the men with a glare that could have felled a prizefighter.

'Gentlemen, for the past few months I've been involved in training some very brave young women to blow up bridges and kill with their bare hands,' she stated in a voice of intimidating calm. 'Yesterday I sent the first group of them off to France where a terrible death may await every one of them. I think you'll find I'm not in a mood to be put off.'

29

THE ADVERSARY

The long train ride north to neutral Tangier proved mercifully uneventful, though I remained, as ever, alert for any sign that the enemy might have picked up our trail. Because of the strict controls at the border of Spanish Morocco, we could not have any sort of weaponry with us. This left us largely defenceless, but we could not take the chance of being detained by the border police, not while the clock was ticking so loudly on the fate of Malta.

We had no sooner emerged from the bustle of Tangier's railway station than we were beset by a mob of hawkers, pressing upon us all manner of wares, including cheap jewellery, treasure maps and hashish. We fought our way through this throng past a perfumery from which issued the popular Arab scents of musk and amber. Ahead of us, the city's whitewashed buildings rolled across its seven hills, dotted here and there with the slender brick towers of the mosques. In the distance, past the battlements of the kasbah, lay the sparkling bay enclosed in a curve of dark blue hills; beyond that, lay the wide blue waters of the Mediterranean and the Straits of Gibraltar.

In 1906 the European powers had signed a treaty which established Tangier as a neutral port to be administered by a multinational committee. The city's international status had quickly gained it a reputation for a laxity that bordered on decadence. As well as being a nexus point for migrant workers passing between Africa and Europe, its many shady bars and cafés were frequented by spies, exiles and smugglers of every stripe.

It occurred to me that we were in more danger here in these boisterous streets than among the storm-haunted peaks of the Atlas Mountains. I took little comfort from the sight of the white-helmeted local police in their khaki uniforms, for they seemed as bemused by the swarming crowds of colourful merchants and entertainers as any newly arrived tourist.

Beyond the palm trees that surround the circular sloping square of the Grand Socco, we found the discreet entrance that leads into the courtyard of the El Mahzri hotel. That antique building had been constructed in a Hispano-Moorish style under the auspices of a notorious Scottish marquis and had retained a certain roguish reputation ever since. Turpin had assured me that no one here would enquire after our business or question whatever names we chose to sign in under.

After our long journey from Fez, we were all grateful for a bath and some basic comforts. Once we were freshened up, we gathered round a table in the hotel bar and ordered drinks and a salver of flatbreads and spiced meats. Karrie had the tablet in a satchel that was slung over her shoulder. She had taken it upon herself to act as the guardian of the precious artefact her mentor had given his life to find, and I was not minded to argue the point. With Dougal keeping as close to her side as he could get away with, I knew our mysterious treasure was well protected.

Dougal took a swallow of local beer and screwed up his face at the taste of it. 'I suppose it will have to do until we can get home to a proper pint of eighty,' he grumbled.

'Where do we go from here, sir?' Jaikie asked me. 'Back to Gibraltar? I suppose we should hand this little mystery over to some code-breaking geniuses and see if they can make anything of it.'

'Right enough,' Dougal agreed. 'I can't make head nor tail of the blessed thing.'

'We must go on to Malta,' Karrie declared firmly. 'That is where the tablet came from and the key to its secrets must lie there.'

'I agree with Karrie,' I said. 'And if everything Stannix told me is correct, then there's precious little time to waste.'

The bar, which had been mostly empty when we arrived, was gradually filling up with customers, but we paid them little mind as we gratefully devoured our simple supper.

'Malta it is then,' said Jaikie, sipping from a glass of iced water. 'But how are we to get there? A ship would be too slow. Is there a chance we could hire a plane?'

'I don't know that any civilian pilot would willingly fly into the middle of a war zone,' said Karrie.

'Turpin gave me the names of a few people I can approach,' I said, 'but we'd better watch our step. Tangier has a reputation for intrigue and double-dealing second to none.'

At this point I noticed the waiter standing at my shoulder, clearing his throat to get my attention.

'Many pardons, sir,' he apologised, 'but the gentleman at that table over there invites you to join him for a drink.'

'Thank you.' I dismissed the waiter and glanced over at the table he had indicated. The man seated there wore a broad-brimmed hat that partially concealed his features and was dressed in a long leather coat. He raised his glass in salute, leaving me in no doubt at all as to his identity.

The others were looking in the same direction.

'I can't say I like the look of him,' Dougal growled.

'It's Ravenstein,' I informed them. 'All of you please stay calm.'

Jaikie's sharp eyes darted about the room, assessing the other customers who had recently arrived. 'What are you going to do?' he asked.

'I suppose I had better go and have a chat with him,' I replied with an air of casual irony. 'Don't make a move until we know just where we stand.'

As I stood up, Karrie laid a hand on my arm. 'Please be careful, Richard. I'm quite sure he's not alone.'

I sauntered over to the table and sat down opposite the enemy, who greeted me with a smile devoid of either warmth or amusement. I suspected at once that he did not actually need the gold-rimmed spectacles he was wearing, but that he felt compelled, when facing me, to mask himself behind even this most minimal of disguises. The eyes beyond the polished lenses were as cold and pale as Arctic ice. Beneath his straight, patrician nose the tight line of his mouth was formed by full lips suggestive of a sensual appetite only held in check by a rigid self-discipline.

He placed a glass in front of me and filled it from a bottle of spirits. 'Schnapps,' he said. 'It was a pleasant surprise to discover that they serve it here.'

'I've never cared for the taste of it,' I said, pushing the glass aside.

Ravenstein took a sip of his own drink. 'I'm so glad

we have this chance to talk, Mr Hannay. Our last meeting was so rushed.'

'It's very hospitable of you to invite me over, but I don't believe we have anything to discuss.'

'Oh, I think you know that is untrue. And by now I am sure you are well aware of the sort of man you are dealing with.'

'I hear you're the last of the old Black Stone gang,' I remarked casually. 'I thought I had put paid to all of them, so I suppose I should regard disposing of you as a sort of mopping-up operation.'

'Ah, you are trying to provoke me.' He gave an indulgent nod. 'Very good. But you mistake your adversary, Hannay. I am not one of the cosh-wielding thugs you are used to dealing with. I am a knight of the new order.'

'A knight, eh?' I looked him over with disdain. 'I'm sorry to tell you, old man, that from where I stand your armour's looking more than a little tarnished.'

'Whatever you think of me, I have an impressive knack of getting results against all the odds. You, I believe, have demonstrated a similar prowess on numerous occasions.'

'The difference is that I don't preen myself on my successes. I just thank God I came through alive.'

'Ah, there is that famous English modesty,' Ravenstein observed. 'It is so dishonest. It is merely a form of inverted vanity.'

'Perhaps so,' I agreed. 'But take it from me, no one admires a braggart.'

Ravenstein folded his hands on the table in front of him and leaned forward an inch or two. 'Let me explain myself, without bragging. I come from a long line of

Prussian aristocrats. My family was intensely loyal to the Kaiser, and with his downfall the whole structure of our society collapsed. Germany's flirtation with democracy ended in utter ruin, but out of the ashes a new aristocracy has arisen, one based not on bloodlines but on will. In this new world, those extraordinary men who have the will to rule will do so.'

'I take it that you are one of those men?'

Ravenstein took out a pack cigarettes and tapped it on the table. 'Demonstrably. My position in the new order will be one that I have won by my efforts and my ingenuity.'

'This all sounds very grand, but I feel obliged to point out that you are being led by a madman.'

Ravenstein dismissed this quibble and lit his cigarette. 'When a man embodies the will of an entire nation, he is bound to be prey to a few flights of fancy. But even those serve a purpose. War with the Bolsheviks was inevitable, so why should it not come now rather than later?'

'If your quarrel is with the Russians,' I said, 'I rather wish you hadn't dragged us into it. I suspect you're going to regret it too.'

Ravenstein took a long draw on his cigarette and eyed me through the smoke. 'Hannay, you, like me, are a man of the old school. You know what the rule of the mob has done to Russia, where every man is a slave, even those at the top. A man there has not a handful of earth to call his own. Is that the sort of land you would choose to live in?'

He spoke with such bald sincerity, I could almost believe that he genuinely wished to convert me.

'I want to live in a land where no man has to call

another his better,' I told him, 'where, whether rich or poor, a man's worth is judged by his courage and compassion, and where a sense of personal honour is valued above all else.'

Ravenstein appeared to be assessing my words. 'Our visions then are perhaps not so far apart, after all.'

'On the contrary,' I retorted. 'I believe they diverge considerably. I hear there's damnably little compassion in this Germany of yours and those extraordinary men you're so proud of are nothing but brutes and bullies.'

At this his jaw tightened visibly. 'You should not speak so unkindly of your future allies, Hannay.'

'Allies? I hardly think so.'

'Listen to me. With the removal of Malta from the board, Gibraltar will fall, and so will Egypt. With Egypt in our hands, we shall have possession of the Suez Canal, the very lifeline of your precious empire. At that point, you and your American friends will have no choice but to make a bargain with us. It is then that we shall all work together for the extermination of the Bolsheviks.'

'So far Malta has held out stubbornly,' I pointed out, 'and I don't believe you have the means to change that.'

Ravenstein pursed his lips in thought for a moment, then stubbed out his cigarette.

'Very well then, let us come directly to the matter at hand. You have in your possession a certain item which I must insist you turn over to me.'

'You can insist all you want, old man,' I retorted, 'but I'm afraid you're deluding yourself.'

Ravenstein leaned back in his chair and sighed heavily. 'Please drop this pretence of ignorance. I know very well that with the help of Dr Adriatis you made your way into the Atlas Mountains and found the tomb of the man referred to as Redfalcon. From it you extracted the object that had been hidden there. I know this just as I knew from my informants at the hotel in Fez that you would be travelling to Tangier. My agents have been watching out for you from the moment you arrived at the train station.'

'You do seem to know quite a lot,' I admitted.

'No doubt the object is contained in that satchel that Dr Adriatis is keeping so close to her person. If you could prevail upon her to surrender it to me, then we can all walk away peacefully and no one need be harmed.'

I answered the implied threat with a hard stare. 'I have to say that you've given me very little reason to want to oblige you.'

'Then let me give you a reason. If you look around you will see that most of the men in this room are in my employ.' He lifted one hand and in response eight or nine tough-looking customers rose slowly from their seats. They were a mixture of Arabs in fezzes and Spaniards in grimy white suits. When Ravenstein waved them back down, I realised that only a handful of the clientele could be regarded as innocent bystanders.

'I can't say they look like any improvement on the slovenly toughs you hired back in England,' I commented.

'All that matters is that there are enough of them to take what I want by force and leave you and your friends very much the worse for wear. Possibly even dead. A heavy price to pay for something that is no possible use to you.'

None of his henchmen looked to me to be armed, and I judged that here in a public place in neutral Tangier

Ravenstein would wish to avoid the sort of gunplay that might bring the local police down on his head. Even so, the odds were heavily stacked against us.

Something about his attitude puzzled me. 'If this object is of no use, why are you so determined to have it?'

Ravenstein leaned forward, as though disclosing a confidence. 'I already have what I need. You see, when I failed to recruit Dr Adriatis to my cause, I pursued a different avenue to the secret of Redfalcon. I had my agents track down the original journal of Don Rodrigo d'Alcantara, the sole survivor of the three shipwrecked knights.'

He paused long enough to watch me absorb this information, then continued in a self-satisfied manner. 'It was stored in the deepest recesses of the archives of the National Library in Madrid, a city in which, as you can understand, I have many friends. That journal is now in my possession, and you will be very impressed with what I found tucked inside the leather cover.'

He reached into his coat and brought out a folded sheet of yellowed parchment. Opening it up, he presented it to my gaze.

'As you can see, Hannay, I already have Redfalcon's secret.'

30

THE TURN OF THE CARDS

Even at the brief glance that was all he would grant me, I could see at once that what he held was a perfect copy of the markings on the tablet, exactly to scale, with the same irregular positioning of the symbols.

'It states here quite clearly,' said Ravenstein, pointing out some handwritten words down the side of the paper, 'that this is an authentic copy of the message buried in Sir Thomas Easterly's tomb.'

He folded it up and slipped it back into an inner pocket with a smirk of satisfaction. 'You see, Hannay, all I want from you is something I already have. You do not even understand its meaning, so to you it is quite worthless.'

The fact that Ravenstein already possessed the mysterious message we had travelled so far to lay our hands on came as something of a shock, and I found my mind racing to assess the significance of this unexpected development.

'And I suppose you do understand it?' I queried, keeping my voice flat and steady to conceal my unease.

'I do.' He lit a fresh cigarette and drew on it pensively. 'In a spirit of friendly cooperation, I will even explain to you what those symbols are.'

I could hardly believe he was speaking the truth, but I was nonetheless intrigued to hear what he had to say. 'Please enlighten me.'

'When properly decoded, those symbols form a prayer, a prayer that summons the power of God to one's aid.' He smiled patronisingly. 'You see, just a piece of empty superstition, whether written on paper or engraved on that tablet you possess.'

'Which begs the question, why do you want it?' I was at this point genuinely puzzled as to his motives for risking this confrontation.

'As you know, the Führer is an avid collector of historical and religious artefacts.' He quirked his mouth to show that he was somewhat embarrassed to discuss such a matter. 'It would gain me great favour if I were to bring him this new addition to his private museum.'

'Far be it from me to disappoint Uncle Adolf,' I responded, 'but I'm not inclined to do you any favours.'

'Regardless of your feelings,' said Ravenstein, his manner now hardening, 'you are outnumbered and without friends here. Let us settle this matter without violence. I am sure you would not wish any harm to befall the lovely Dr Adriatis.'

'I think she can stick up for herself,' I asserted confidently.

Ravenstein's eyes roved around his hired thugs and I calculated that any moment now he would signal them to attack. 'I'll tell you what,' I suggested, rapping a knuckle on the table to get his attention, 'why don't we cut cards for it?'

'Cut cards?' He gave a sceptical sneer. 'What on earth are you talking about?'

I took Blenkiron's veteran deck out of my pocket and placed it on the table between us. 'Whoever cuts the higher card wins the prize. Is that all right with you?'

He stared at me, dumbfounded, and I could tell that my startling offer had briefly knocked him off balance. 'You cannot be serious.'

'I'm absolutely serious,' I assured him. 'It will avoid a lot of that unpleasant violence you were talking about. Since we're both men of our word, I'm sure I can trust you to abide by the rules.'

A narrow smile spread across his lips and a mocking amusement glittered in his eyes. 'It is true what they say about the English – you are all quite mad.'

I began to shuffle and riffle the cards. 'We are also famed for our sportsmanship, aren't we? So what about it? Are you game or not?'

He regarded me curiously for several seconds before nodding. 'Very well, let us indulge this silly fancy of yours. But you must let me shuffle the cards also.'

He held out his hand and I placed the deck on his palm. 'By all means,' I agreed. 'We must play fair.'

Ravenstein shuffled slowly, never taking his eyes from me the whole time. Then he laid the deck down and asked, 'Who draws first?'

'I think it's only right that you have first cut,' I answered amiably.

His eyes flickered briefly to the cards, then back to me. He placed his fingers around the top half of the deck and carefully raised it, inspecting the card he had drawn. He displayed it for me with smug satisfaction. 'The king of diamonds. I believe the advantage is very much with me.'

He replaced the cards and patted the deck together.

'That is a strong draw,' I admitted with a rueful sigh. 'Let's see what lady luck has in store for me.'

I rolled my shoulders, as if preparing for a feat of strength, then moved my left hand tentatively towards the deck, keeping it off to the side. When Ravenstein's eyes shifted momentarily to follow the movement, I laid my right hand upon the deck and made my cut. I raised the cards and turned them to him. An irritated muscle twitched at the side of his nose at the sight of the ace of spades, which I had palmed earlier and slipped into the deck without his noticing.

'Sorry, old fellow,' I sympathised. 'It looks as if the luck just isn't with you today.'

Then I performed my second trick, bending the cards in my fingers and shooting them directly into his face. When he reflexively flung up his hands to ward them off, I grabbed the edge of the table and rammed it into his midriff.

With the breath knocked out of him, I continued to shove, bashing him right back into the wall. His men, being mere riff-raff, sat frozen, uncertain what to do without a direct command. In complete contrast, Jaikie, Dougal and Karrie had leapt from their seats and rushed to my side.

'Get out now, while we have the chance!' I ordered them, waving towards the exit.

We made our move in a group, but a few of Ravenstein's minions had enough initiative to throw themselves in our way. A brief scuffle forced us back and I heard Ravenstein rasp out a vicious command in Spanish. Now the whole ugly crew were moving in on us.

I snatched up a chair and smashed it into the face of one Moroccan, while Dougal treated another to a hefty crack on the jaw. As soon as they toppled, two more toughs took their place.

Those innocent customers who were not part of Ravenstein's gang made a swift exit from the field of battle, while the two pale-faced waiters crouched quaking behind the bar. One of them grabbed a bottle of vodka and took a hefty swallow before passing it to his companion.

The fight was going full tilt now, with chairs and tables being knocked over in all directions. Dougal stood firm as an oak, his fists lashing out like twin hammers. Taking a fighting stance at his side, Karrie repeatedly swung her weighted satchel hard enough to crack the skull of anyone who dared to come within range.

Nimble as a Scottish hare, Jaikie darted among the enemy, delivering a flurry of well-placed blows. Though lacking the youthful energy of my companions, I was no less determined, and knocked down my fair share of opponents. But sheer weight of numbers was against us, and it was clear we could not hold out for long – until there came an unexpected intervention.

As if from nowhere, we were suddenly reinforced by four burly young men in leather flight jackets and scarves, the distinctive garb of military fliers. Seeing us hard pressed and outnumbered, they immediately weighed in on our side and set about laying our opponents flat to right and left with fists, knees and headbutts.

The tide began to turn, and while I grappled with a lanky Moroccan I saw Ravenstein reassess his situation.

He spotted Karrie wielding her satchel as a weapon and instantly moved with the flashing speed of a predator. Ducking behind her, he snatched the bag from her grasp in one powerful, whip-like motion.

'Out! Out!' he yelled to his men, making a swift beeline for the exit. 'Get to the cars!'

Breaking off from the fight, his bruised and bloodied gang tumbled out after him. With a furious bellow, Dougal moved to pursue them, only to find Karrie holding him back.

'What are you doing, you daft lassie?' he protested. 'He's got the tablet!'

'No, he hasn't,' Karrie assured him with a grin. 'When nobody was looking, I swapped it for the sandwich platter. That's all he'll find when he opens my satchel. The tablet's over there under the table.'

Dougal gaped at her in utter astonishment. 'What are you like, woman!' he exclaimed. Still flushed from the heat of battle, he waved a finger in front of her face and struggled to find adequate words to express his adoration. 'You . . . you . . . you're a *gazelle*!'

Karrie grabbed his hand and, yanking him forward, planted a solid kiss directly on his lips. While he was still reeling with astonishment, she examined his knuckles. 'Look, they are skinned and bloody from the fight,' she said, leading him away. 'Come out to the courtyard and we'll bathe them in the fountain.'

Now that I could take a proper look at our rescuers, I was taken aback to see that two of them sported the insignia of the Luftwaffe. The man who appeared to be in charge of the group wore RAF wings, and beneath his luxuriant handlebar moustache he grinned from ear to ear as he greeted Jaikie with the familiarity of an old comrade.

'Well, Nipper, you're never far from trouble, are you?' he said laughing.

'Binnsy! I hardly recognised you with that bush on your face,' Jaikie exclaimed. 'Sir Richard Hannay, this is Harry Binns. We played rugby for Cambridge together.'

'Jaikie here was the weediest specimen on the squad,' said the airman, 'but by God he could move fast.'

'And that's why you called him Nipper,' I guessed.

'Binnsy here was a pretty fair centre half,' said Jaikie. 'Bit of a butterfingers with the ball, though.'

'Careful, Nipper, I can still tackle like a charging bull,' Binns warned.

He presented the RAF man standing next to him, whose boyish face was clean shaven. 'This chap here is my wingman, Flash Bolton. And this pair are Dieter and Willi. They're Luftwaffe, but good chaps, all things considered. We ran into them earlier and rather hit it off. We've been doing the rounds of the bars trying to outdo each other in outrageous flying stories.'

Bolton snapped off a jaunty salute while the two Germans attempted a swaying, military bow. I was aware that there existed a special bond between pilots of whatever nationality, and even in time of war it clearly persisted when they encountered each other on neutral ground.

'I certainly appreciate your showing up in the nick of time,' I said. 'We were in a pretty tight spot.'

'We would not stand by and see your brave little band overwhelmed by such a filthy mob,' Dieter declared with the hearty geniality of a man well buoyed by alcohol. 'Cowards of their sort deserve a good thrashing.'

'Enough thrashing,' slurred his fellow German, pulling him away. 'We get drinks now.'

They strolled unsteadily to the bar and loudly placed a command for beer. The two waiters, emerging timidly from cover, made haste to oblige them.

Binns placed his fists on his hips and made a shrewd appraisal of Jaikie and myself. 'Nipper, I know the game sort of chap you are,' he declared, 'and I've heard one or two tales about General Hannay. I've a solid hunch that you and your party aren't here to enjoy the sights and those bleeders who set about you didn't do it just for the exercise.'

With a sidelong glance, Jaikie deferred the question to me.

'You're right, Captain Binns,' I confirmed. 'We're here on important military business, and now that we've got the enemy on our necks the sooner we get out of Tangier the better.'

'Fair enough,' said the airman. 'Where are you bound for?'

'Malta,' Jaikie replied, 'and as soon as we can manage.'

Binns let out a hearty laugh and clapped his companion on the shoulder. 'Hear that, Flash? We've got ourselves some passengers.'

'You're going to Malta?' I asked, scarcely able to believe it.

'We're stationed there,' Binns informed us cheerfully. 'We flew here in a Wellington for a few days' leave on neutral ground.'

'We were aiming to head back soon anyway,' said Flash Bolton, with a bleary-eyed grimace. He slipped a hand under his cap and rubbed his head. 'I don't think I can actually drink any more.'

'Grab your kit,' Binns exhorted us, 'and we'll head for the airport right now. Get the old girl fuelled up then it's off into the blue.'

'Here, sir, let me give you a hand picking up those cards,' Jaikie volunteered. 'It looks to me like they bring you good luck.'

A pair of taxis whisked us off to Tangier airport, which was located in mountain country behind and above the city. Binns and Bolton passed through the glass doors of the airport station and quickly cleared their flight papers with the authorities. The two pilots then went off to inspect their plane, while Jaikie and Karrie tried to scrounge up some food and drink for the trip. Once we were alone, Dougal approached me in a conspiratorial fashion that was very unlike his usual straightforward manner.

'I wanted to ask you for a piece of advice, sir, if you wouldn't mind.'

'I wouldn't mind at all,' I responded. 'I hope I can be of some help.'

'Well, the thing is this – it occurs to me that I'm very likely in love with that Greek lassie, and it might well be that she's grown a mite fond of me.'

'I would agree with you on both counts,' I assured him.

'The trouble is, this isn't like Jaikie and his lass Alison,' he continued awkwardly. 'She's back home in Scotland, so he doesn't need to fash himself about her safety. But here we are, me and Karrie, sticking our necks out on this dangerous caper. It might be that in worrying overmuch about each other we'll take our minds off the business at hand and put the whole party at risk. So it's maybe not such a good idea to be giving in to these romantic notions.'

Dougal scowled down at his grazed knuckles and I could see he was genuinely troubled. I laid an encouraging hand upon his shoulder.

'Dougal, when I first met my wife Mary, she was already an agent for military intelligence at the height of the Great War, and in her time she placed herself in just as much danger as I did. I had to believe that she could take good care of herself, even without me around, and she had to trust that I too would find my way out of any number of scrapes.

'Now, I think Dr Adriatis has proved herself just as capable as you or I, and I'm sure she trusts that you too can handle any situation that's thrown your way. That trust may come hard, but it will see you through, and it's a lot better than letting any sort of fears rob you of a future happiness.'

Dougal beamed gratefully at me. 'To be honest, sir, many's the time over these past few days I've wished the great McCunn were here to give me sage advice. But I think it's fair to say that you're nearly as wise a man as he is.'

I was well aware of the exalted opinion all the Die-Hards had of the retired Glasgow grocer who had been their guardian and their mentor, so it was with absolute sincerity that I told him, 'Dougal, I don't believe I've ever been paid a higher compliment.'

Karrie and Jaikie rejoined us just as Binns and Bolton returned from the plane. Both fliers looked grave and more than a little angry.

'Rotten news, I'm afraid,' Binns reported. 'Some dirty blighters have yanked out our fuel lines and taken a hammer to one of the engines.'

'It's going to take at least a full day to fix the damage,' Bolton added with a scowl.

We turned at the sound of propellers bursting noisily into life. I could only watch in helpless frustration as a plane with German markings accelerated down the runway and lifted off into the sky. Whatever Ravenstein was up to, he'd bought himself a good head start over us.

31

KNIGHTS OF THE AIR

———

The thirteenth of August had dawned hazy and bright over Takali airfield, with the promise of blistering heat to come in the fullness of the day. The ground crew led by chief engineer Dennis Whitstable rolled the twelve planes of 249 Squadron out of their pens – crude shelters built from concrete blocks salvaged from Malta's many ruined buildings, or out of empty oil cans filled up with sand – and checked that they were fuelled up and ready for action. Despite their makeshift nature, the pens offered the planes some protection from the relentless German bombing.

Once they were strapped into their cockpits, the Spitfire pilots went through their lengthy start-up procedure and the Merlin engines choked into life, coughing out dust as usual. There was dust everywhere you went on the island of Malta, much of it carried in by the sirocco wind sweeping in from Africa, but this was augmented by the debris tossed into the air each day by the German bombing raids.

Seated in his plane and awaiting the signal for take-off, Peter John Hannay took from his pocket a much worn but highly cherished photograph of a blonde girl whose smile seemed to light up the entire cockpit. This was Anna Halverson, the Norwegian girl on whom his heart had been set since they shared an adventure some years before, while they were still in their teens. He fixed the photo to the dashboard. He then kissed the tip of his forefinger before pressing it to the lips of the lovely face smiling back at him. So far, he reflected, this little ritual had brought him more luck than he probably deserved.

His other good luck token was tucked inside his tunic. It was an old copy of Bunyan's *The Pilgrim's Progress* passed down to him by his father, who had inherited it from his old friend and mentor Peter Pienar. Old Peter had been an expert flyer and had died in action bringing down one of Germany's most renowned and deadly aces. Only recently had Peter John begun to leaf through the well-worn volume and mark certain passages that struck him as pertinent to his life in the air. One read, *I seek a place that can never be destroyed, one that is pure, and fadeth not away*, and he thought of this as he gazed at Anna's picture. She and her father were now safe in Scotland, beyond the reach of the Nazi invaders who had occupied their country.

He taxied into position, forming a diagonal queue with the rest of the squadron as one by one they took to the air, led by Squadron Leader Oliver Markham. As he watched his comrades lift off from the ground, Peter John was reminded, as always, of the grace and power of the hunting birds he had prized in the days of his youth, when he had been all but obsessed with the sport of falconry. He had trained goshawks, sparrow-hawks, merlins and innumerable kestrels, and through them he had become well acquainted with death.

Those noble birds, for all their beauty and strength, had seemed doomed to perish at the least provocation. Sometimes they died of apoplexy or a clot, sometimes one would become lost, tangle its jesses in a tree and die of starvation. Upon occasion death quickly followed a clash with a rival bird. It was his love of these birds and their power of flight which had prompted him to take flying lessons at the earliest possible opportunity, and then enlist in the Royal Air Force upon the approach of war. He learned all too soon that like a bird of prey's, the life of a fighter pilot could be tragically short.

Now he was on the runway, driving forward with mounting speed, the blood rushing in his veins as the roar of the engine grew louder. There was a series of bumps as the wheels bounded over potholes newly filled in after the last bombing raid had once again pockmarked the whole field with craters. Then came that moment, that lurch as the wind caught the wings and the plane lifted clear of the confines of earth to ascend into the freedom of the skies.

That brief moment of exultation gave way to the familiar routine of checking speed and altitude and moving into a V formation with the rest of the squadron. Off to his left was Canadian Russ Hollingsworth, commonly known as Hollywood on account of his North American accent and his matinee idol looks. Next to Squadron Leader Markham, he was the most experienced flyer of them all and claimed he had once flown upside down over Buckingham Palace.

On his other wing was T. Jack Westerbrook, or Jacko, who came from Norfolk farming stock and had a habit of describing the Germans as foxes or some other form of vermin. Once, after downing a Junkers 88, he declared with unfeigned vehemence, 'And that pays you back for Aunt Hettie's henhouse!'

Markham's confident baritone came over the radio,

ordering everyone to confirm by number that they were in position. He then scrutinised the formation and barked out instructions.

'Cuthbert, straighten up, you incessant dandy! You're not on the dance floor now! Emersby, you're wobbling like a jelly! What would your lady friend say if she saw you making such a hash of things? Get a grip, man!'

These were both newly arrived replacement pilots and they had learned right away that no fuel could be spared for practice flights. Their training took place in the full blaze of battle, and Markham told every fresh pilot, 'You need to learn as fast as if your life depends on it – because it bloody well does!'

This morning's briefing had been anything but cheery, not that the pilots needed much reminder of their tightening resources. The convoy ploughing its way across the Mediterranean had been subject to every form of attack the Axis forces could bring to bear, including bombers, submarines and torpedo boats. According to the latest reports, of the fourteen merchant vessels carrying vital supplies no more than half a dozen remained afloat and a couple of those could not be located. Those that were left were strung out over five miles of sea along with their hard-pressed destroyer escort.

There was some good news, however. Cooperation between the Germans and the Italians had broken down amid long-festering distrust and mutual recrimination. The result was that the Luftwaffe refused to provide air cover for Italian naval actions while the ships of the Regia Marina declined to offer support to the Germans' aerial campaign. On top of this, a series of bogus messages from the British commanders persuaded the Italian admirals that a force was being sent against them much more formidable than anything Malta could actually muster. As a result, they chose to withdraw to the relative safety of their own coastline, leaving the destruction of the convoy in the hands of their overbearing allies.

The squadron banked right over the bomb-scarred landscape of Malta and headed west over the waters of the Mediterranean, which today looked an ominous gunmetal blue. Communications with the convoy were sporadic, but the position of the ships had been determined closely enough for the RAF planes to zero in and provide them with protection on this last leg of their long voyage.

'Ten o'clock low, boys,' Markham announced at last.

Glancing down, Peter could see a merchant vessel, possibly the *Rochester Star*, which bore the scars of a recent attack but at present was sailing safely towards its destination. Markham led the way along the trailing route of the convoy until puffs of smoke and vapour trails were visible in the skies to the west.

'Trouble up ahead, lads,' he informed them grimly. 'We'd better get in there and lend a hand. Watch your backs and make your bullets count!'

The squadron climbed rapidly to three thousand feet, carrying them above the enemy, who Peter could now see were attacking the great American tanker the *Ohio*. Her escort of three destroyers was putting up a barrage at the incoming Junkers 88s, and as a result several German bombs were falling into the sea around the target, sending explosive showers of spray washing over the vessel's deck. The *Ohio* was already blackened with fire, and broken chunks of twisted metal stuck out from her decks in places where she had taken a direct hit. She was moving very slowly, and plumes of black smoke testified to the fact that her engines were labouring mightily.

The Malta squadron now plunged into the enemy formation, peeling off to engage in a deadly aerial ballet. Darting through the screen of nimble Messerschmitt 109s, Peter targeted one of the Junkers, laying a stream of fire directly along her fuselage. Flames erupted from the burning scar and a wing sheared off as the plane tilted violently, completely out of control. She plunged downward in a sickening spiral and hit the sea with an explosive crash.

Peter John barely had time to take any satisfaction from the kill before a hungry Messerschmitt came roaring down on his tail. He threw his plane into a wild corkscrew intended to shake off the pursuit as a stream of bullets streaked by, narrowly missing the Spitfire's fuselage, and then the German pilot suddenly swerved away. Hollywood was coming at him out of the sun, his guns chattering in a staccato rhythm. The Canadian's aim was true, piercing the German's cockpit and sending the stricken enemy down into the waves.

'Close one there, PJ,' Hollywood called over the radio. 'Look out, here comes another bandit!'

While the RAF men duelled with the German fighters, the Junkers, their payloads having been delivered, began to withdraw northward. They appeared to have added little further damage to the *Ohio*, but the attack was not yet over. Like a bat out of hell, a Stuka, the deadly demon of the skies, came swooping down towards the beleaguered tanker. Jacko was on his tail, blazing away to bring him down before he could reach her.

Peter saw his wingman score a direct hit on the enemy pilot, who slumped forward, releasing his bomb too soon. The explosive detonated in the sea, tossing up a frothing cascade, but the danger was not past, for whether it was an accident or the German pilot deliberately sacrificed himself, the Stuka was headed straight for the ship. The *Ohio* was too slow and bulky to manoeuvre out of danger, and the defensive guns blazed in a desperate frenzy, but the incoming dart could not be stopped. It smashed directly into the deck and exploded in a horrifying fireball.

Reeling back from the blast, the sailors recovered from the shock in time to close in with fire extinguishers. They battled hard to bring the flames under control, and as Peter passed overhead he could see the gnarled shell of the Stuka sticking out of the deck like some ghastly artwork in blackened metal. Yet the *Ohio* remained afloat, like a stubborn boxer who takes punch after punch and still battles on to the next round.

The attacking force was now fleeing back to their airfields in Sicily, and Markham called his squadron back together.

'Time to head home before we run dry,' he announced. 'Everybody check in.'

One by one each of the pilots called in their status, but one voice was missing.

'Looks like we lost Emersby,' Markham concluded solemnly. 'We'll raise a glass to him tonight, boys.'

Peter John had lost count of how many comrades he

Knights of the Air 263

had lost since the storm broke over France, but each fresh loss still hurt like a wound. He only hoped Emersby's sacrifice was worthwhile, because if the battered hulk of the *Ohio* could not find a way to reach the Grand Harbour at Valletta, then the island must fall and with it the hopes of free men everywhere.

Shaking off such gloomy thoughts, he gazed once more at the picture of his sweetheart and projected his mind forward to a joyous reunion. He had no suspicion that another reunion, one he had not foreseen coming so soon, was waiting for him back on Malta.

32

THE BESIEGED

Thanks to the hard work and determination of our new pilot friends, we were able to take off from Tangier at first light in their twin-engined Wellington. Flying low over open water to avoid drawing the attention of the Axis coastal defences of Algeria and Tunisia, we reached Malta seven hours later and descended towards the airfield at Takali, a few miles to the east of the ancient capital of Mdina.

Seen from the air, the base was a roughly circular sprawl of landing strips, blast pits and slit trenches where relays of mechanics worked round the clock to keep the bombers and Spitfires ready to fly at a moment's notice. Batteries of anti-aircraft guns ringed the perimeter, their upturned barrels glinting in the blazing summer sun.

Months of relentless aerial bombardment had left the main runway seamed and scarred like the face of a quarry. As we made our approach we passed over a repair party feverishly toiling to fill in the gaping bomb craters with rubble salvaged from fragmented outbuildings. Our landing was a rocky one, involving some tricky manoeuvring that would have taxed even Archie Roylance's capabilities.

I accompanied Binns and Bolton to the command post, where they reported in to the officer on duty. Here I learned that Peter John's squadron was en route back from their latest sortie. Rejoining my young friends outside, we all four scanned the skies to the west, eagerly awaiting the first sight of the returning fighters. All the while Karrie held the tablet in its satchel tightly in her arms, clinging – as I was – to the hope that here on the island it might finally give up its secrets.

We did not have long to wait before the squadron appeared, sweeping towards us in a disciplined formation. One by one they touched down, each plane being greeted with cheers from the men on the ground. From some of their sombre comments, however, I understood that at least one fighter had not made it home.

Flight crews swarmed to help the pilots out of their cockpits and there was a frustrating delay before I was able to spot Peter John peeling off his goggles. He moved stiffly away from his plane and paused to flex his neck. It was then he sighted me, and his face lit up with surprise. With a whoop of delight, he stripped off his flight helmet and rushed to meet me. Clapping both hands on my shoulders, he exclaimed, 'Dad! By heaven, are you a sight for sore eyes! What on earth are you doing here?'

'No need to worry, Peter,' I reassured him. 'I'm not here to talk about your school report.'

He laughed at this private joke of ours. He had never really taken to school and had sometimes worried about his marks. For my part, I had always made it clear to him that his academic performance was less important to me than his honest character, sharp mind and courage on the sporting field.

'I suppose I should have expected you,' he said wonderingly. 'It's just like you to pop up exactly where the action's at its hottest.'

'It seems some of us aren't destined for the quiet life,'

I said. 'Maybe when we've finished toppling the Reich we can slip away for a spot of salmon fishing.'

At close quarters I could see that the shortage of food and the strain of constant warfare had taken their toll on my son. His face was noticeably thinner and his well-worn flight suit hung loose on his frame. Despite these privations, his eyes were as bright as ever and his air of resolve undiminished.

'Look, I'd better go and have a word with Markham,' Peter said, pointing out his squadron leader, 'explain to him who you are. I suppose I can tell him truthfully that you're here on some important business?'

'I think it's fair to say that.'

Once he had permission from his officer to join me, I introduced Peter to the other members of my party. I explained to him as briefly as possible what it was that had brought us here, and couldn't help but note the scepticism with which he greeted my story.

'I've got to tell you honestly, Dad,' he stated apologetically, passing his gaze across Dougal, Jaikie and Karrie, 'and the rest of you, but with all we've been going through here, it's hard to see how this treasure hunt of yours is going to do us any good.'

'It's a puzzle to us as well,' Dougal agreed gruffly.

'I suppose we must have faith that our journey has a purpose,' said Karrie, touching a hand to the satchel at her side. 'I cannot believe we would have come through so many dangers and difficulties if it was not somehow meant to be.'

At this point Harry Binns came jogging up to us. 'I've had a word with the chaps here,' he reported, 'made a big noise about you being a general, Mr Hannay, and they've agreed to let you borrow one of their cars for the trip to Valletta. They've phoned ahead to let HQ know you're coming.'

'Give me a minute to get out of my flying gear and I'll come with you,' said Peter John.

Soon we were headed north with Dougal at the wheel, Jaikie beside him and myself squeezed in at the back between Peter John and Karrie. Like the airfield at Takali, the road had been badly damaged, forcing Dougal to steer an erratic course through potholes and rubble. My son gave us a brief and self-effacing account of his time on Malta, displaying more concern for the sufferings of the civilian population than for his own safety. The hospital at Valletta, he told us, was working flat out to deal with the constant stream of casualties.

'Our old friend Peter Paterson is a doctor there,' said Jaikie. 'I'll bet he's happy as can be at having his hands full.'

'And Thomas Yowney's got himself stationed here as a chaplain,' Dougal added. 'It seems like the Gorbals Die-Hards are here in force.'

'I believe your gang did a pretty good job of pulling my old man out of a pickle when you were all in Paris,' said Peter John.

'Och, that was nothing,' said Dougal. 'Your father did all the hard work on that caper.'

It did boost my confidence to know that the whole group was here on Malta, as Stannix had assured me they would be when we spoke back in London. These four young Scots seemed to have between them a range of talents that made them equal to any challenge.

Peter John told us that medicines were in short supply and food was running low. Rationing was made stricter every week so that hunger pangs were just part of the daily routine. He added that we were lucky to be given the use of a car, as fuel was such a rarity that the bicycle was the most common mode of transport for soldiers and civilians alike.

The farms and villages we passed along our route bore all the hallmarks of deprivation and heavy bombardment. In spite of this the people seemed to hold themselves proudly and waved cheerfully at our military vehicle as it rolled past.

'You could hardly blame the locals for wanting to be rid of us,' said Peter John, 'and yet the more they suffer, the more pride they take in their alliance with us. We may be short of many things here, but there's plenty of guts and nerve to go round.'

We all fell silent at the sound of sirens in the distance. This was soon followed by the drone of aircraft high above and before long we heard the first bomb burst some distance ahead.

'Better pull over under cover,' I advised.

Dougal turned into a grove of olive trees, concealing us beneath the drooping branches. The thunder of aircraft engines grew louder as the raiders swept in from the coast, accompanied by the hideous din of exploding bombs. To my horror I realised that we were directly in the enemy's flight path. Instinctively we crouched low in our seats as the heavy bombers roared overhead. As the last one passed over us, from a couple of hundred yards to our left there came a sickening detonation that rocked the ground beneath our wheels.

Now, in addition to the rumble of the bombers, we could hear the drone of our own fighters, which had been launched into the sky. Then there came repeated bursts of anti-aircraft fire, like a series of sharp punches. Gradually the din abated as the enemy planes were forced to disperse. The sound of the all-clear was as welcome to our ears as sweet music.

Climbing out of our car to survey the aftermath of the attack, we discovered that the farmhouse overlooking the grove had taken a direct hit. In its place was a blackened crater surrounded by smouldering rubble. An old man staggered out from the shelter of a nearby barn and shook a furious fist after the departed raiders. Neighbours converged to offer him what help and comfort they could.

Seeing there was nothing we could do, we climbed back into the car and continued on our way in a grimmer mood following this demonstration of the punishment being inflicted on the brave little island. Soon we could see the rooftops and ancient fortifications of Valletta directly ahead.

Four centuries earlier, to guard the entrance to the Grand Harbour, the Knight of St John had built forts on the twin promontories of Senglea and Birgu. Following the great siege of 1565, they celebrated their victory over the Turks by constructing a magnificent town along the ridge on the other side of the water with richly ornamented churches and splendid fortified towers.

The new town was named after Jean de Vallette, the Grand Master who had commanded the Order during that long battle. In the old town the ramparts of bastions which had withstood the Ottoman assault still reared up in all their strength, a testament to the men who built and defended them.

As we drove down the main street we saw heaps of rubble everywhere and buildings reduced to fire-blasted shells. The length of the Great Harbour was dotted with the skeletal hulls of ships destroyed by the incessant German bombing, but now that the raid had passed the quayside was swarming with well-organised teams unloading a recently arrived merchant ship, presumably an outlier of the Pedestal convoy, most of which still lay beyond the reach of safety.

We reported in to headquarters, once an elegant manor, now fortified with sandbags and turned to military use. When I requested a meeting with the governor I was informed that he was busy inspecting the submarine pens and would not be available until the next day. Knowing how odd my tale must sound to the officers on duty, I decided not to press the urgency of my mission, since it seemed advisable not to stretch their goodwill.

On a positive note, they found accommodation for us, this being some cramped rooms in the Kevala Hotel, one wing of which had already been reduced to rubble. The remaining walls were riven with cracks, and the windows covered over with paper, so that the whole place gave the appearance of being held together with sticking plaster and prayer. The staff could not have been more hospitable, and appeared to take pride in carrying out their duties as if there was no danger to be feared and all their guests were simply here for a restful holiday.

When we had checked in, Dougal and Jaikie announced they were going to the hospital to surprise their fellow Die-Hards, and Karrle and I sat down with Peter John to try, unavailingly, to decipher the ancient tablet. It was no good – the meaning of the symbols remained closed to us.

That night my thoughts were once again of Mary, wondering how she was coping with the burden of sending those newly trained young women off to France where they would face danger on every side. Would a day ever come, I wondered, when all of this would be over, when the just and lasting peace we thought we were fighting for would finally become a reality? In my sleep my dreams were filled with those taunting symbols. They appeared to dance before my eyes, seeking some sort of pattern that would speak whatever message it was that had been left to us by Redfalcon.

In the morning, I left the rest of my party to their breakfast while I smartened up as best I could and marched over to headquarters. I was kept waiting for only a half-hour before being admitted to the office of the governor, Viscount Gort. Lack of sleep and the heavy weight of his duties had made him short on patience, and when I told him what had brought me here he gaped in blank disbelief at my tale of knights, tombs and ancient codes.

'Hannay, let me get this straight,' he barked. 'I was led to believe you were here on some intelligence mission, perhaps with new information on enemy movements that might be of help to us, help we sorely need.' He paused, almost choking on his indignation. 'Instead,' he resumed with redoubled scorn, 'you come to me with some preposterous yarn out of the tales of King Arthur and expect me to have my cipher officers waste hours poring over a brass plate. Have I got this right?'

I was not prepared for so hostile a reaction, and did my best to placate him. 'I fully appreciate how hard pressed you are, governor, and how fantastic this might seem, but I can assure you that the Germans are taking this business very seriously.'

'Seriously?' Gort spat with contempt. 'I've heard Hitler's taking advice from astrologers and mystics. Do you want me to do that too?'

I did my best not to bristle at his provocative tone. 'Granted, it might be a long shot, but if there's any possibility that this tablet holds some clue to a crack in Malta's defences we'd be fools to ignore it.'

'Let me tell you, Hannay,' Gort informed me brusquely, 'that I already feel a fool for having sat here and listened to this nonsense. If this hodge-podge of myths is all you have for me, I'll thank you to waste no more of my time.'

It was clearly all he could do not to call his guards and have me thrown out on my ear. I stood and did my best to make a civilised exit.

'Thank you for your time, governor,' I said from the doorway. 'And thank you for listening to me.'

As I closed the door behind me, I heard a loud snort of displeasure. With a sinking heart I realised that the Die-Hards and I were on our own, with the fate of the island in our hands.

33

THE SPARK OF HOPE

——

When I returned to the hotel, I spotted Karrie, Dougal and Jaikie in a corner of the dining room sharing a pot of tea with Peter John. When I joined them, they looked up at me enquiringly.

I shook my head. 'No go, I'm afraid. When I told the governor about Redfalcon and our discovery in the Atlas Mountains, he looked at me as if I'd gone completely off my rocker. He thinks the whole business is utter humbug.'

'I had a feeling it might go that way,' Peter commiserated, as I sat down beside him. 'Governor Gort's a hard-headed, practical chap, just the sort you need to steer you through a crisis. But he's pretty much set in his ways and not exactly hungering after new ideas.'

Seeing that I was worn out after my fruitless meeting, Karrie poured a cup of tea and handed it to me. 'Here, you should drink this,' she insisted. 'It's strong enough to bring a mummy back to life.'

I took a swallow and she was right – it was certainly bracing. I was trying my best not to be disheartened, but it seemed unfair on my comrades, who had been through so much, that I had no better news to offer them.

'Would he not even let his intelligence officers take a look at the tablet,' asked Jaikie, 'to see if they might come up with any insights?'

'We don't rate even that much assistance,' I replied.

'Look, I don't want to put a damper on things,' said

Peter diffidently, 'but could it be that he's right, that this tale of Redfalcon's secret is just a myth, like the Loch Ness Monster?'

'Don't you be so quick to dismiss Nessie,' Dougal warned him. 'I've heard tales.'

'Ravenstein hasn't travelled across Europe and Africa and activated so many of his resources because of a myth,' I said. 'He believes that this tablet is the key to victory on Malta.'

'But if this Ravenstein already has a record of the symbols, as you told me,' said Peter, 'why would he go to the trouble of trying to get his hands on the tablet? Was he really just trying to butter up the Führer?'

'No, I don't believe so,' I said. 'What he wanted was to keep the tablet out of our hands so that we couldn't work out what it signifies.'

'Well, so far he need have no worries on that score,' said Jaikie gloomily.

'I'm sorry to go,' said Peter, rising to his feet, 'but if I don't get back to the squadron Markham will have me on latrine duty for the rest of the year.'

As I watched him leave, I reflected that if nothing else came of this long journey, I had at least enjoyed a reunion with my son before he faced the coming German assault. I looked around at my young friends and I could see that we were all struggling with our thoughts, searching for some way forward.

Karrie laid the tablet down on the table and frowned at it. If the fury of frustration in her eyes had burned any more fiercely, it might have scorched the metal.

'I have compared these symbols to every hieroglyph,

every sacred language I know, and still I have come up with nothing.' She clenched her fists and gave an angry shake of her head.

'Don't fash yourself,' said Dougal, laying a comforting hand on her arm. 'The dratted thing has got every one of us baffled.'

'It's too bad Thomas Yowney's laid up in the infirmary,' said Jaikie.

'The infirmary?' I echoed, immediately voicing my concern.

'That's what we found out when we went looking for him and Peter yesterday,' said Dougal. 'A few days ago he was conducting a wedding between one of our sergeants and a girl from operations control when the air-raid sirens sounded. The happy couple insisted on sticking it out and completing their vows.'

'A bomb hit the chapel,' Jaikie went on. 'Nobody was killed but half the roof came down on Thomas. We tried to see him, but Doc Paterson sent a message that he mustn't be disturbed. Says he needs rest and quiet if he's to recover.'

Dougal snapped a hard biscuit in two and tossed half into his mouth. 'Talk about rotten luck. Just when we need a first class mind to tackle this puzzle.'

'How about that!' exclaimed Jaikie, suddenly beaming all over his face. 'Sometimes all you have to do is wish.'

I followed his eyes and saw a pair of familiar figures entering the dining room and walking towards our table. One was the jaunty, round-faced doctor, Peter Paterson; the other was the tall, slim figure of Thomas Yowney. The parson's head was heavily bandaged and he was limping along with the aid of a stick.

Dougal and Jaikie leapt out of their seats to meet their old comrades and boisterous greetings were exchanged, with much hand shaking and back-slapping all round. The bonds of friendship formed by the four young Scots during their impoverished childhood had clearly only grown stronger during the enforced separations of wartime.

'Well, Thomas, I must say you don't look too bad for a man who's had a building fall in on him,' Jaikie observed with a grin.

'It's just as well you pulled through,' said Dougal, 'or we'd have had to invade Berlin and give Herr Hitler a sound thrashing for having the gall to drop a bomb on one of the Die-Hards.'

'He should still be in bed,' Paterson observed disapprovingly, 'but when the nurse told us who it was who'd come calling, I couldn't hold him back.'

'You've kept me cooped up long enough,' Yowney declared defiantly. 'Without my kindly guidance, there're boys out there whose spiritual welfare will go gurgling down the drain like dishwater.'

Dougal helped Yowney into a chair and the chaplain greeted me with a smile. 'It's good to see you again, General Hannay. It seems that whenever the Jerries have their eye on a juicy target, there you are standing in their way.'

'That job would be a lot easier if I had any idea what they're up to,' I said.

'And this young lady will be Dr Adriatis,' Yowney went on. 'I hope you've not found it distasteful to be travelling in company with these hooligans.'

'You and your friends are the noblest gentlemen a

lady could ever meet,' Karrie responded. 'It seems they all expect great things from you.'

'Do they indeed?' the chaplain responded with a twinkle in his eye.

'I've kept him in bed for a few days' rest,' said Peter, his tone making it clear just how challenging an endeavour that had proved to be. 'We can't risk any damage being done to the best brain ever to outwit the Glasgow constabulary.'

'I'll thank you not to taunt me about the scandalous days of our youth,' Yowney complained. 'It was galling enough to be cooped up like a prisoner and dosed with castor oil. So, lads, is it words of Christian wisdom you're wanting?'

'We're in need of a lot more than an uplifting sermon, padre,' I told him.

'I've got to go back to my rounds now,' said Paterson. 'This chap is still a patient of mine and I'm entrusting him to your care. All of you keep an eye on him and make sure he doesn't do himself another injury.'

Once the doctor had gone, I left it to Karrie to tell Thomas the history behind Redfalcon's tablet. She then placed it before him so that he could give it a proper examination.

'Unless we and a very clever German have been completely misled,' I told him, 'something about this tablet holds the key to whether Malta will stand or fall.'

With a sober nod the clergyman bent his gaze on the tablet. The rest of us could only look on in suspense as he carefully scanned it, inch by inch, pausing now and then to tap a finger on one or another of the cryptic symbols.

After several long-drawn minutes he raised his head.

'I believe I've a pretty shrewd idea what these symbols are,' he announced. 'And if I'm right, I can make a canny guess at what they're hiding.'

I was astonished that he appeared to have cracked it so easily. For the first time since our arrival on Malta I felt a spark of hope that there was a brain on our team who was a match for Ravenstein.

'For heaven's sake, Thomas, let's have it,' Dougal blurted out.

Yowney answered with a slow shake of his head. 'If I tell you, you'll just think I'm daft. No, I'll need to show you. First, though, we'll need to scrounge up some torches and a crowbar.'

34

THE PATH OF SALVATION

Shortly thereafter, armed with the requisite equipment, we set out through the streets of Valletta. Thomas Yowney led us through a maze of streets littered with fallen masonry where the broken walls of bombed-out houses reared against the sky. Dust lay everywhere, baking under the August sun.

Yet despite the widespread destruction, there were people abroad: shopkeepers patching up their storefronts, workmen clearing away rubble, women gossiping in doorways while their barefoot children played amid the ruins. Soldiers and civilians on bicycles whizzed past us, their bells ringing out a warning to clear the way.

Yowney's air was one of deep preoccupation with his own thoughts. When we pressed him to name our destination, he waved our questions impatiently aside and quickened his pace. For a man hampered by a stick, he made remarkable progress. The agility with which he negotiated his way around every obstacle in his path testified to his determination to penetrate the heart of the mystery that lay before us.

Our course brought us to the steps of the church of St Agnes. Miraculously, its handsome façade was still largely intact. Pausing on the threshold of the nave, I could see three black-clad women kneeling before the high altar in attitudes of mourning, murmuring prayers as they ran beads through their fingers.

'The Maltese people are Romans, of course,' Yowney explained quietly, 'not staunch Presbyterians like myself, which means their faith grants them the particular comfort of praying for their dead. I sometimes envy them that, even though it's something they've had to do entirely too much of, of late.'

The bereaved worshippers did not raise their heads or pay us any mind as we entered. The interior of the building was like a highly ornamented jewel-box. Its rib-vaulted ceiling was supported by fluted columns of finely carved stone, its walls embellished with richly painted reliefs.

Yowney waved his stick at our surroundings and continued to speak in a reverent hush. 'During my time here, I've taken a liking to their churches and have visited most of them. In some cases a friendly priest has given me a guided tour. Which leads me to what I hope is the answer to your conundrum.'

He led us into one of the ornate side chapels where there hung a portrait of the church's patron saint framed in gold. Sweeping his gaze over the floor, Yowney pointed his stick towards one of the flagstones at the portrait's base.

Peering down, I saw that it was incised with the image of a sword. With a sharp gasp of recognition, Karrie pulled the tablet from her satchel and made a swift comparison.

'Yes!' she confirmed excitedly. 'This device matches one of the symbols on Redfalcon's tablet.'

'And it's not the only one,' said Yowney. Using one long finger as a pointer, he directed our attention to other images on the tablet. 'I've seen this one on the floor in the church of St Elmo, and *this* one in the church of St Publius. And this *other* one, I'm pretty sure, is in the church of St Thomas. I'll bet the ones I don't recognise will turn up as well if we look for them.'

'So it's just about some carvings in a church,' Dougal grumbled. 'What good does that do us?'

'For that you need to get your shoulder behind the crowbar and prise up this slab,' said Yowney. 'Have you not heard the phrase X marks the spot?'

'Are you saying there's treasure under here?' Jaikie asked. 'Like *Treasure Island*?'

'I think what we'll find is a sight more interesting than pirate loot,' answered the chaplain.

I noticed that the three praying women were on their way out and I signaled the others to wait until they were gone. As soon as we had the place to ourselves, we set to our task.

Together Dougal and Jaikie worked the crowbar under the edge of the slab and raised up one side, then gripped it by hand and lifted it off all the way. They had opened a square hatch to reveal a stone stairway leading down.

'This is a hiding place, then,' Karrie speculated, 'one of many at different locations where relics and other valuables could be hidden from invaders?'

'Do you not see the truth yet?' Yowney wondered. 'We'll need to get down there to be sure, of course.'

'I'll go first,' said Jaikie, switching on his electric torch and setting a foot on the topmost step just as a priest came sweeping up the aisle towards us from the vestry.

'What is this? What are you doing to my church, Chaplain Yowney?'

'Don't you worry yourself, Father,' Yowney reassured him. 'We're just checking the drains, you know, in case there's been any bomb damage.'

With that he followed Jaikie down into the gloom, lighting his torch as he went. Karrie went next, then Dougal, then myself, leaving the priest to stand over the hole, scratching his head and muttering about the strange ways of these Scots.

'Beneath our feet lies a world of wonders,' I heard Karrie murmur as we descended.

At the bottom of the stairway we found ourselves in a large cellar that had been carved out of the limestone. Engraved into the wall was the image of a sword, the same as the one on the flagstone above. Two open tunnels led out of the cellar, one marked with the symbol of a ship, another with the sign of a tree, both of which had their counterparts on the tablet.

'Unless I'm losing my wits,' said Yowney, 'that way will take us to St Elmo's, where we'll find a flight of stairs leading up. This other direction will take us directly under the church of St Catherine.'

He had already set off that way, his stick tapping on the bare stone floor.

'Hold on there, Thomas,' said Jaikie, catching him up. 'Should you not be taking it easy? You're supposed to be in hospital.'

'I'll manage fine,' said Yowney. 'So I've taken a wee knock on the head. That's no excuse for lying in bed all day.'

'Look here,' Dougal remonstrated with him, 'Doc Paterson told us that—'

Yowney cut him off with a scornfully raised hand. 'Peter means well, but sometimes he takes on like an old wifey. Now come on. Do you not see yet what we've found here?'

'Of course,' said Karrie, passing her torch beam over the walls as we walked. 'It's a complex of underground tunnels connecting key points in the island's defences.'

'That's right, lass,' Yowney enthused, 'and we're the first folk in ages to find our way down here.'

'I have to say, I feel a bit dim for never having thought of it,' I confessed.

'None of us had an inkling,' said Jaikie, 'and to be honest, I'm still having a hard time believing it.'

'It all makes perfect sense now,' said Karrie, as she thought back over the history she had studied so carefully. 'How was Fort St Elmo able to hold out for so long? Because it was supplied by means of these tunnels. How did reinforcements evade the Turkish army to reach the city? And how did a raiding party appear out of nowhere to attack the Turkish camp? It was these tunnels constructed in secret by Sir Thomas Easterly that made it possible.'

'After the siege, when they were constructing Valletta, they must have extended the tunnel system to include the new town,' I guessed.

We now found ourselves in another cellar like the first. There was a stone stairway leading up and the symbol of a tree engraved on the wall.

'You see?' exclaimed Yowney in almost boyish delight.

'It's as I told you. These stairs lead up to the church of St Catherine. This other tunnel will take us on to the old abbey of St Gregory's.'

Once again he was pressing onward without a pause. I reflected that either Doc Paterson had exaggerated the severity of his injuries, or he was so energised by his discovery that he had healed himself in part by a sheer act of will.

As we followed, Dougal observed, 'This must have been an unholy amount of work, to dig out all this without any sort of drilling equipment.'

'The knights were skilled engineers,' Karrie reminded him, 'but also, if you look closely at these walls, you'll see that some of them must have been formed naturally, probably by water flowing underground over thousands of years.'

'I suppose then that our friend Redfalcon found a natural tunnel system,' I guessed, 'and extended it, linking it up to key points on the surface.'

'And that tablet you discovered,' Yowney explained, 'although the distances are compressed, will have all the entrances marked in the correct positions relative to each other. It's like a map without which you'd have no idea where you're going.'

'If you don't mind me asking, Thomas,' said Jaikie, 'where exactly are we going?'

'Ah, now there's the thing,' said Yowney, rubbing his chin with one bony hand. 'I can see pretty much what locations those tablet symbols represent, and they're all churches or fortresses. There's one, though, that's not like the rest, the one like an upside-down letter U.'

'Yes. It might be an arch,' said Karrie.

'Well, the puzzling thing is,' Yowney went on, 'that if the tablet is a map, then that symbol is on a spot where there's no church or any other sort of building, just a barren stretch of land overlooking some cliffs.'

'Then why would they have bothered extending their tunnels out there?' I wondered.

'That's the question, isn't it?' said Yowney. 'We'd better find out. It will be a bit of a trek.'

'In that case we'd better just use one torch at a time,' Jaikie suggested. 'Otherwise the batteries might all run out and leave us stranded in the dark.'

We adopted Jaikie's suggestion and pressed on with only one beam penetrating the tunnel ahead.

'I hope we're not going down into Hades,' Dougal intoned grimly. 'I hear things get a bit hot down there.'

Yowney's smile was barely visible in the torchlight. 'Just stay close and let's hope we're on the path of salvation.'

We were at the end of the second hour of our long trudge through the dark when the tunnel ahead began to widen into something much larger. We advanced into a vast yawning blackness and switched on all five of our torches to illuminate the space ahead. We had entered a huge cavern large enough to contain a cathedral or two. Our beams flickered across a smooth watery sheen, the surface of a long subterranean lake that stretched off far into the distance.

Overhead the arched roof was barely visible, but I could see limestone stalactites dangling like crude swords.

The shore of the lake was scattered with rocks and broken shards that had over time fallen on to a surface of gritty sandstone granules.

'This explains the symbol,' breathed Karrie. 'Not an arch but a cave.'

'A cave and a half!' said Dougal.

Having driven himself on to this awesome destination, Thomas Yowney finally became aware of his fatigue and slumped against the cavern wall.

'Here, Thomas,' said Jaikie, taking him by the shoulders. 'You have a seat on this flat rock here.'

Once he was seated the chaplain waved away any further assistance. 'I'll be fine,' he declared. 'I'm just needing a wee breather.'

'I think you've earned a rest, padre,' I told him. 'If not for you we'd still be blundering around up top without a clue. This cave is a bit of a puzzle, though.'

'I see what you mean,' said Jaikie. 'What on earth has this place got to do with the defence of Malta?'

Karrie was making her way along the grey, rocky shore, probing the ground with her torch. After a minute or two she cast the beam far ahead, peering intently at the piles of stone littering the far end of the cavern, and suddenly uttered an excited cry. 'I can see something over there! It looks like a carving – or even a statue.'

Without another word she set off at a run along the shore, leaping over rocks and dodging around stalagmites.

'Where are you going, you daft lassie?' Dougal called, darting off in pursuit. 'You don't know what's out there!'

They disappeared into the shadows, leaving the rest of us to ponder the mystery of this subterranean chamber.

Gazing out over the dark waters of the lake, I couldn't help thinking of Jules Verne's famous story in which the underground realm was inhabited by monsters from the days of prehistory. Turning my gaze upward, I beheld the vaulted roof of the cavern with its numerous spiked stalactites poised above our heads.

'This tunnel system is a magnificent piece of engineering,' said Jaikie, staring about him at the cavern walls, 'but even if Ravenstein has tumbled to its existence, I still don't see what good it would do him.'

'There doesn't appear to be any way up to the surface from here,' I observed, 'so I can't see what use this part of the complex would be to the Knights.'

'No, it wouldn't be any use,' Yowney agreed, 'unless this pool connects to the sea. The Maltese, being an island folk, have always been braw swimmers.'

'To the sea.' As I repeated his words, an awful possibility arose in my mind, one almost too horrific to contemplate.

Just then I became conscious of a deep rumbling sound and from Yowney's startled expression it was clear that he heard it too. Jaikie, who had advanced curiously to the water's edge, now made a rapid retreat.

'I think we might have walked into some serious trouble,' he told us.

The noise had now resolved menacingly into the rhythmic throbbing of engines.

'That's either a loch monster,' the clergyman murmured, 'or . . .'

'Or . . .' I echoed.

Before I could complete the thought, lights appeared

beneath the water, and then a conning tower broke the surface. Moments later the hull of a U-boat rose up from the depths, like a monstrous sea dragon erupting into its lair.

35

THE FACE OF THE ENEMY

———

Water sloshed over the rocky shingle that marked the shore of the lake as the raider vessel came to rest. I glimpsed Dougal and Karrie, a pair of distant shadowy figures, diving for cover among the rocks at the far end of the lake, snapping off their torches as they did so. Jaikie, Yowney and I swiftly withdrew into the tunnel behind us, covering our torches with our hands. Crouching low, I kept a furtive watch on the enemy vessel, realising that this secret infiltration behind our defences had been Ravenstein's plan all along.

The hatch in the conning tower clanked open and the captain's bearded face rose into view. Hauling himself up to stand atop his vessel, he removed his naval cap and wiped a braided sleeve across his brow before taking a good all-round look at his surroundings. Satisfied that they had the cavern to themselves, he began issuing orders to his men down below. In response a pair of hatches opened up in the deck and a group of seamen clambered out. They rolled out a gangway, connecting the boat to the lake shore, and began unloading supplies, having placed oil lanterns round about to provide illumination.

The next group of men to emerge from the bowels of the sea beast were a very different sort. They wore the uniforms of the elite Kriegsmarinen and had about them the hard-bitten air of veterans who had fought their way through hell and back on more than one occasion.

Yowney took a peek over my shoulder and muttered, 'Damnably bad luck, Dougal and that Greek girl getting stuck at the other end of the lake.'

The unaccustomed strength of his language testified to the depth of his feeling where our comrades were concerned.

'They could try swimming back to us,' Jaikie murmured, 'but it would be a mad risk.'

'They'll be safe enough so long as they keep out of sight,' I told them quietly. 'Those soldiers won't stick around down here for long. They'll be coming this way as soon as they're organised, so that they can head up to the surface.'

The marines, about two dozen of them, were forming up on the shore and checking over their weapons. Well equipped with machine guns, pistols, grenades and mortars, they were big men, each one of whom looked more than capable of hefting his own personal arsenal. Only the most ferocious resistance would be capable of giving them pause, and that was something we were in no position to muster.

A single figure paced up and down the shore before them, issuing orders and checking the supply of ammunition. In his wide-brimmed hat and long leather cloak, even from afar I had no doubt that it was Ravenstein. Not content with devising this operation, he had come along in person to supervise the attack and glory in his triumph.

The sailors were now unloading cases of explosives, all of which looked ready for immediate use, and stacking them up beyond the stern of the submarine. The urgency of the captain's commands made it clear how anxious he was to get this dangerous cargo well clear of his boat.

'You two need to get topside as fast as you can and raise the alarm,' I told my companions.

'You go, Jaikie,' Yowney said in a low voice, clapping his friend on the shoulder by way of a farewell. 'I'll stay here with the general and see if there's any way we can stall these chaps until you bring us help.'

Jaikie gave a quick nod and set off back up the tunnel at a brisk trot. With his nimbleness and unwavering sense of direction, he was the best messenger we could possibly have hoped for, and yet, no matter how fast he ran, there was no way he could reach our people in time to stop the German attack force in its tracks.

'Well, padre, you have a well-earned reputation as a bit of a bright spark,' I told him, 'so I'm open to any suggestions you can come up with.'

Yowney's eyes took on the blank look I had seen before, as if all his thoughts had turned inward to review every possible option. After a few moments of contemplative silence he said softly, 'Perhaps if they could be persuaded to believe we're several steps ahead of them, that the tunnels behind us are already guarded by our troops . . .'

I considered the notion. It was a long shot, to be sure, and would probably buy us only a minute or two at best before Ravenstein and his men called our bluff and mowed us down. Then I spotted something which gave me hope that a minute or two might be all we needed.

Out at the far end of the lake, beyond the lights of the U-boat, I could just make out a pair of shadowy figures slithering through the rocks unseen by the enemy. Instead of withdrawing well out of sight, or even taking the chance of swimming under the water to rejoin us, Karrie and Dougal were edging ever closer to the Germans' supply of explosives.

Back in Casablanca Karrie had described to me how she had grown up watching her father use dynamite in his mining operations. Knowing this, I felt certain that she would attempt exactly what I would do if I were in her place. So long as there were detonators among those supplies, there was a slim chance that she might pull it off. But she and Dougal were going to need time and a distraction to ensure they weren't spotted.

'Padre, you keep out of sight and follow my lead,' I ordered.

Leaving Yowney under the cover of darkness, I stepped forward into the light and presented myself before the face of the enemy. Spotting me at once, Ravenstein advanced on me and whipped out his pistol.

'Hannay!' His mouth twisted into an expression of undisguised malice. 'Why is it that wherever I go, there you are, dogging my tracks?'

'It strikes me, Ravenstein,' I retorted with all the bravado I could muster, 'that you're the one who keeps dropping in without an invitation. This time you've taken a step too far and there's no way out for you.'

The battle-hardened men at his back seemed amused to see a lone civilian standing in their way, though I could also hear murmurs of unease that their arrival had been detected so soon. The important thing, as far as I was concerned, was that their attention was fixed solely upon me and not upon whatever might be going on behind them. Ravenstein impatiently waved them to silence.

'I don't know how you managed to find your way down here, Hannay,' he sneered, 'but you are far too late to stop me.'

'Oh, I know what you have planned,' I informed him coolly. 'You aim to move unseen through these tunnels, striking at our command and communications centres and preparing the ground for your airborne troops. Very bold, but it's not going to work.'

'Why not? Because of you?' He snorted. 'You may have stumbled down here by chance, still blinded by your own ignorance, but you are quite unprepared. Look at you – you are not even armed.'

'Did you really expect me to swallow that rot about a magical prayer?' I retorted. 'No, while we were stuck in Tangier, my friends and I put our heads together and figured out that what we had in our hands was a map to this underground maze. From then on it was perfectly clear what you had in mind and we've been streets ahead of you all the way.'

Ravenstein's pale eyes were as hard as steel. 'You're lying. You had no clue, not even the slimmest conception.'

'On the contrary, old man. The tunnels behind me are well guarded by our troops, as are all the entrances to this complex. You haven't the remotest chance of reaching any of your targets.'

'And yet, here you stand,' said Ravenstein, waving his pistol at me, 'one lone man, armed with nothing but empty bluster.'

'There's a whole squad behind me,' I warned him.

'They're ready to storm this place at my command and wipe out your little crew.'

The German barked out a short, dry laugh. 'Wipe us out, eh? So why haven't you done so?'

'Because we believe in something called civilisation, which means we have to show a degree of mercy even to our enemies. That's why I'm giving you this chance to surrender.'

I heard angry growls among the German soldiers and the harsh clatter of guns being cocked for action.

'Surrender?' sneered Ravenstein. 'I was right all along, Hannay. Your much vaunted courage is mere stupidity. You are quite mad.'

Faced with his hardening scepticism, I knew he was on the point of gunning me down. I did not dare to peer into the darkness beyond him to see what progress Karrie and Dougal were making, and there had not yet been time for Jaikie to organise any sort of resistance. Ravenstein's elite strike force, with the advantage of surprise and moving invisibly beneath our defences, might cause untold havoc. And then, once they had reached their initial objectives, I was quite certain he would send the signal that would bring an airborne invasion down on our heads. I had only one card to play and I would have to count on Yowney to back me up.

'Captain Jenkins!' I called into the tunnel behind me. 'Tell your men to prepare to attack!'

'They are ready and eager, sir,' the unseen parson called back in a voice bristling with military efficiency.

'Sergeant Higgins!' I added, pressing my luck. 'Bring up the Bren guns.'

'Fully loaded and awaiting your command, suh!' Yowney answered in the belligerent tones of a bullish sergeant major.

The hesitation in Ravenstein's face was barely a flicker, and his men were straining at the leash to charge into action. My heart was hammering and my insides were twisted into knots with sheer tension. Every second I could buy for Karrie and Dougal was worth the risk and it was vital that I keep the eyes of the Germans focused entirely upon me, even at the cost of my life.

'I'm afraid I have even more bad news for you,' I informed Ravenstein. 'Two of our submarines are now guarding the entrance to this place, so there's no retreat or escape for you and your men.'

At that moment I saw one of the commandos at the very rear of their formation glance back and spot the would be-saboteurs at work among the explosives. Even as the man turned and unslung his machine gun, Dougal launched himself at him. His momentum carried them both over the edge of the shore and down beneath the dark, freezing waters.

The rest of the squad were now looking round for the source of the disturbance and I knew I could not let them spot Karrie.

'Captain Jenkins, order your men to attack!' I yelled at the top of my lungs.

The whole German force swung about to face me and beyond them I saw Karrie slip down into the lake unobserved. Ravenstein aimed his pistol directly at my face.

'There is no army, Hannay,' he spat. 'All you have at your back is a couple of your foolish young Scottish friends. At least you will have the satisfaction of dying together.'

I braced myself for death, hoping that Karrie had succeeded in setting the detonators. If so, then my life was not given in vain.

Ravenstein began to squeeze the trigger and raised his hand to signal the advance. At that exact moment the entire cavern exploded.

36

SAFE HARBOUR

I was knocked off my feet by the force of the blast and engulfed in a choking cloud of smoke and dust shot through with flashes of flame. My ears were ringing as I wrapped my arms protectively round my head and pressed myself flat to the ground until the shock had passed. For a moment I wasn't even sure if I was alive or dead, but with an effort I pushed myself up on my elbows and peered through the flaming murk.

Most of the men who were assembled on the shore, hardened warriors all, were killed outright by the blast. Those who were not howled in agony as they were consumed by the swelling inferno. Grenades, mortars and bullets exploded amid the fire, adding to the man-made storm that was already bringing the walls of the cavern tumbling down in crashing sheets of rock.

The U-boat lay tilted on its side, its hull gashed open by the blast. Its engines were ablaze, flames belching from its innards as a series of detonations boomed through its tortured length. Even through the thunderous din, I could hear the dying screams of trapped sailors.

Ravenstein, on his knees, struggled to shake off his concussion. Leaning on one arm, he stretched out a hand towards the pistol he had dropped. I watched him turn the weapon towards me, preparing to take a final revenge for the utter ruination of his plans. With one eye closed, he took careful aim, and I had not the strength to move.

All around us, smoke swirled while rocks pattered down on to the bodies of the dead and the dying, and made splashes all across the surface of the lake. Then, in the midst of the debris dropping from the cavern roof, a spiked stalactite broke loose to plunge downward like a giant dagger. As though guided by the hand of some higher justice, the pointed rock drove itself right through the body of my enemy. With an astonished grunt and a last convulsive shudder, Ravenstein died. The thought flashed through my mind that while some men in time might find their Jerusalem, he had surely found his hell and been consumed by it.

I felt Yowney's hands grab my arms and haul me backwards out of the cavern, which was now in a state of total collapse. Huge boulders were dropping from above to smash into the lake, where a rapidly spreading pool of oil was blazing like the fires of perdition.

Suddenly, to my great relief, I saw Dougal and Karrie hauling themselves dripping out of the water. Once on shore they stumbled towards us and we all four staggered as far up the tunnel as we could drag ourselves. Finally we sank down on to the stone floor, exhausted and amazed. Behind us there came a gargantuan rumble as the entire roof of the cavern came down, closing it off for ever and burying the dead invaders in an unhallowed tomb.

'Karrie,' I panted, 'you've saved the day. If that gang had got loose they'd have made havoc of our defences.'

'I think you've fickled them good and proper,' said Yowney, heaving himself up into a sitting position.

Karrie's face in the faint light of our torches was weary and sad. 'I thought I would be glad of the chance to take revenge upon the despoilers of my country,' she said, 'but I feel nothing but horror. A great empty horror.'

Dougal put an arm round her shoulders. 'It's a terrible thing to fight and kill,' he said, 'but if we hadn't been here, our own people would have been slaughtered without mercy and the war might have been lost.'

'I suppose you're right,' the courageous young woman agreed, her head drooping so that her long damp hair fell across her face like a veil. 'But I think I won't sleep well for a long time to come.'

'It's a sad thing to have taken a hand in such killing, however necessary,' said Yowney solemnly. 'Maybe I'll take a leaf out of the book of my Maltese friends and say a prayer for our dead enemies.'

'Given what's happened to them, I couldn't begrudge them that either, padre,' I concurred.

Once we had all recovered our breath, we picked up our torches and began the long trek back.

'I feel a bit foolish asking this after all we've been through,' I said to Karrie, 'but what was it you had spotted when you went dashing off to the far end of the lake?'

She forced a tired smile. 'It was a crude statue of some primitive goddess, dating back to when the cave was being used as a temple. Her name was lost to history long ago, and now her shrine is lost too.'

'Given all that was at stake,' I said, 'I'm sure the old girl won't mind too much.'

Suddenly we spotted lights flashing before us. It was Jaikie at the head of a well-armed squad of soldiers.

'Thank God!' he exclaimed, clapping his hands on each of us in turn. 'Thank God you made it out of there!'

'General Hannay,' said a young captain, giving me a smart salute, 'we've got explosives here to block off the tunnels.'

'You won't need any of that,' I informed him. 'The Germans brought enough to seal their own destruction.'

'Dick! Oh, Dick,' called a familiar voice from further up the passage. 'Thank heaven you're safe!'

Emerging from the band of soldiers, as radiant and unexpected as a vision of angels, came Mary, her arms outstretched towards me. We met in an embrace that said more about the love between us than could ever be put into words.

'Mary!' I gasped, astonished and ecstatic. 'How . . . how on earth do you come to be here?'

'Oh, I pulled a few strings,' she answered, joyful tears sparkling in her eyes. With a gentle hand she wiped some of the grime from my cheek. 'I knew that whatever you were up to, you'd need me here to clean you up at the end of it.'

Later, when there was time to talk in private, Mary told me that within an hour of her arrival on Malta she had run into Jaikie, who was rounding up a rapidly organised defence force. Reunited with her in such circumstances, I felt as if I had climbed out of the depths of hell to find myself on the very threshold of paradise. To be with those I loved, my family and my friends, to know that they were safe, was to be blessed beyond words.

Peter's squadron had scrambled to meet incoming enemy aircraft. They found the German transports and their escort holding position out at sea, waiting in vain for a signal from Ravenstein that his force had accomplished its part of the invasion plan. As our fighters moved in, the Germans decided against risking planes loaded with paratroopers in a pointless battle, and made a rapid retreat to their Italian bases.

Early next morning we joined the crowd packed in tiers around the Grand Harbour. It looked as though the entire population of Valletta had gathered here. Some waved flags, British and Maltese, others just waved white sheets as a mark of victory. Four surviving merchantmen had already made it to port, but there was one left still to arrive. The cheers as it lumbered into view must have shaken the clouds.

Battered, holed and burned, the *Ohio* and her courageous crew had battled on against insuperable odds to come at last to their safe haven. Her engines ruptured, her steering wrecked, she was lashed between two destroyers, which kept her afloat and steered her laboriously into the harbour.

In her vast hold was fuel for our planes, food for our people, everything Malta needed to continue its resistance to the enemy. Soon, I knew, our American allies would pour across the northern shores of Africa to join our own troops. It was the turning of the tide and it was possible now to think of a day when the war would be over and the hard-won peace would begin at last. After a long journey through the darkest of nights, we could finally see before us the first glimmerings of dawn.

I had learned that this day, August 15th, was one of the island's most important Catholic feast days, that of Santa Maria. For many of the more devout Maltese, their miraculous deliverance had been brought about by the intercession of the Mother of God. Given all that my friends and I had been through, I was in no mind to question their faith in the miraculous.

At the start of this journey I had had my doubts as to whether I had it in me to complete one last adventure. Now, as we watched the *Ohio* limp into the Grand Harbour to the echoing cheers of the crowd, I saw that it was never too late to fight, never too late to hope. Some lines from Tennyson's *Ulysses* rose in my mind as a fitting commentary on all we had been through.

> *Tho' much is taken, much abides; and tho'*
> *We are not now that strength which in old days*
> *Moved earth and heaven; that which we are, we are;*
> *One equal temper of heroic hearts,*
> *Made weak by time and fate, but strong in will*
> *To strive, to seek, to find, and not to yield.*

AUTHOR'S NOTE

When I was granted the immense privilege of writing a tribute to John Buchan and his hero Richard Hannay, *The Thirty-One Kings*, I expected it to be a one-off, and the last chapter was intended to be a farewell to those characters. Many people, however, critics included, expressed a strong desire for more. Seeking to oblige them, I rolled ideas around in my head until I came up with the notion of uniting Hannay with the heroes of Buchan's much-loved novel *John Macnab*. This meant going back in time to the 1920s, rather than writing a sequel to that first World War II adventure. In the course of writing *Castle Macnab*, however, the thought occurred to me that there was a fine yarn to be made from linking up the great siege of Malta in 1565 with the equally heroic siege of 1942. This was a mission worthy of Richard Hannay and the Gorbals Die-Hards, and a chance to explore a pivotal moment in the war, of which Operation Pedestal formed a vital part.

Sending Hannay and his team on an epic journey to Gibraltar, Casablanca, the Atlas Mountains, Tangier and Malta involved a huge amount of research, and I am very grateful to all those authors and historians whose works provided me with information and inspiration. Special mention, however, must be made of my fellow Scot Alice Morrison, author of *My 1001 Nights: Adventures in Morocco*. Her writings and films (available on YouTube) brought Morocco vividly to life for me and contributed hugely to that part of the novel. Truly, she is a gazelle. Anyone who was rather taken aback to find British pilots sitting down to drinks with their German counterparts in Tangier will find in the pages of wartime memoirs that such outbreaks of mutual goodwill did occur while they were on neutral ground. An example can be found on page 169 of *Fortress Malta* by James Holland.

The First Aid Nursing Yeomanry was the actual organisation which provided some of the first female agents for the SOE. For the purposes of the story I have fictionalised it as the Royal Nursing Auxiliary and placed Mary Hannay in charge of it. I should also mention that Kamsoura will not be found on any map as it is a fictional town combining elements of a number of real Moroccan locations.

Many thanks as always to my wife Debby who lends me invaluable help as a researcher and editor. Thanks also to fact-checker Kirsty Nicol and my editors at Polygon.

RJH